ARKSTORM

THE OTHER BIG ONE

BOBBY AKART

THANK YOU

Thank you for reading **_ARkStorm,_** a novel by author Bobby Akart.
Join Bobby Akart's mailing list to learn about upcoming releases, deals, and appearances. Follow this link to:
BobbyAkart.com

PRAISE FOR BOBBY AKART AND ARKSTORM

"Read one of his books and you are hooked!" ~ Amazon review for Perfect Storm 4

"He has a way of taking real life scenarios and combine them with believable characters to create an amazing story." ~ Amazon review for Perfect Storm 3

"Bobby Akart continues to give his readers spellbinding scenarios that are so close to real life, it's scary as all get out." ~ Amazon review of Black Friday

"He's right up there with James Patterson, David Baldacci, Brad Thor and others that write thrillers.

To me he actually surpasses them." ~ Amazon review for Nuclear Winter series

"I cry for the injured and defenseless, rage at the bad guys, and scream with impotent rage when one of my favorite characters are hurt or killed! Such is the artistry of the author. Such is the realm of Bobby Akart." ~ Amazon review of Black Gold

"Love the intensity of his stories, his through research, his creativity, the characterizations and the abundant action and realistic locations." ~ Amazon review of New Madrid Earthquake

ARKSTORM
THE OTHER BIG ONE

by
Bobby Akart

OTHER WORKS BY AMAZON CHARTS TOP 25 AUTHOR BOBBY AKART

The California Dreamin' Duology
ARkStorm (a standalone, disaster thriller)
Fractured (a standalone, disaster thriller)

The Perfect Storm Series
Perfect Storm 1
Perfect Storm 2
Perfect Storm 3
Perfect Storm 4

Black Gold (a standalone, terrorism thriller)

The Nuclear Winter Series

First Strike
Armageddon
Whiteout
Devil Storm
Desolation

New Madrid (a standalone, disaster thriller)

Odessa (a Gunner Fox trilogy)
Odessa Reborn
Odessa Rising
Odessa Strikes

The Virus Hunters
Virus Hunters I
Virus Hunters II
Virus Hunters III

The Geostorm Series
The Shift
The Pulse
The Collapse
The Flood

The Tempest
The Pioneers

The Asteroid Series (A Gunner Fox trilogy)
Discovery
Diversion
Destruction

The Doomsday Series
Apocalypse
Haven
Anarchy
Minutemen
Civil War

The Yellowstone Series
Hellfire
Inferno
Fallout
Survival

The Lone Star Series
Axis of Evil
Beyond Borders

Lines in the Sand
Texas Strong
Fifth Column
Suicide Six

The Pandemic Series
Beginnings
The Innocents
Level 6
Quietus

The Blackout Series
36 Hours
Zero Hour
Turning Point
Shiloh Ranch
Hornet's Nest
Devil's Homecoming

The Boston Brahmin Series
The Loyal Nine
Cyber Attack
Martial Law
False Flag

The Mechanics
Choose Freedom
Patriot's Farewell (standalone novel)
Black Friday (standalone novel)
Seeds of Liberty (Companion Guide)

The Prepping for Tomorrow Series (non-fiction)
Cyber Warfare
EMP: Electromagnetic Pulse
Economic Collapse

Copyright Information

This is a work of fiction. Names, characters, organizations, places, events, and incidents are either the products of the author's imagination or are used fictitiously. Any resemblance to actual persons, living or dead, or actual events is purely coincidental.

The author and publisher have provided this eBook to you for your personal use only. You may not make this eBook publicly available in any way.

Copyright infringement is against the law. If you believe the copy of this eBook you are reading infringes on the author's copyright, please notify the publisher at

CrownPublishersInc@gmail.com.

© 2023 Crown Publishers Inc. All rights reserved. Except as permitted under the U.S. Copyright Act of 1976, no part of this book may be reproduced, distributed or transmitted in any form or by any means including, but not limited to electronic, mechanical, photocopying, recording, or otherwise, or stored in a database or retrieval system, without the express written permission of Crown Publishers Inc.

DEDICATIONS

ARkStorm was written at a time when my heart was heavy with sorrow and grief. Our beloved English Bulldogs, Bullie and Boom, had brought us joy and laughter for thirteen-and-a-half years. The princesses of the palace, as my long-time readers know them, passed away within two weeks of one another several months ago. While they'll be missed our journey as a family will continue.

This novel is devoted to our sweet girls as they were always our family's calm in the storm.

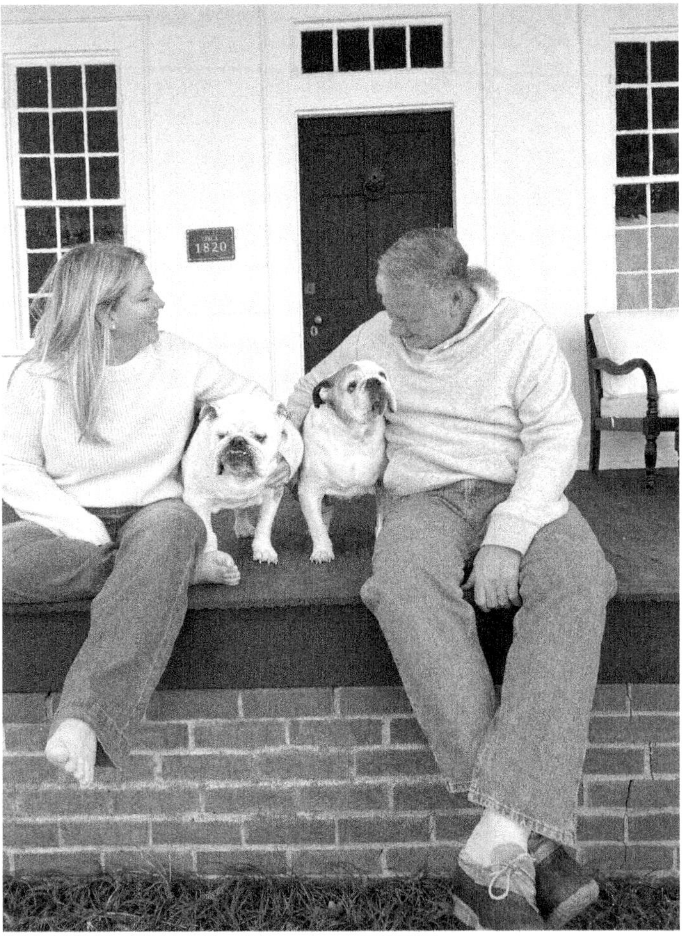
1820

EPIGRAPH

There's always a calm before the storm.
~ Heather Graham, American Actress

The greatest of floods begin with a single raindrop.
~ Unknown

Survival is the ability to swim in strange water.
~ Frank Herbert, Author of *Dune*

Rain doesn't count; building arks does.
~ Warren Buffett, American Financier

I am going to bring floodwaters on the earth to destroy all life under the heavens, every creature that has the breath of life in it. Everything on earth will perish.
~ God speaks to Noah, Genesis 6: 17

PROLOGUE

Late October
Station II Emergency Operations Center
Crescenta Valley, California, USA

That summer had brought drought and fire to California. Not unusual for the region, but certainly cataclysmic even for the Golden State. It had been two decades since the Station Fire had scorched its way through the neighborhoods of Pasadena, the hillsides of the Crescenta Valley, and the Angeles National Forest. Nearly two hundred thousand acres had been consumed by the blaze, as were hundreds of buildings. Station Fire I, as it had been renamed now, took a month to extinguish.

Today, Station Fire II was nearing its forty-five-day rampage across the Crescenta Valley once again. History was repeating in a big way. The media had anointed it the worst fire in decades. Its devastation was measured in economic terms, as was often the case when reporters and pundits attempted to compare one natural disaster to another. For the firefighters from across the country, the tragedy was viewed through the eyes of the weary, the injured, and the families of those who lost loved ones.

Deputy Chief Finnegan Fergus O'Brien, a mouthful of a name to be sure, stood on the ridge overlooking his beloved neighborhood of La Cañada. An Irishman, he'd immigrated to America with his family from Dublin when he was a boy. They'd lived in Boston for a few years before they'd uprooted and headed to the Los Angeles area.

Growing up, the other neighborhood children had immediately been drawn to him, especially because of his accent. They'd quickly corrected him when he mispronounced the name of his new community as "la-Canada," like the country. "Lah-can-ya-da," they'd explained, was the way to say it. Finn had shrugged, as he'd had little experience with the Spanish language or the reasons why towns in California seemed to be named using Spanish words.

Then he'd learned the history of the state and understood.

Finn, as everyone called him, had always wanted to be a fireman. He had been a throwback as a kid, shunning video games and MTV. He'd loved to play outdoors, especially riding his bike and visiting the many mountainous parks north of LA. As he'd advanced through school, his entire focus had been on a career as a fireman.

And so he was. He'd learned and undertaken virtually every aspect of the job, from battling structure fires in the city to search and rescue missions. However, he'd gained a particular expertise in battling the many wildfires that plagued the state each year. The summer fires were an annual occurrence for California.

However, this one was different. It was devilish in its ability to reconstitute itself. It was monstrous in its destructive capability. Now, Station Fire II, an absolute beast of a blaze, was threatening his home.

He'd led Region 1, North Operations Bureau, Division 3 of the Los Angeles County Fire Department for just over ten years. With retirement coming like a freight train at the end of December, those he'd established relationships with throughout the fire department as well as civic leaders in the Crescenta

Valley promised they'd miss his devoted service. None of that was on his mind that day as he commanded units from battalions 4, 6 and 22 as they battled Station II.

A hot gust of wind pushed its way up the valley, smacking him hard at the top of the ridge with a combination of ash, smoke, and debris. It seemed to remind Finn his work was not done.

The first flames had been reported much farther to the north, most likely caused by a lightning strike or a campfire left unattended. The investigation would take place later. The fire had to be contained first. Due to the hazardous terrain, containment was challenging enough without attempting to extinguish the blaze. Eventually, Finn knew, the fire would run out of fuel. Unless, of course, it made its way into the valley. There, homes would feed the fire's hunger.

To fight any wildfire, you have to remove one of the factors of the so-called fire triangle. Heat, oxygen, or fuel. It had been hot well into late October, and there was no forecast of rain in sight. The fire was too large to smother, so the only option was to remove its fuel.

He'd been leading a group of firefighters across the ridge, searching for flashy fuels, easily ignitable grasses, leaves and pine needles that carpeted the forest floor. Finn worked with his team to create a series of fuelbreaks, strategically locating strips of bare earth where the combustible plant material once lay.

Take away the fuel; starve the fire. A simple concept that was a nearly impossible task on the side of a ridge. Using two bulldozers the fire department borrowed from the California National Guard, they cut a swath through the forest threatened by the fire. They'd been carving their way through using chainsaws, axes, and the dozers' blades for more than twenty-four hours without stopping.

Above the fuelbreak, Finn marveled as powerful indrafts of air generated fire whirls, also known as firenadoes. The fire was drawn upward, burning towards the sky, throwing flames and debris into the air. This was indicative of an extremely strong wildfire. Superheated air changed the dynamic of any blaze.

Coupled with the efforts of other firefighters and the planes dropping water from the sky, Station Fire II was gasping for air as it began to die down. Finn wanted to breathe a sigh of relief as he saw the battle turn in his favor. However, he knew he and his crew would be building backfires for days to draw the flames toward the top of the ridge in order to lure them away from the homes below.

His home. The one he grew up in with his long-deceased parents. The one in which his beloved wife had passed away following a fight with breast cancer before they could have children.

As he prepared to order his team home to get some rest, he paused. For the first time in over twenty-four hours, he removed his helmet. He desperately wanted to smell the clean air that part of the Crescent Valley afforded him. Instead, his nostrils were filled with rancid smoke and the smell of charred wood.

Despite the effort his sense of smell demanded, his ears picked up a sound rising from the valley.

Faintly. In the distance. Surreal.

It was a lonely saxophone playing a tune he couldn't quite make out, conjuring up images of the emperor Nero playing his violin as Rome burned. The inability to discern the song being played or the direction from which it came haunted him for weeks until it washed from his memory when the rains came.

And so it begins ...

PART 1

DECEMBER

In spite of all the marvels the hand of Man has wrought,
He yet stands impotent before the fury of flood and fire,
No matter with what courage these great Forces may be fought,
They leave in their path destruction, inevitable and dire.
~ Kate H. Wright, La Crescenta Women's Club,
January 12, 1934,
following the Great Crescenta Valley Flood

ONE

**Monday before Christmas
Los Angeles International Airport
Los Angeles, California, USA**

Samantha Hendrick leaned forward in her white Tesla S, squinting her eyes through the windshield as it was being pummeled by the incessant rainfall California's Central Valley had experienced for the last week. Whoever said *it never rains in Southern California* was sadly misinformed.

The Bosch Aerotwin wipers heralded by Tesla as cutting-edge weren't doing squat-diddly as the torrents of water swept over the windshield. If it hadn't been for the fact her nieces were unaccompanied minors who required a handoff by the airline to an adult, she would've exited the 110 Freeway and returned home. She'd let Uber or Lyft do the heavy lifting, pardon the pun.

Her husband Tyler's family had suggested they keep the girls while his brother and wife flew to Hawaii for their ten-year anniversary. *It would rekindle our marriage,* they'd said. *We'd only be gone ten days,* they promised. *Plus,* they suggested, *it would give you guys a chance to experience parenthood with our girls.*

Subterfuge, Sammy had thought to herself. The whole second-honeymoon trip idea had probably been orchestrated by their families to nudge Sammy and Tyler into having children. Certainly, their families had had plenty of ammunition to throw in the couple's faces at Thanksgiving when they'd gotten together in Pennsylvania.

Countless times, they had been reminded of the couple's so-called five-year plan. Tyler's family had talked about *the plan* for most of Thanksgiving dinner. Five years had come and gone, and there were no grandchildren or new nieces or nephews in their future.

What the couple tried to explain, which their families couldn't grasp, was the love they shared was so strong they couldn't imagine adding a child into the mix. The two were mostly inseparable, both working remotely from home with the exception of an occasional business trip.

They'd grown up in rural Central Pennsylvania before moving to the Orlando, Florida, area. Tyler had been an athletic trainer who'd been hired by the USA Baseball National Team. The squad had trained and played exhibition events at Champion Stadium located at the ESPN Wide World of Sports at Walt Disney World. It had been a dream job for Tyler, one he swore he'd never leave. Then the University of Central Florida came knocking.

He accepted the position of associate head athletic trainer for the UCF football program. Four games into his first season, he became the head athletic trainer when his boss was fired due to a doping scandal. Tyler not only cleaned up the mess, but he was also instrumental in turning the program around through his disciplined training regimens.

As Tyler advanced his career, Sammy was impressing her corporate superiors. She'd been hired by a multinational food and beverage corporation as an analyst. Using her accounting and business management skills, she quickly rose up the corporate ladder of success by providing accurate sales forecasting for new products developed by the company.

However, she'd reached a crossroads. The company offered her a promotion that required her to relocate to the tiny hamlet of Purchase, New York, where the corporation's headquarters were located. She'd receive a substantial raise and cost-of-living increase. A dream job in many respects. However, there was a catch. Sammy would have to move to Westchester County, just north of New York City.

Like many couples, Sammy and Tyler sat down to weigh the pros and cons. Weather was a factor. An important one, in fact. Having lived in Florida for several years, they didn't miss the endless, harsh winters of Central Pennsylvania. New York would be no different. They'd have the option of maintaining two residences, as Tyler's job required him to remain in the Orlando area. After being used to spending much of their days together, being separated for weeks at a time was almost a deal-killer.

And then the phone rang.

Tyler was being courted for an upward move. Not with his beloved Penn State University's football program. No, it was much worse. It was their archrivals calling—the University of Southern California in Los Angeles.

Initially, he walked around their home muttering, *Hell no, no way,* and *I'd rather die.* Despite his misgivings, he and Sammy flew to LA to meet with athletic department and school officials. They were wined and dined and impressed. Yet they still faced a major obstacle because of Sammy's career. Now they would be thousands of miles apart. So USC sweetened the pot.

They'd learned through conversations with the couple that Sammy had always dreamed of going to law school. She'd already earned her master's degree, so her educational successes made her a prime candidate for any doctoral program. School administrators made her an offer: "We'll hold a spot at the law school for you." Years ago, California had abandoned the need for graduate and doctoral applicants to pass tests like the LSAT and the MCAT. Now it was mostly based on admission committees and internal school politics.

Big changes. Big opportunities. Five-year plans cast aside.

Sammy was now a corporate attorney, and Tyler was part of the USC Trojans team, playing in the college football playoffs, with their first game held at the Rose Bowl against, you guessed it, Big Ten rival and Tyler's alma mater, Penn State.

As she wheeled the Tesla around the curves of World Way leading to the myriad of parking options at LAX, she shook her head in disbelief as the water poured across her car. She began to wonder how she was going to entertain the girls. The forecast for Christmas through New Year's was rain, rain, and more rain.

Suddenly, she longed for Florida, the Sunshine State.

TWO

Monday
LAX
Los Angeles, California

Inside the terminal, Sammy waited somewhat impatiently for the flight to arrive. Her brother-in-law could've flown with the kids from Pittsburg through LAX. Heck, it was just a hop, skip, and a jump to Hawaii, with the skip being LA, where they could have dropped their daughters off with Sammy. Instead, they'd flown through Dallas and sent their daughters to LA. As unaccompanied minors, the kids had to wait until the flight was unloaded before a Delta Air Lines *red coat*, as gate supervisors were called, escorted the girls to the unsecured area of the terminal.

Naturally, the pressure she'd put on herself to navigate the Tesla through traffic in her rush to LAX was unnecessary. Flights in and out of most California destinations had been delayed for weeks, causing major headaches for airlines around the country. It was amazing how weather issues at one or two major airport hubs wreaked havoc across the entire system.

Her mind wandered as she watched the planes land and take off in the pouring rain. She was glad she wasn't flying anywhere. Her law firm represented several international conglomerates that required her to attend merger and acquisition negotiations. Sammy had a knack for cutting to the chase, frequently sitting in a boardroom filled with men who tried to upstage one another. She was adept at cutting through the BS and posturing typical during these types of negotiations. It was a stressful job but one that paid very well. She'd earned the two weeks off during the holidays.

Yet she wished she could hide in her office as she thought about the task at hand. When this ten-day visit had been put into motion over Thanksgiving, Tyler hadn't been expecting to be preparing his team for the Rose Bowl at New Year's. The long days would keep him away from home except for Christmas. At the time they'd agreed to watch the girls, Sammy never imagined being cooped up at the house amidst interminable rainfall. Her mind continued to wander until a pair of voices rose above the shuffling passengers.

"Sammmeeeee!" the girls yelled in unison, breaking free of the gentle grasp the Red Coat had on their hands, allowing them to race down the concourse toward their aunt. For some reason, the girls were on a first-name basis with Sammy and Tyler, dispensing with the formalities of aunt and uncle.

"Hi, guys!" Sammy responded cheerily. She really did love the girls and had looked forward to the visit, although she wished it were half as long. Her well-thought-out itinerary, which included a trip to Disneyland, the beach, and visits to nearby Millard Falls, was scuttled. They'd have to find ways to be entertained until the weather cleared.

"We are sooo ready to have some fun!" shouted Sophie, the older of the two girls by all of eleven months. Sophie had been born in January, and her sister, Olivia, whom they called Livvy, had been born later that year in December. A quick turnaround most new mothers wouldn't wish for.

"We're going to Disney, right, Sammy?" Livvy asked. She had just turned six and joined her sister in the cute, I-wanna-be-a-Disney-princess-someday phase of their lives. Livvy pulled away and looked up to her aunt. "Did you know that I'm the same age as Sophie right now?"

"Only for a few weeks," protested Sophie. "Sammy, I'll be seven on January 12."

Sammy laughed. "I know that, girls. I have all the important dates on my calendar." She winked at the Delta Red Coat, who'd caught up to the girls with some paperwork for Sammy to sign. Because the girls had checked their luggage, the Delta representative turned over their boarding passes and baggage claim stubs.

Hand in hand, the trio walked amongst the masses of passengers heading toward the luggage carousels. Sammy expected it would take some time for their bags to find their way from the plane, across the rain-swept tarmac, onto the carousel.

While she waited, she let go of the girls' hands to send a text to Tyler.

Sammy: The eagles have landed. LOL.

Tyler: Are they behaving?

Sammy: So far, so good.

Tyler: It'll go by fast, I swear.

Sammy and Tyler were used to being alone with their dogs, Carly and Fenway. The lovable pups joined them for everything from trips into the mountains to leisurely nights on their dual recliners, with each getting a lapdog. Tyler understood keeping up with two young girls would be somewhat taxing on Sammy since he'd be occupied with work.

Sammy: We'll have fun. How is Malachi?

Sammy was referring to the Trojan's star quarterback, Malachi Nelson, who'd won the Heisman Trophy as a senior. He'd suffered a hamstring injury during practice a week ago, placing Tyler under a lot of pressure to treat the young man and nurse his multimillion-dollar legs back to health.

Tyler: You have no idea how many times a day I'm asked that question. The answer to the public is "game-time decision." Truth? I'll have him ready.

Sammy: I'm proud of you.

Tyler: LOL. I have the easy job. Good luck. Love you!

Sammy: Love you back!

"Rain, rain, go away. Please come back another day!"

Sophie and Livvy had slipped away from Sammy

and were standing near the airport exit, staring through the windows at the downpour. Conflicted, Sammy debated whether to wait for the girls' luggage or hustle over to retrieve them.

With a wary eye on both tasks, she eventually spied their bags and snagged them off the carousel. By the time she joined the girls, they were belting out another nursery rhyme.

"It's raining, it's pouring, the old man is snoring!" They began laughing so hard at their silliness they forgot the rest of the words to the Mother Goose rhyme.

Sammy smiled as the girls giggled and hugged one another. She surmised their bond was stronger by being so close in age. Whether that was part of their parents' plan or not, it seemed to work for Sophie and Livvy. Suddenly, despite the gloomy weather, Sammy was warming up to the idea of time with the girls.

"Come on, girls. My boat is parked just across the street."

"Really?" asked Livvy.

"No, goober," her sister shot back. Then, after another glance at the water filling the access road, Sophie scowled. "Right, Sammy?"

THREE

Tuesday
Off the coast of Manawai
The Hawaiian Archipelago

Frankie Alama was a descendent of a Hawaiian fishing deity. Before the Pacific Islanders were introduced to *haole* foods from the U.S. mainland, their cuisine primarily consisted of vegetable-based meals like poi or the delicacies of the sea.

Every culture had its collection of fishing stories, and the Hawaiian Islanders were no exception. Ku'ula-kai was revered as a fisherman with almost supernatural powers. Not only was he celebrated for his enormous catches but also for his battles with sea creatures like eels, sharks, and octopuses.

The blood of Ku'ula-kai coursed through the veins of Frankie Alama. Frankie's knowledge of the fishing areas and seasons throughout the Hawaiian Archipelago had been handed down to him over several generations. While modern techniques had been introduced to displace the ancient fishermen's use of lines, lures, nets and spears, Frankie still was still a master of the old ways.

He also had an innate ability to sense when a storm was brewing. Perhaps it was his weary joints beginning to ache after nearly seventy years. Or it was some form of sixth sense handed down through the DNA of the great Ku'ula-kai. But on that afternoon in December, he sensed Lono, the Hawaiian god, had conjured up a mighty *ino*.

He was certainly familiar with the subtropical moisture that formed off the northern coast of the Hawaiian Islands during December. Meteorologists on the local news stations spoke of the storms often, not that Frankie noticed, as he rarely watched television. He didn't need advanced forecasting equipment to know when the moisture was gathering and the winds were picking up. He could stand onshore and look across the dark waters of the Pacific Ocean and watch the *ino* form.

These warm-water storms would almost appear to rain upside down, at least from his perspective. The high concentrations of moisture should, by the laws of nature, release a deluge upon the ocean and any land masses nearby. However, Frankie knew these rainstorms were different. They appeared to evaporate, and the prevailing winds seemingly sucked them into the heavens.

That Tuesday began like any other. For days, dark clouds had gathered over the water while Frankie and his sons fished for yellowfin tuna. Their yield was abundant, as always. When Frankie was a child, his family only caught what they needed for their village. Now it was his business, as the cost of living in Hawaii had grown exponentially over his lifetime. His days on the water were longer, as he worked diligently to catch enough to fill his boat. As a result, he found himself away from shore as the storms built.

Despite being short on their day's quota, Frankie suddenly told his sons to prepare for their return to shore. He walked to the bow of his fishing boat and watched the clouds grow darker. Their shape was ominous.

Ghostly. Angry. Almost supernatural.

This *ino* would be different, he informed his sons, who had joined him. He tried to explain the folklore behind the so-called rivers in the sky. The Pineapple Express, as the *haole* weathermen called them. No, this storm appeared to come directly from Maui, the keepers of the winds.

Maui, one of the Islanders' most famous demigods, had been credited with many things, including pulling up the island chain from the ocean with a magic hook as well as creating fire. Maui had used his powers to conjure up a strong wind to lift a kite high into the heavens, only to unknowingly cause terrific damage to the islands he'd created. The experience taught Maui there were forces in nature far stronger than he was.

Frankie nodded to himself as he relayed the story to his sons for likely the twentieth time in their lives together. As the storm across the Pacific grew in intensity, Frankie surmised that the demigod Maui had overdone it this time.

FOUR

Tuesday
National Oceanic and Atmospheric Administration
Regional Offices
Sacramento, California

"Come on, you guys. The governor's office is up my ass, and I'm over it." Howard Brown paced the floor in the National Weather Service's offices that shared space with NOAA in Sacramento. The representatives from the National Oceanic and Atmospheric Administration, who'd been brought into the Sacramento offices years ago, allowed the NWS regional director an opportunity to vent before addressing his concerns.

"I mean, do you have any idea the number of oh-so-many-important events the state has coming in the next ten days?" Brown continued to stomp around the office; his nearly three-hundred-pound frame seemingly caused the concrete floor to shudder underneath him. "Concerts. Parades. Football games. Statue dedications. Jesus, he wants us to forecast—no, *guarantee* that there won't be any rain on New Year's Day for the Rose Bowl parade and the freakin' football game."

With a huff, Brown paused and stared at the downpour that beset Sacramento. People who had the unfortunate job of going about their business on the streets of California's capital donned raincoats and umbrellas. He rolled his eyes and shook his head as a gust of wind turned one mini umbrella inside out. The woman who held it struggled to fix the problem before slamming it onto the sidewalk out of frustration. Within seconds, the tattered umbrella became tumbleweed, bouncing off the other pedestrians.

He spun around and addressed Bekki LaMarre, the team leader for NOAA in Sacramento. She'd been transferred there when the prior governor pitched a fit that California was being slighted by the federal government when it came to matters of the environment. She had been allowed to pick her own team, so she drew from fellow University of California, Berkeley grads Gregory Entremont and Tomas Stoppkotte.

"Bekki, what should I tell Governor Pappas?"

"Mr. Brown, it's simply that time of year," she replied. "You know how these rain events are. They'll last for a couple of weeks, providing a brief respite in between. Then, by the end of January, they'll be over it, and the governor will have his sunny skies again. Well, except the Bay Area, of course."

"You don't think I know that? I've told his chief of staff the same thing. Isn't there anything I can say to give him hope?"

LaMarre sighed. She wasn't going to lie simply to satisfy the newly elected, high-strung governor. "Forecasting can be fickle, as you know. That said, we could tell him what he wants to hear. If we're wrong, what's he gonna do, fire us?"

"He can't fire us," chimed in Stoppkotte, who had a tendency to take statements literally.

"She knows that," added Entremont, who shot his boss a glance with an accompanying eye roll. He made a suggestion. "I have a computer model that can interpolate these unique and otherwise unpredictable weather patterns outward for at least two weeks, maybe longer."

"Two weeks will be fine," interjected Brown. "Just get me past the damn Rose Bowl on New Year's Day. That seems to be his hot button."

Entremont looked at LaMarre and nodded. She responded to Brown. "We'll begin working on it this evening. I think we can have you something by tomorrow morning. Right, guys?"

Her cohorts nodded.

Brown dismissed them and instructed his assistant to inform the governor's chief of staff to expect a response by early afternoon the next day.

LaMarre led her associates up the emergency stairwell to their offices above the NWS. They spoke in hushed tones as they made their way upward.

"We're sticking our neck out by relying upon your modelling program," she began. "We haven't even proposed its use to Miami yet." The primary offices of NOAA were located in Miami, Florida.

Entremont whispered in response, "I know, but we have to pretend like we're doing something to satisfy Brown and that douchebag governor."

"Hey!" exclaimed Stoppkotte with a chuckle. "At least he's our douche."

"Good point," said LaMarre. "One with powerful DC connections. We'd better couch this forecast with a lot of holes and determinations subject to conjecture. He probably could have us fired, you know."

They entered their offices. It was after hours, and the minimal staff employed at NOAA's Sacramento office had left for the day. Entremont tasked LaMarre and Stoppkotte with information gathering while he prepared the model for the difficult task at hand.

Trying to forecast the timing and intensity of atmospheric rivers.

FIVE

Tuesday
Hendrick Residence
La Cañada, California

Sammy fell backwards onto the bed, causing Tyler's laptop to bounce upward off his thighs. She lamented the end of her busy day. "I'm exhausted. They exhaust me. I mean, where does the energy come from?"

"You were six once," he mumbled, trying to stifle a grin. He felt guilty for not being more present during the first two days of his nieces' visit. He'd inwardly promised his wife to make it up with a long-overdue vacation. Maybe to Italy, something they'd often discussed during their runs through the Angeles National Forest.

"I'd have to ask my mom, but I'm pretty sure I wasn't this energetic," she said as she rolled her head around her shoulders to relieve some tension. She took a deep breath and released an equally deep exhale, utilizing Dr. Andrew Weil's 4-7-8 relaxation breathing technique. Four seconds in, hold for seven seconds, and then releasing for eight seconds. It was so very California, although Sammy had utilized it since college.

She snuggled up against her husband, who adjusted his body to allow her to have a view of his laptop.

"I don't know, Sammy. I have a bad feeling about this."

"The game?"

"Well, not so much the game but Malachi's ability to perform."

Sensing Tyler's concern, she gave him some room and sat cross-legged in bed. "You said his knee is fine."

Tyler, deep in thought, scratched at his beard without taking his eyes off his computer screen. "After practice this afternoon, I went over to the stadium to assess the field conditions. Like always,

West Coast Turf in Palm Springs was overseeding the playing field with Bermuda rye grass. They've done it that way for years because it grows fast and holds paint well."

"So what's the problem?" asked Sammy.

"I talked to Martin Rodriguez, the owner of the company. They know their stuff, both good and bad. Sure, they've been able to tweak their process in the past to deal with the weather. However, he reminded me that unpredictable variables like rain and growth spurts can throw the delicate balance off. When you think about it, the field at the Rose Bowl is a large, rectangular living plant. All of this rain coupled with cooler weather can bring fungus to the turf, which in turn makes it susceptible to being ripped up from the root system."

"Football cleats are rough on the ground, right?" asked Sammy.

"Yeah, and when the field gets sloppy, recently rehabilitated hammies can pull again."

Sammy had seen her husband stress over games before, but this one was different for obvious reasons. As much as he loved his alma mater, he'd take great pleasure in USC beating them on New Year's Day. She reached across his chest and seized the television remote from the nightstand. Tyler, a classic movie aficionado, generally watched at night using his AirPods while Sammy read a romance novel on her Kindle.

She turned on the TV and navigated through channels to KTLA, Channel 5. The weather segment was just beginning. Evening news anchor Cher Calvin was discussing the historic rainfall with former Weather Channel meteorologist Chris Warren.

Calvin's face reflected the concern that many of KTLA's viewers were feeling. "Let's turn now to our storm team meteorologist. Chris, you're no stranger to covering storm events during your days with the Weather Channel. And, certainly, your personal connections to Seattle make you familiar with rainfall. However, what do you make of this?"

Warren nodded as she completed the news anchor segue, handing off the broadcast to the seasoned meteorologist. "Cher, without a doubt, Southern Californians have been surprised by the consistent rainfall that has beset the Central Valley all the way to the City of Angels. While it is highly unusual in its persistence, the amount of rain is hardly unprecedented."

"What do you mean by that?" she asked.

Warren moved slightly to his right to stand in

front of a large television monitor. "Let me direct our viewers' attention to this graphic provided by NOAA. Then I'll put it into context."

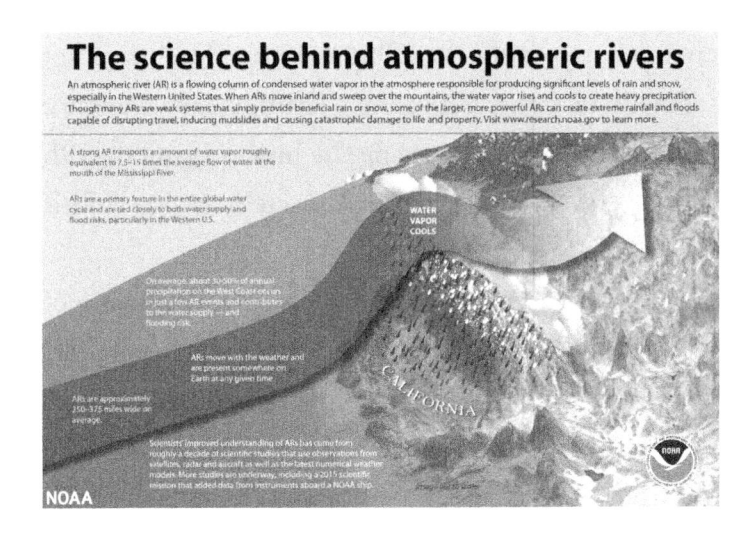

The science behind atmospheric rivers

An atmospheric river (AR) is a flowing column of condensed water vapor in the atmosphere responsible for producing significant levels of rain and snow, especially in the Western United States. When ARs move inland and sweep over the mountains, the water vapor rises and cools to create heavy precipitation. Though many ARs are weak systems that simply provide beneficial rain or snow, some of the larger, more powerful ARs can create extreme rainfall and floods capable of disrupting travel, inducing mudslides and causing catastrophic damage to life and property. Visit www.research.noaa.gov to learn more.

NOAA

Warren stood to the side of the screen and gestured as he spoke. "What we have experienced in recent days is a series of atmospheric rivers. It would be easy for me to use a lot of scientific terms to explain this weather phenomenon. However, I want our viewers to gain an understanding of this recent rain event. As I'll explain, what we've experienced thus far is not all that different from the rain events occurring nearly every year at this time."

He paused to study the graphic on the massive ten-foot-by-ten-foot monitor. He explained, "Atmospheric rivers are long, narrow regions of the atmosphere that transport condensed water vapor from tropical and subtropical areas to our west. This wide swath of water vapor, ranging from two hundred fifty to nearly four hundred miles wide, follows normal upper-level weather patterns across the Pacific to the nation's West Coast.

"When the water vapor in the form of an atmospheric river makes landfall in California, it cools and is released in the form of rain or snow."

Calvin interrupted Warren. "Was an atmospheric river responsible for the unexpected snowfall in the San Gabriel Mountains?"

Warren nodded. "As we've reported, San Francisco and the Central Valley have been in the midst of a two-decades-long megadrought. It's increased the risk of wildfires and definitely contributed to the severity of the Station Fire II last fall.

"Cher, this is a direct result of the rise in global temperatures. As December arrived, our winter was poised to be wetter and colder than years past. Everything is getting more extreme. It's wetter and drier, hotter and colder. Until a week ago, we'd experienced three out of the four in SoCal. Now, with unusually cold temps, we were hit with a massive snowfall."

"When will it end, and what can we expect in the coming days or weeks?" she asked.

"Well, these atmospheric rivers, commonly referred to as the Pineapple Express because of where they are formed and how quickly they can come ashore, vary in size and shape. Frankly, what we've experienced this month is not that unusual other than the fact the temperatures were lower, resulting in the snowfall. Each time an atmospheric river makes its way to California, its impact is dependent on many factors, ranging from temperature to wind speeds. It makes the rainfall event extremely difficult to predict."

"How bad can it get?" asked Calvin.

Warren ran his fingers through his hair. "Climatologists and meteorologists have warned about the potential of an ARkStorm."

"Wait," interrupted Calvin. "Ark, as in Noah's ark?"

Warren managed a smile because it was a common misnomer when discussing the unusual weather event. "No, not exactly, although the ARkStorm scenario, as it's been referred to, would certainly be biblical in nature. A double entendre, if you will. In the term ARkStorm, the letters *a* and *r* stand for atmospheric river. The letter *k* refers to one thousand, as in once-in-a-thousand-years storm.

"To put this in perspective, consider the rainfall we've experienced in the last week. Now, that pales in comparison to an ARkStorm. An ARkStorm would dump water the equivalent of twenty to twenty-five times the volume of the Mississippi River. Imagine this. The Mississippi River runs from Minnesota to the Gulf of Mexico. The entire water volume, times twenty, could be dropped on California's Central Valley."

"My gracious," said Calvin. "But of course, to ease our viewers' shock, this is all hypothetical."

Warren grimaced. "Well, sort of. It's happened before."

"In California?" she asked as her eyes grew wide.

"Yes, actually," he replied. "In the winter of 1862, from December into January, more than ten feet of rain was dumped onto California over a period of six weeks. Immense amounts of snowfall, not dissimilar to what we've seen of late, built up a massive snowpack. Toward the end of the six weeks, the weather pattern warmed somewhat, but the rains kept coming. The snowpack quickly melted.

"The combination of heavy rains and melting snow caused an area of the Central Valley to be under thirty feet of water from Sacramento to LA, and in between the mountain ranges. The water remained for nearly a year, creating a massive lake."

Calvin was overcome with the possibilities. "Do you mean Los Angeles could flood?"

Warren nodded and furrowed his brow. "The term flooding denotes an amount of water that can be controlled by our system of channels and storm drains. The ARkStorm scenario envisions something of a much greater magnitude. LA would be underwater, with the likelihood that the waters rushing through the Central Valley would merge with the Pacific. The resulting lake would split the state in half."

Warren paused and walked closer to the news anchors, whose faces reflected their fears. He added, "For many, many years, Californians have referred to the *Big One*, a catastrophic earthquake likely along the San Andreas fault. Climatologists refer to an ARkStorm as the *Other Big One*. Its geological impact could be the same as, if not worse than, a major quake along our many fault lines."

Sammy muted the television and, after a second, turned it off. Tyler closed his laptop and tossed it on the bed beside him.

"Kinda puts it all in perspective, doesn't it?" he asked.

Sammy had no words. She thought about the life they'd built in the foothills of the San Gabriel Mountains just north of LA. It was hard for her to imagine it washing away into the Pacific. Yet it could happen.

She grasped Ty's hand and laid her head on his chest. For several minutes, they held each other in silence until they fell asleep.

SIX

Wednesday
Hendrick Residence
La Cañada, California

Tyler was out the door early that morning. Sammy tossed and turned, waking him up frequently until, finally, he found himself staring at the ceiling, listening to the raindrops pelting their roof.

Until they weren't.

He slipped out of bed and slowly opened the curtains to peer outside. Although it was before dawn, the ambient light of their neighbors' might wake up his wife. He studied the flooded street, which had held an inch or more of rainwater for about a week. An occasional drop caused a corresponding ripple, but the deluge they'd experienced had ceased.

It was gonna be a good day. His first stop would be the Rose Bowl to check in with the grounds personnel. Then off to USC, where he would attend the morning team meeting.

"Is it Christmas Eve?" Sammy's sleepy, muffled voice quizzed him in the dark. Ty had to think about it for a moment. All of his days seemed to run together now as the team prepared for the big game. There were no days off. Well, except for Christmas. After the bowl championship series, he'd have more than a month of free time to spend with Sammy before early weight training sessions prior to spring practice.

"Tomorrow," he whispered as he bent over to kiss her on the cheek. "Today, it looks like you might have a break in the rain. No promises on sunshine, but maybe."

"Good. That weather guy gave me nightmares. Love you." She feigned a smooch and rolled over to catch a few more winks.

Tyler hadn't gone for a run in almost ten days. The pause in the consistent rainfall tempted him. He donned his Patagonia, lightweight rain gear just in case he got caught in a shower. He quietly slipped out of the house without waking their young guests. He regretted not being able to spend more time with them. After setting his Apple watch to outdoor run, he took off at an energetic pace.

For Tyler, running was a way to either start the day to gather his thoughts or to end his day to unwind. It was therapeutic and not necessarily about exercise. He'd always suspected the couple's jogs together were about exercise for Sammy. She never complained and always joined him. Yet he got the sense she'd consider other, less strenuous means of working out except for his love of fishing. That was his alone time. Tyler was a deep thinker, and in order to think, fishing was the perfect outlet. It was just him, his rod and reel, and the elusive underwater creatures, which were both confounding and rewarding to the angler.

When it came to running, he'd learned early on that she didn't need encouragement. He recalled one occasion when they had been training for a half-marathon. "You've got this, babe," he'd said encouragingly as they approached the ten-mile mark. "I know I've got this!" she'd hollered back.

He'd sensed a tone. Later, she insisted there was no tone. However, he knew there was a tone. He never did it again. Aloud, anyway. He preferred the subliminal messaging approach. It usually worked.

He only ran a few miles that morning, preferring to stretch his legs rather than head into nearby Flintridge. Technically, their home was located in La Cañada, a community located adjacent to Flintridge. In the 1970s, California had experienced a rate of suburban sprawl during which cities like LA spread outward and small communities like La Cañada merged with others nearby.

La Cañada, which translated as *the canyon* in Spanish, had officially incorporated with Flintridge in 1976. Over time, the hyphenated reference to La Cañada-Flintridge had been abandoned, as it became too wordy.

The climate there was typical of Southern California, with mild winters and hot summers. Unlike Central Florida, where they'd lived through summers of daily afternoon waterings, as they called it, rainfall in SoCal came predominantly during the winter months.

The couple's home was located in the North Arroyo neighborhood adjoining La Cañada, overlooking the Brookside Golf Course. Their views extended through the valley to the south where the Rose Bowl was located and to the north where the

Devil's Gate Dam created a reservoir for floodwaters out of the San Gabriel mountains.

Because of its beauty and proximity to LA, the La Cañada community, sprawling through the Crescenta Valley, was densely populated with twenty thousand people in just eight square miles squeezed in between the mountains. It offered the couple everything they wanted in a place to live as well as being conveniently located near their jobs. The population of Los Angeles County was ten million, making commuting to anywhere an annoyance, to put it mildly.

Not that traffic would be a problem for Tyler on New Year's Day, the day of the game. The Rose Bowl was only two and a half miles from their home in Pasadena. The USC campus was on the other side of downtown LA, an absolute pain in the ass of a commute.

By the time he reached Harbor Freeway, a hint of sunshine was peeking through the gray skies, and Tyler was in good spirits. He texted Sammy a couple of emojis, including a sunshine and a yellow face blowing a kiss.

SEVEN

Wednesday
NOAA
Regional Offices
Sacramento

The sunshine peeking through the overcast skies was all the trio of climatologists needed to get the governor's office and Brown from the NWS off their backs for a few days. As requested, they'd created a forecast model that painted a rosy picture for their much-ballyhooed Rose Bowl game on New Year's Day. Once delivered, they'd shut their offices down until after the new year.

"Okay, guys, today we appear to have a break in the waves of water vapor coming onshore," began LaMarre as she passed out the Starbucks soy lattes they'd ordered.

An ordinary atmospheric river experienced by the West Coast transports water vapor equivalent to the volume of water flowing into the Gulf of Mexico from the Mississippi River. Every winter, meteorologists struggle with predicting their impact on California's weather, making forecasting difficult. While at Cal Berkeley, Entremont had written his graduate thesis on atmospheric rivers and their impact on the global water supply. He'd placed a particular emphasis on climate change and how it might cause the atmospheric rivers to intensify.

Entremont would take the lead on the project because he'd created the forecasting program. LaMarre and Stoppkotte would gather data at his direction. As Entremont worked through his program, he gave his associates a primer on the work performed by the United States Geological Survey, or USGS.

"Most of the public view the USGS as being involved with earthquake and volcanic activity. Fifteen years ago, they assembled a team of scientists to design a large, hypothetical storm similar to the one that hit California in the winter of 1861 into 1862. With the scientific precedent being set, they envisioned a similar wind and precipitation event in modern times. The idea was to provide a worst-case scenario for emergency responders and government planners to use to prepare for this potential catastrophic event. Just as importantly, they wanted the public to know that this ARkStorm scenario, as it became known, was scientifically and historically plausible."

LaMarre stood over Entremont's shoulder as he began to insert information into the blank data fields. "How does your forecasting model differ from what they produced?"

He continued to bang away on the keyboard as he spoke. "Well, for one, they underestimated the impact of climate change on their findings. Consider this. When the USGS team created the ARkStorm scenario, they were working off global climate data from over twenty years ago.

"Earth has gotten hotter with heat-trapping gases. By low estimates, global temps have risen six-tenths of a degree since '06. As a result, sea levels have risen three inches, and extreme weather patterns in the U.S. alone have increased by thirty percent."

LaMarre wandered away from Entremont's workstation and studied a large relief map of the planet that hung on a windowless wall. "At NOAA, we produced a study for Congress that proved climate extremes—through an index of hot and cold, wet and dry—had jumped thirty percent in the last twenty years. And that excluded the number of hurricanes in those averages."

"I remember," said Stoppkotte. "All they wanted to do was focus on the economic impact because that's what politicians do. Control the money."

"Right," LaMarre agreed. "Does it really matter if a Category 4 or 5 hurricane makes landfall or not? It formed as a result of climate change. Luckily, it didn't destroy homes and lives."

"They always wanna focus on what's newsworthy," Stoppkotte added. "Heck, in Greenland and Antarctica, ice sheets have lost over five trillion tons of ice. Report that."

Entremont nodded as he continued, "Other factors have to be considered. The planet's population has grown substantially, nearly two billion people since '05. That means more carbon pollution and more people vulnerable to climate change.

"It's unsustainable. The numbers don't lie. Greenhouse gases are rising steadily, and the cause is fossil fuel burning and other human activities. I mean, simply put, we're rapidly reshaping our planet without regard to the consequences that we're beginning to suffer. Something has to give."

The three stayed silent for a moment as they contemplated their warnings. LaMarre knew they were preaching to the choir, so to speak. So many scientists like herself were frustrated by the lack of care and concern of ordinary Americans who appeared to live in the moment rather than take into consideration the impact their lifestyles would have on their children or their grandchildren.

Entremont leaned back in his chair, which drew LaMarre's attention back to the task at hand. "Okay, I've already plugged in the demographic data as part of the program's assumptions. You know, things like population concentrations by county. For example, if an ARkStorm came ashore in the center of the state, Sacramento and Contra Costa counties would bear the brunt of the storm. Merced County, north of Fresno in the San Joaquin Valley, would be affected the least."

LaMarre pulled up a chair next to Entremont. She pointed at the monitor. "I assume that this could be modified to come closer to Los Angeles and Orange counties?"

"Well, yes, although it wouldn't be likely," replied Entremont. "Weather patterns, temperatures, and upper-level winds play a factor, preventing a southern trajectory."

"It is possible, though?" she asked.

He nodded and began typing on the keyboard again. The modeling map changed in appearance as it depicted a large wavelike graphic taking a serpentine shape across California's coastline.

"Landfall here near the point at Lompoc all the way up to San Luis Obispo would be devastating for SoCal. Points as far south as Orange County would experience forty inches of rainfall. Winds along the coastal areas would reach hurricane force, especially along the mountain ranges. In lower-lying areas, winds would hit fifty to sixty."

"Okay. Let's work with your default assumptions on impact areas. What do you need from us next?"

Entremont chuckled. "This is gonna be tricky and will require Stoppkotte's other skills."

"Huh?" the nerdy scientist asked.

"You're going to hack into the *Hi'ialakai*," he replied with a smile.

"The old research vessel?" asked a confused LaMarre. "It was decommissioned back in 2020.

Remember? It was replaced by the *Oscar Elton Sette*."

"Renamed and reflagged, not decommissioned," said Entremont. "It's CIA now."

"Sweet Jesus," said LaMarre.

EIGHT

Wednesday
Hendrick Residence
La Cañada, California

"Rise and shine, ladies! We have important business to attend to." Sammy was moving cheerfully through their Spanish hacienda-style home, enjoying the freedom the days away from the office had afforded her. She loved her job. The stress associated with it, not so much. Participation in a typical merger or acquisition was somewhat akin to babysitting adults. Or acting as the referee in a mixed martial arts fight. The participants often lost control. Sammy would find herself calming people down and soothing bruise egos. The legal aspect of the negotiations was the easy part.

"Is it still raining?" asked a sleepy-eyed Sophie as she emerged from the guest bedroom. Sammy had decorated the space by being true to the Mexican architecture. Light-colored walls were adorned with artwork found at the many antique stores in the area. She combined neutral walls with warm furnishings oftentimes handmade by local craftsmen.

"That, young lady, is the good news," replied Sammy as she gave her oldest niece a hug. "We've caught a break. It looks like we might even get a little sunshine today."

"Yes!" exclaimed a much-too-chipper Livvy. It was still too early to turn somersaults and cartwheels despite Sammy's lighthearted mood.

"I have a big day planned for us," said Sammy as Livvy joined the morning group hug. "First, I'm gonna make you guys one of my specialty breakfast bowls."

"Cereal?" asked Sophie.

"No. This is a different kind of bowl. It's very California. Egg whites, avocado, and brown rice."

"Ewww."

Livvy echoed her sister's sentiment. "Yucky!"

Sammy frowned and then let out a laugh. She

recalled having the same reaction when she first moved to California. Just as she'd embraced the California way of living, she'd adopted the healthy cuisine most of her health-conscious neighbors enjoyed.

"Okay, I'll make you a deal. If you promise to try it, then I'll buy you lunch at In-N-Out Burger. It's everybody's favorite."

"We love burgers!" said Sophie enthusiastically.

Sammy tickled her, causing both girls to roar with laughter. "But you have to promise to eat a healthy breakfast. You need to be ready for some big-time shopping."

"For presents?" asked Livvy.

"That's right. We'll pick out something for your parents, and wouldn't you like to find something for Tyler?"

"Yes," said Sophie. "May we buy you a present, too?"

"Of course."

"Sammy, can we borrow some money to go shopping?"

Sammy let out a hearty laugh. She leaned down next to the girls and replied, "Absolutely, it's the American way. Now, get dressed and meet me in the kitchen. I want to teach you how to cook."

The girls bolted for the guest room, hitting the arched door opening at nearly the same time, causing a traffic jam.

Sammy took a deep breath. She'd found ways to entertain the girls for the initial part of their stay by playing games and watching television. Now she'd be venturing out into the wild with them in tow. She chuckled as she talked to herself.

"You're going to the mall two days before Christmas with two six-year-old girls. You must be certifiably cray-cray."

Breakfast went smoother than expected, with both girls pretending to like the dish that was wholly foreign to their regular diet, which probably consisted of sugary cereals and frozen Jimmy Dean sandwiches. Not that it mattered at this stage in their lives. Their energetic bodies most likely burned off more calories than they consumed.

The skies were gray as they entered the shopping complex at Eagle Rock Plaza. It was in a busy section of LA where the Glendale and Ventura Freeways intersected. Either the break in the weather or the close proximity of Christmas brought out masses of Angelenos.

Having lived her entire life on the East Coast, Sammy's visualization of LA included palm-tree-lined streets, beaches, endless bungalow-style homes and Hollywood. Well, also the smog, but once she'd committed to moving to the area, the smog magically dissipated from her vision.

After officially declaring herself to be an Angeleno, the dominant visual experience was the freeway. At nearly five hundred square miles, the City of Los Angeles was a global metropolis that could swallow several major U.S. cities within its borders. The millions of inhabitants had to get from point A to point B. Cars, trucks and buses scurrying about in all directions needed freeways, and LA boasted some of the most famous in the world.

The 405 was also known as San Diego Freeway. I-10, which ran from LA to Jacksonville, Florida, was commonly known as the Santa Monica Freeway in the city. Then there was the aforementioned Glendale and Venture Freeways as well as the Hollywood Freeway. However, the most famous was Interstate 5, which ran north and south along the coast. The Golden State Freeway, as it was called, stretched fourteen hundred miles.

Sammy hated the interstate system. All of them. People drove like bat-out-of-hell maniacs in LA. There was nothing chill about their driving habits. This was one of the reasons she and Ty had chosen

La Cañada to purchase a home. It was close to her office, making her commute short and allowing her to avoid the freeways. Today was a rare exception. Shopping on short notice required a visit to the mall.

The shoppers had a great time. For the most part, the girls behaved, although they had a tendency to run off when something of great interest caught their eye. Sammy carried the shopping bags, allowing her nieces to have free rein to enjoy their shopping experience. However, she had to admonish them repeatedly to stay close and not wander too far.

By the time their shopping day was done, they'd spent more than planned, but the gifts the girls had picked out for their family, each other, and themselves were thoughtful. By the time they exited Eagle Rock Plaza, the sun was peeking through the clouds, a rare sight in the last several weeks.

Sammy had an idea. "Girls, what would you think about a picnic in the backyard?"

"What about In-N-Out burgers?" asked Sophie, who had a memory like an elephant and a similarly voracious appetite.

"We can still do burgers, fries and anything you want from there. I was thinking, since the sun is starting to come out, let's eat in the backyard and get some fresh air."

"You've got a deal!" agreed the adorable Livvy. Sammy smiled at the just-turned-six-year-old with blonde hair and hazel eyes. She was gonna be a man slayer when she grew up.

After a lengthy wait in the drive-thru at In-N-Out, which was anything but, they made their way back to La Cañada without a hitch. The sun cooperated and actually cast its healthy rays for more than an hour that afternoon.

With lunch out of the way, the girls ran around the fenced backyard with Carly and Fenway. The four players rustled and tussled and tumbled around in the rain-soaked grass, covering themselves with mud towards the end. Sammy let them enjoy themselves, already considering hosing them down outside before allowing any of them to enter her well-kept home.

Then things went horribly wrong, at least from Sammy's perspective.

She'd climbed into the hammock and allowed the sunshine to soak into her face, arms, and toned legs earned from years of swimming. She was gently rocking, and despite the mayhem generated by the girls and the pups, she found herself drifting off to sleep. That was when the attack began.

In her half-sleepy state of mind, she thought

she had an itch on her upper thigh. Then, inexplicably, the itch began to move. Slowly at first. Like a crawl.

Sammy's heart raced, and her eyes popped wide open. The itch was on the move and had invaded her shorts. She rolled out of the hammock and landed in the wet grass. She immediately jumped to her feet, swirling around and swatting at the front of her shorts. It was more than an itch. It was a cold, wet interloper of some kind.

The girls had stopped playing as they looked on with genuine concern. Sammy was so shocked, neither screams nor words came out of her mouth.

Frantically, she struggled to unbutton her shorts and pull them over her hips. Thinking the creepy critter that had crawled into them was gone, she stood still for a moment, looking downward. Then she saw it.

The lizard had attached itself to her panties. She swirled around again, a near-perfect pirouette that almost landed her butt in the mud. The lizard held on to the fabric with its sharp, curved claws.

Sammy, usually the cool-headed, unflappable attorney, was panic-struck. Without thinking of her circumstances, she pulled down her panties and raced into the house, naked from the waist down.

Her trauma was over, although it was just the beginning of the embarrassment.

Carly grinned. Fenway barked. And the six-year-olds taunted her. Endlessly.

"I see Sammy's fanny!"

"She's nekkid!"

"Wait 'til I tell Tyler!"

She'd never live it down.

NINE

Wednesday
NOAA
Regional Offices
Sacramento

"Come on, Tomas," Entremont appealed to his former college roommate, who hacked into U.S. government computers just for sport when not studying. He used to boast about how easy it was, and he was right. More recently, he'd helped his fellow climate activists annoy oil companies by hijacking their Zoom calls during the COVID pandemic.

"Listen, even though I have the skill set to do it,

I'm not hacking into CIA servers on a secret spy ship that isn't supposed to exist," he said defiantly. He'd crossed his arms in front of himself to wall off his persistent friend.

"Okay, hear me out," Entremont continued. "The *Hi'ialakai* was decommissioned, right? Replaced by the *Oscar*." The NOAA ship *Oscar Elton Sette* had originally been built for the U.S. Navy. The two-hundred-twenty-four-foot ship conducted research by surveying fisheries, marine mammals, coral reefs, and marine debris like the debris floating across the Pacific following the tsunami that had struck Japan many years ago.

"We've established that," said LaMarre. "How do you know *Hi'ialakai* was turned into a spy ship for the CIA?"

"I have a friend," he replied with a subtle smile. "Okay, listen. Once it was decommissioned and mothballed for a year or so, it was sailed out of the Pacific Islands Fisheries Science Center in Honolulu for Guam. There, it was retrofitted to suit the CIA's purposes, including keeping an eye on the Chinese and protecting our shores from their so-called weather balloons full of surveillance equipment.

"However, the *Hi'ialakai* needed a cover story. Something that Washington could claim as research related just like those stupid weather balloons spying on us."

"Let me guess," LaMarre interrupted. "It still appears to be a functioning research vessel with some special gadgets added on."

"Well, yes and no. Sure, we spy on their spies. We also have the capability of shooting down their phony weather balloons. However, to advance the ruse, it's still capable of conducting oceanic and weather-related research."

"Remotely?" asked LaMarre.

"Yes."

"What's the point?" asked Stoppkotte. "Gregory, why don't we just contact NOAA – Miami to request access to their data."

"Because we're making this shit up, that's why," he quickly replied. "I'm trying to save our jobs here. You know, in case this loose cannon of a governor decides to shift the blame for a rainy-as-hell bowl game on us. Our modeling forecast needs to be plausible. For that, we need real-time data. If we produce a result that differs from what NOAA's numbers suggest, we will absolutely get fired."

LaMarre sighed. "He's got a point."

"Okay, let's say I can do it," said Stoppkotte, who was warming to the idea. He was studying side-by-side photographs of the two vessels. They were virtually identical. "How do we know the computer equipment is still on board and capable of being accessed?"

"Get to hackin'," said Entremont with a laugh. He placed a lot of confidence in the capabilities of Stoppkotte. "Once you're in, let me know. Meanwhile, Bekki and I will plug in the data that's public knowledge."

"What am I looking for, specifically?" asked Stoppkotte. "And where?"

"These storms, like most severe precipitation events that impact California, form over the mid-latitudes in the north Pacific. Look north of the Hawaiian Islands for areas of high levels of vertically integrated water-vapor currents. It's similar to what modelers do when assessing the formation of a tropical cyclone. Only, an intense low-pressure system is not required. It's all about water vapor.

"We'll take your observations of the atmospheric conditions, plug them into my modeling program, and allow the laws of fluid dynamics and thermodynamics to fill in the gaps between what is currently known and what is on its way."

LaMarre smiled and patted her subordinate on the back. "I get it now. We know these atmospheric rivers come in waves. Once they form up, eyes on the ground, and in space, can make their own analysis. However, if I understand you correctly, your program can take the earliest available data and extrapolate it into a forecast."

Entremont cracked his knuckles before leaning over the keyboard. "That's correct, and importantly for the task at hand, the computer model we generate will provide a pretty accurate timeline of when the next AR will make landfall."

The trio got to work. Each time Stoppkotte breached another layer of security of the *Hi'ialakai*'s computer servers, he let out a cheer as if he were rooting for himself at a craps table in a Las Vegas casino. The deeper he went, the louder the cheer, much to the chagrin of his cohorts.

LaMarre and Entremont did their best to ignore him. They went as far as they could with information discerned from a variety of sources within readily accessible programs.

"That's as far as we can go at this point, Bekki," he explained. "I've inserted the known parameters of temperature, pressure, moisture content, and windspeed. The display reveals the calculations at twenty-four increments from tomorrow for a period of seven days."

"Christmas Eve through New Year's Eve," she mumbled.

"Yes. A seven-day forecast is the best most modelers can provide. Meteorologists can basically do the same thing I can, albeit less accurately. Then they pass the information around to the media for regurgitation on the nightly news."

"Why is it less accurate?" she asked.

"Well, laziness, for one. Accuracy has been sacrificed for speed of results. They want answers immediately so they can be the first to break the news to their viewers or online subscribers. What I do is include all the parameters and shorter time steps. The program, which I've never shared with anyone, can better depict the intensity of the storm, especially in terms of timing, rainfall amounts, and wind speed."

LaMarre was impressed. She adjusted her chair and pointed toward the four monitors stacked into a square. "While we wait on Tomas, can you tell me how this next AR compares to what California has gone through in the last two weeks?"

"From the data we have so far, it'll be the strongest one this cycle. I imagine that by tomorrow as the rains pick up in earnest, the forecast will reflect a significant atmospheric river coming ashore that'll remain steady for several days before it begins to dissipate."

Stoppkotte clapped his hands once, startling the other two climatologists. "Guys, I'm in!" Then his demeanor changed to reflect his solemnity. "I hope that what I'm looking at is wrong."

TEN

**Wednesday
NOAA
Regional Offices
Sacramento**

"Talk to me," Entremont implored his friend. He and LaMarre rushed to Stoppkotte's side.

"Okay, first of all. Yes, I'm in, and yes, everything is fully operational. What I've found may be an anomaly, so Gregory may correct me. However, it appears that another atmospheric river, other than the one you just forecasted, is coming hot on its heels."

"May I trade places with you?" asked

Entremont. Without replying, Stoppkotte stood and moved to the side.

Entremont slowly made several entries as he navigated through the NOAA-designed computer, careful not to raise awareness of their unauthorized presence. He turned slightly to make eye contact with LaMarre, who fidgeted as she waited for an explanation. He pointed at the monitor as he spoke.

"Look at this macro-scale hydrology model," he began before pausing to make several more keystrokes. "Actually, this variable infiltration capacity model will add context. But first, back to the hydrology." He stopped and ran his fingers along the monitor as he spoke.

"Tomas was correct in his observations. Check out this marine hydrology level. All of this moisture is rising straight into the atmosphere to form the basis of the next atmospheric river. It's the volume that is striking. Unless the monitoring equipment is faulty, what's forming is a hundred times the amount of water vapor that you and I just forecasted."

"A hundred times?" LaMarre asked.

"Almost. Hang on a moment while I check something," he replied. Now, as adrenaline fueled his desire to confirm his hypothesis, Entremont typed furiously on the keyboard. Then he suddenly spun around and rushed to his workstation to study a graphic.

"What is it?" she asked.

"I wanted to cross-check the hydrology numbers from the three AR events that swept over California since the end of November with the data recorded by the *Hi'ialakai*. They're identical."

"Holy crap!" exclaimed Stoppkotte. "That means …" His voice trailed off as Entremont finished his sentence.

"These numbers are accurate. Let me check the other available parameters, although some of them won't be available until the atmospheric river fully forms in the next twenty-four to forty-eight hours." He grew quiet and furrowed his brow. He was hunched over the keyboard, alternating his attention between the entries he was typing and the corresponding results coming from the *Hi'ialakai*.

As he worked, he took screenshots of the results. The Canon printer began spitting out page after page, hitting the floor due to the sheer volume of data Entremont was requesting. Finally, after the furious interaction between man and artificial intelligence, he stood and motioned for Stoppkotte to return to his seat.

"I'm done, and frankly, anything else I need will

develop over the next several hours. My modeling program doesn't require actual formation of the atmospheric river. Once I have the formation data, the other parameters can be extrapolated from historical information and assumptions."

LaMarre had remained stoic during the flurry of activity, moving only to retrieve the many documents Entremont had generated during his work. She stacked them neatly and set them on his desk near the keyboard. Then she waited as Entremont walked through their office, running his fingers through his hair. His stress was apparent.

"Gregory, please tell me what's on your mind. Do you need to plug in the data first? Do we need to wait until—"

He cut her off. The tone of his voice was low and ominous. "Bekki, this is serious. I can wait for more data, but I'm certain based on what we've uncovered."

"Certain about what?" she asked.

"This is an ARkStorm in the making. The Other Big One. The big Kahuna. The amount of water vapor this system is flushing into the atmosphere is like nothing I've ever seen. When the USGS generated their ARkStorm scenario, they based it upon the back-to-back atmospheric rivers that occurred in 1969 and 1986. I mean, sure, they were actual, intense AR events that would be devastating if they took place consecutively.

"However, what's forming off the northern coast of Hawaii is as strong as both of those modeling samples combined, times fifty. This AR is at least as strong as what scientists know about the ARkStorm of 1861 and 1862."

LaMarre held her hands in front of her with her palms facing downward in an attempt to tamp down the tension in the room. She took a deep breath herself and exhaled. She glanced around the large, open space, which was devoid of staff. Everyone at the NOAA offices had been given time off for the holidays. The trio would've been enjoying themselves as well had it not been for the governor's demands of the National Weather Service, which trickled down to them. To ensure their privacy, she locked the door to their offices.

"Bekki, what's wrong?" asked Entremont.

Instead of answering, she motioned for them to join her in the comfortable seating in the small reception area. It was rarely used except for employees who gathered there in the morning to trade stories about their off-duty activities.

"Gregory, based on what you know, what does this ARkStorm look like when it makes landfall?"

Entremont took a deep breath as he answered, "It will cut a wide path as it reaches shore. Easily a hundred miles wide, much like a large hurricane. However, unlike a hurricane in which the eye is clearly defined and distributes the worst of the storm, this entire ARkStorm will have the destructive force of a hurricane.

"If, and it's likely based upon its proximity to the upcoming atmospheric river that's coming into the state beginning tomorrow, the ARkStorm stalls, the results will beyond comprehension. The amount of rainfall could be measured in feet, not inches. Further, if the temperatures remain seasonably warm, the collision of the subtropical precipitation meeting the snowpacks in the mountains will generate flooding of biblical proportions."

"A thousand-year flood event?" asked Stoppkotte.

"Absolutely," he replied.

"California's system of earthen levees, concrete dams and flood-control alluviums would never handle it," added Stoppkotte.

Entremont continued, "Listen, the historical record from the 1860s is considered accurate. The

Central Valley flooded, creating a lake that remained in place for a year, permanently in some places. Today would be far different."

"Why?" asked LaMarre.

"Mudslides, erosion and debris accumulation," he replied before going into more detail. "Consider this. From late summer into November, California experienced severe drought conditions. Grasses and plant material from last year's fires did not regenerate in the spring like normal. The Station Fire II destroyed what underbrush there was and took acres upon acres of trees with it. It's as barren as we've ever seen it, and all three of us were born in Cali."

"The mudslides are already occurring in parts of the state," added Stoppkotte. "The kind of rain event you're describing will reshape mountains."

"Yes. These landslides will carry fallen trees down the mountains and ridges into the reservoirs. The dams, both earthen and concrete, will be overwhelmed. All the homes built below them will be swept up in a roaring river of debris until it arrives at a choke point. Then a new dam will be constructed, containing all of this debris."

"Just like in the 1860s," Stoppkotte surmised.

"Only more permanent," added Entremont. "The Central Valley will become so flooded a permanent lake could form. It would be an environmental disaster like no other. And it goes without saying, the economic losses would be in the trillions, and the loss of life would be in the millions."

His words hung in the air as the trio contemplated the gravity of the situation. LaMarre's mind had been racing since Entremont first relayed the likely magnitude of the ARkStorm. She'd heard enough. She gathered her nerve to make a proposal that would shock the guys to their core.

ELEVEN

Wednesday
NOAA
Regional Offices
Sacramento

LaMarre closed her eyes. The look of consternation on her face was obvious. After letting out a long sigh, she studied her subordinates, who were also her dearest friends. She hesitated, knowing that what she was going to propose might destroy the close bond they'd developed at Cal Berkeley.

"Please bear with me as I progress to my point," she began. The guys sensed her angst, so they simply nodded their heads in agreement. "Gregory, can you create a forecasting model, as they've requested, based on what's readily known to others in the meteorological community?"

He remained calm. "Sure, but it won't be accurate. You know, based on what we've discovered."

"Understood. Now, when will the severity of this ARkStorm be discovered by others?"

"Probably, um, midweek. Next Wednesday, maybe Thursday, I'd say."

"If the weather forecasters start throwing around terms like ARkStorm and thousand-year floods, what do you expect the reaction to be? You know, in the general public?"

Entremont thought for a moment and shrugged. "With the attitude of many Americans toward the sensationalistic media, they'll shrug it off."

"Like Chicken Little saying the sky is falling," added Stoppkotte with a hint of snark.

Then Entremont added, "In the media, as we all know, the saying goes like this: if it bleeds, it leads. Heavy rains may be something the weatherman discusses, or maybe the anchors if it's a slow news day. When people start to die, it gets more attention."

"Attention," LaMarre muttered. "That's the key. These people don't listen. They ignore all the evidence. It doesn't affect them directly, so it's ignored."

"Whadya mean?" asked Stoppkotte.

"Climate change and how it's destroying our planet. The only planet we'll ever have. The politicians use it as a fund-raising tool or to gain more power over the budget. Large corporations knock each other over to prove they're more *green*. Activists chain themselves to oil wells, lie down on interstates, or even hang from bridges like they did in Houston. And look what that got 'em. They think they're fighting the good fight, but the public either ridicules the annoyances they create or mock them for their perceived foolishness.

"The only thing that gets the public's attention is death and destruction. If somebody blew up an oil rig in the Gulf, causing an environmental disaster, that would be in the news for weeks. Remember Deepwater Horizon? Shoot up several electricity substations, causing a widespread blackout, and the cameras would be rolling as cities burn at night from societal unrest.

"Now, I want you to imagine the death and destruction this ARkStorm will cause. The destruction of property and infrastructure is inevitable. The economic loss measured in dollars will suit the politicians just fine. They'll be knocking each other over in a fight over how to spend the money to clean up and rebuild.

"However, what if millions died?" She let her words hang in the empty offices.

Entremont tilted his head. He was puzzled and unsure where LaMarre was headed with this. "Well, we have the ability to mitigate the loss of life with my forecasting model. I mean, we could save a lot of people's lives."

LaMarre tilted her head back and forth like a pendulum. "Maybe. Sure, we'd be heroes. What would we get for it? A raise? No. Pat on the back? Maybe. Congressional Medal of Honor? Nah."

Entremont had to know. "Bekki, what are you thinking? We have to ring the clarion bell, right?"

She furrowed her brow and shook her head from side to side. "No, actually, we don't. This is not an officially mandated project. We're really just doing a favor for the NWS and the governor."

"People's lives will be at stake," countered Entremont.

"A few sacrifices for the greater good," interjected Stoppkotte unemotionally. He made eye contact with LaMarre. He understood. She allowed a slight smile.

Entremont was incredulous. "What? Are you kidding me? Do you want to sit on this and let people die? They'll never be able to react in time, if at all."

"It's the only way to raise awareness of climate change so people will not only listen, but act," argued LaMarre.

"She's right, Gregory," said Stoppkotte. "For decades, going back to the days of Severn Suzuki to Greta Thunberg, environmental activists have tried to raise awareness. Think about it, since the first Earth Day in 1970, people like us have fought for people to recognize climate change as an existential threat to our planet. People responded by driving electric cars, but the damn government didn't build enough charging stations. As a result, we're backsliding to gas-guzzling SUVs."

"Gregory, you have to understand the magnitude of what I'm proposing," said LaMarre. "This will be the largest natural disaster in modern history. It will be covered by media around the globe. The blame for the ARkStorm will not be on us or anyone else in the scientific community. It will fall solely on the atmospheric changes that created it and the climate change that exacerbated those atmospheric changes. Our decision will be the catalyst the world needs to make tough decisions and real change."

Entremont wiped away a tear. He couldn't believe he'd been embroiled in this scheme. "So tell no one," he muttered as he stared at the polished linoleum floor.

"That's right," said LaMarre.

He was crying now. He looked toward the ceiling in an effort to draw the tears back into their respective ducts. "There will come a point in time when they figure out what's coming."

"Perhaps," said LaMarre. "However, if the developing ARkStorm is following the coming atmospheric river closely, will they be able to discern when one event ends and the Other Big One begins?"

Entremont shook his head from side to side. Without his forecasting model, they'd be blindsided.

LaMarre sat next to her friend and wrapped her arm around his slumping shoulders. He was defeated. She knew he'd go along with the scheme and not disclose their decision to anyone.

"Do you need some time to gather yourself? We need to produce a mundane forecast for the governor's office."

He wiped the last of his tears and nodded. "I can do it. It'll take an hour or so."

Entremont rose and returned to his workstation.

LaMarre whispered in Stoppkotte's ear, "Keep

an eye on him. I'll be right back, and then you can take off."

"I don't mind waiting."

"Nah, not necessary. You're headed back to New Jersey to visit family, am I right?"

"Yeah, flight leaves first thing in the morning. Ten days of my mom's cooking. Blissful, actually."

She laughed and slapped him on the back. "Just give me a minute while I give the NWS a heads-up that a report is coming. Then we'll get you started on your culinary bliss."

LaMarre left, and Stoppkotte took up a seat near Entremont, where he could study his computer activities. He wanted to trust his friend, but the opportunity the coming ARkStorm presented was bigger than their friendship or co-worker status.

It was bigger than all of them.

TWELVE

Thursday
Christmas Eve
Hendrick Residence
La Cañada, California

Sammy had done everything she could to maintain the couple's Christmas tradition despite the inclusion of their nieces, Tyler's extraordinary work schedule, and the constant rainfall. For many families, Christmas revolved around meals. It was the one time of year the couple allowed themselves to stray from the health-conscious diet and exercise program that most assuredly would afford them a long life together.

Christmas Day, their tradition was to eat out at their favorite Chinese restaurant. Since their arrival in California, they'd tried more than a dozen restaurants featuring Chinese cuisine that included bourbon chicken for Tyler and honey garlic chicken for Sammy. After a taste-testing tour of the area, they'd found the Eagle Rock Green Dragon in Glendale. Their excellent lo mein noodles and wonton soup earned them a five-star rating by the couple.

Selling the girls on Chinese food for Christmas dinner was not easy, so Sammy promised she'd have Tyler cook on the grill, not that he'd object. However, under the circumstances, she felt guilty for asking him.

Tyler was running on empty by the time he arrived home on Christmas Eve. It had been a stressful day at the John McKay Center, the 110,000-square-foot athletic facility built for the football program and named after the Trojans' famed head coach. The team had gathered for a recap meeting before being dismissed for the three-day holiday weekend. Many of the players and coaches would stay in LA, likely hanging out at the McKay Center, utilizing the weight room and studying game film of their opponent, Penn State.

In addition to the stress and anxiety associated

with preparing these stellar athletes for the Rose Bowl, the team's coaches and staff had been discussing the rumors swirling around campus.

Earlier in the day, the USC president had joined the chairman of the Pasadena Tournament of Roses Association at Tournament House, the building where the organization was headquartered. The heavy rain and the potential for it continuing was a concern. They told the media if the forecast didn't improve by Monday, the parade and the game would be postponed indefinitely. The parade might even be cancelled.

This announcement sent shock waves through the sports world and the corporate sponsors of the two big events—Honda and Prudential. Since its inception, the Rose Parade had only been cancelled four times, including three times during World War II. The fourth was during the height of the global pandemic of 2020. The game itself had been played continuously since 1916, hosting over ninety thousand faithful fans to cheer on their teams, except the New Year's Day game of 2021, which had been restricted to eighteen thousand fans due to California's pandemic restrictions. Even then the game hadn't been cancelled or postponed.

The decision would have an economic impact on

LA, resulting in millions of lost tourism dollars. Local officials quickly reacted by inundating the governor's office with demands to force Rose Parade and bowl officials to retract their statement. The governor, it appeared, was ready for them with rosy news.

"Ty! The governor's making a statement."

Tyler had pulled his gas grill under an awning shading their patio so he could use it despite the rain. He'd become the proverbial grill master, adeptly preparing to perfection a wide variety of meats, chicken and vegetables. Shrimp on the barbie? Not a problem. Chicken fajitas with sauteed onions and green peppers? Pshaw.

He quickly flipped the burgers and reduced the heat on the grill before hustling inside. The girls were playing a heated game of Sorry! that threatened to turn violent, as neither appeared to be good sports when it came to competitive board games. Sammy had just pulled a loaf of beer bread out of the oven, which would be thinly sliced for use as the adults' burger buns.

The reporter was standing just inside an airport hangar at the Sacramento airport in front of the governor's plane, a Cessna Citation Longitude. He was filling in airtime as they waited for the governor to make his remarks.

"The governor and his family will be taking a well-earned vacation through the holidays to Rancho Pescadero, the posh resort on the lower end of Baja California in Mexico. The ten-day trip will follow a quite successful first legislative session for Governor Pappas. The governor, who dropped out of the California Senate race after a U.S. congressional investigation, turned his sights on the governor's mansion and won easily. He immediately hit his stride and was able to pass most of his agenda in the past year.

"Meanwhile, the rainy weather that has bedeviled our state has forced a number of closings and cancellations. This morning, officials with the Rose Parade and, the granddaddy of them all, the Rose Bowl announced the potential cancellations, as well. The governor, despite his desire to get out of town for his vacation, wanted to address their concerns. Wait, he's approaching the podium. Let's listen."

The reporter stood out of the way as the cameraman zoomed in on Governor Pappas. His smile was an immediate indication he was prepared to reveal some good news.

Sammy pointed at the television. "Look, Ty. He's smiling."

Tyler shook his head. "He's always got that sh—"

She cut him off before he could describe the governor's grin. She grabbed his arm and whispered, "Watch your language around the girls."

As if on cue, Sophie shouted at her sister, "Kiss my ass, Livvy!"

"I'm tellin' Mom!" her sister threatened.

"You'll forget by then," Sophie countered as the game continued.

Tyler pointed and shrugged. He turned his attention to the governor.

"We've been through a period of unusual weather the past two weeks that simply reconfirms what we all know. Climate change is having a dramatic impact on our planet. Clearly, as most reasonable scientists would agree, the rise in global temperatures has caused storms to be more severe and last longer.

"Now, that said, we have been in constant contact with the National Weather Service in Sacramento. They have worked diligently with representatives of NOAA to generate a forecast that takes us through the New Year's weekend.

"The rain that began this morning is part of an atmospheric river not unlike the ones we've experienced in the last few weeks. Another one began to move onshore today, and it will continue to bring us inclement weather through the next five or six days. Then that glorious California sunshine will return just in time to ring in the new year."

A smattering of spontaneous applause could be heard, which struck Tyler as odd considering this was a press conference. Yet he too wanted to applaud.

"This is good news, right?" asked Sammy, who wrapped her arm through her husband's.

Tyler sighed and nodded. "Yeah. It is. We really need a clean field for the game. Malachi's legs will hold up better. Plus, his running ability gives opposing defenses fits."

The governor took a few questions about his vacation before his press aides cut off the back-and-forth. The news station pulled away from the hangar and returned immediately to the weather desk, where a graphic appeared. The atmospheric river that approached would be more of the same, she reported. Rain in the valleys and snow in the mountains. And, yes, they'd just received a bulletin from the NWS.

At least a partly sunny for New Year's Day was in the forecast.

THIRTEEN

Thursday
Christmas Eve
Home of Gregory Entremont
Sacramento

Entremont hadn't slept. He'd lain awake all night before sliding out of bed to sit at his computer. He generated the accurate forecast for the coming ARkStorm. It was as bad as he'd expected. After the model was completed, he copied it to a flash drive and deleted the original from his computer. Well, he obliterated it using a program called BleachBit, which essentially erased the information without possibility of recovering it. The entire process was very clandestine.

As daybreak came, he watched the local news. Most of the coverage related to Christmas events around Sacramento, including a parade. Weather forecasts called for an increasing chance of rain that wouldn't begin until Christmas morning. Some were giddy with excitement at the prospect of snowfall in the higher elevations. Skiers would flock to Boreal Mountain or Sugar Bowl Resort. Outdoor hikers would find their way to the summit of Mount Lincoln.

Entremont was emotionally spent. He tried to fix a simple meal of bagels and cream cheese, only to burn the bagels beyond recognition. He couldn't bring himself to ride his bike down to Starbucks. Truthfully, he wasn't hungry. He was simply trying to find some normalcy in the whirlwind his frenzied mind had created.

By noon, after watching hours of weather coverage on every possible local and national network, he became so emotionally distraught that he was on the verge of a nervous breakdown. He needed to talk with someone. However, his only sounding boards happened to be his accomplices.

First, he reached out to Stoppkotte, who apparently was on his way to New Jersey, because he didn't answer his phone or respond to text messages. He suspected his friend was one hundred percent on board with LaMarre's conspiracy anyway.

As he became increasingly distraught, he left a tear-filled message on LaMarre's phone. The apprehension in his voice coupled with the revelation he planned on going to their superiors at NOAA – Miami earned a rapid response from LaMarre. She was on her way over.

LaMarre, who lived in walking distance from the office in Broadmoor Estates, required twenty minutes to reach Entremont's remote residence he'd inherited from his parents when they died, near the American River. It was a smallish place with a slight view of the water if you stood in a certain place on the cedar deck and craned your neck to see around the trees. It suited Entremont fine because of its familiarity and proximity to the river, which he frequented just to relax.

That morning, he contemplated finding his favorite spot to think things through, and he might still, but he felt compelled to speak with LaMarre first.

She gently knocked on the door, which stirred Entremont out of his engrossed state of mind.

LaMarre was smiling as she held up a small box of Crumbl cookies for Entremont to see through the door's peephole.

Why's she so cheery? he thought to himself. *I never imagined her to be a masochistic killer.*

In an attempt to feign seriousness, his mood came across as dour. LaMarre noticed it immediately but didn't seem to let on.

"Hey, buddy. I know these aren't Christmas cookies. However, the variety includes birthday cake, buttermilk pancakes, and caramel popcorn. That's your fave, if I recall." Crumbl had enjoyed a meteoric rise around the country, selling one product, gourmet cookies. The flavorful offerings melted in your mouth, making you quickly forget the four-dollar-a-cookie price.

"Yeah, um, thanks. Um, just set them over there. I need to talk to you."

LaMarre tried to study Entremont. She expected to be blindsided with something, so when he spoke, she wasn't necessarily surprised at what he said.

Entremont wandered through his living room, laying out his concerns about the plan LaMarre had proposed. As he walked, he frequently shoved his hand in his right pocket and fumbled around for something as if he'd misplaced a quarter.

LaMarre watched him carefully, immediately noticing the odd behavior he was displaying. Finally, subconsciously, Entremont found what his hand was searching for, and he pulled it out of his pocket for a moment. It was a flash drive.

"Bekki, I ran the simulation over and over again during the night. I tweaked it with the most accurate data points at our disposal. This ARkStorm. This catastrophic event is like no other that America has ever experienced. It ranks up there with quakes along San Andreas or New Madrid along the Mississippi River. I mean, to keep this threat to ourselves is not only irresponsible it's maybe even criminal."

LaMarre gave him an opportunity to voice his concerns without interruption. She could see it would be counterproductive to engage in a heated debate that would force them to be at odds with one another. She didn't want to force him into a corner, so she adopted a different tack.

"You know, Gregory, I think you might be right."

"Huh? You do?"

She managed a fake smile although she was boiling over in anger. He'd freaked out. He planned on ruining the best opportunity any of them would have to raise awareness of the climate-change threat in their lifetimes.

"Yes. Maybe you're right. I couldn't help but notice you have a flash drive. Does that contain the actual predictive model of the ARkStorm's impact?"

He nodded.

"Okay. Good work, Gregory. Let me contact my boss in Miami. Under the circumstances, I'm sure he can arrange for me to catch a military transport to Florida. I'll give him the flash drive and explain the importance of our findings."

Entremont scowled. He continued to fumble in his pockets, nervously rolling the flash drive through his fingers. In his exhausted state of mind, he'd become skeptical and somewhat paranoid.

"Um, I don't know," he began before stopping mid-thought.

LaMarre stepped closer to him in an effort to create a less standoffish posture. "Whadya mean?"

"Um, I think I should deliver it myself. We can go together."

LaMarre had to think fast. She had no intention of delivering the flash drive to Miami. Sure, she might keep it in case she wrote a book at some point under an anonymous pen name. One thing was certain. This flash drive would never make it into anyone's hands but hers.

"Come on, Gregory. Technically, I'm your boss, you know. Miami would question why they went through the extraordinary expense and trouble of making these flight arrangements through the Department of Defense. Besides, don't you trust me?"

Gregory stood still and stopped fidgeting for a brief moment. He was conflicted. He needed to think, and the fact LaMarre was staring a hole through him didn't help. He was unsure how to answer. He gradually turned and wandered to the plate-glass sliding door facing his heavily wooded backyard.

"I don't know, Bekki. I want to. It's just, um." Gregory never finished his sentence. Or began another one, for that matter.

LaMarre was incensed at his sudden distrust of her. She acted impulsively and decisively. As he turned his back to her and voiced his distrust, she picked up a fifteen-inch-high, solid bronze statue of the van Goethem Earth Goddess. With all her strength, she reared back and angrily struck Entremont on the left temple just above his ear.

Blood splattered all over the sliding glass door before Entremont's body fell hard against it. He dropped to his knees in a heap, and his body began to spasm as the brain trauma sent shock waves through his nervous system.

LaMarre stood over him for a moment with a firm grip on the statue, blood oozing through her fingers. After a long minute, the life left Entremont's body, leaving him leaning against the glass door, with his eyes wide open.

Despite the gruesome scene and the brutal murder she'd committed, LaMarre didn't panic. First, she found a garbage bag in Entremont's kitchen. She was careful not to touch anything with her hands. This prompted her to recall every second of her time at the house. It had happened so fast. She hadn't had a chance to leave any prints.

She debated what to do about the cookies. The digital footprint left by his call and voicemail to her phone couldn't be erased. It had to remain. It meant nothing. LaMarre had no motive to kill her friend.

Using another trash bag as a protective barrier between her hands and his pants, she retrieved the flash drive from his pocket. Then she disconnected his computer in the same manner and placed it into the trash bag. Finally, careful not to leave prints, she rummaged through his bedroom drawers to create the appearance of a robbery.

With a final look at the corpse, she was satisfied

her work was done. She slipped through the door into the woodsy front yard, leaving it open just as a burglar would do. She carefully placed two trash bags in her trunk. One had his computer, which she'd later dismantle and destroy. The other had the bloody Earth Goddess statue. She slammed the back hatch of her Subaru and wiped the perspiration off her brow.

In her jeans pocket was the flash drive forecasting the deadliest natural disaster in modern times. She pressed her hand against her pants to feel the device safely tucked away. As she did, she whispered aloud.

"For the greater good."

FOURTEEN

Thursday
Christmas
Devil's Gate Dam
La Cañada, California

La Cañada was located adjacent to the infamous Devil's Gate Dam. The massive concrete barrier, built in 1920, was the first flood-control dam in Los Angeles County. Even before the Charles Manson family used its tubed spillways for satanic rituals, Devil's Gate had a storied history.

As a part of the county's critical infrastructure designed to protect the valley during flood events, the flood basin above Devil's Gate captured the water runoff from multiple mountain ranges. The watershed, known as *Hahamongna*, a phrase meaning flowing waters, fruitful valley, was home to farms, recreation areas, and native species' habitats.

Below the dam, the Arroyo Seco creek ran through the heart of the surrounding neighborhoods and Brookside Golf Club. Most of the creek was contained in a system of concrete channels that contains stormwater and other man-made runoff. This elaborate system of channels and other flood-control structures, like earthen levees, was built after the devastating Los Angeles flood that took place in 1938.

In that year, two massive atmospheric rivers swept across the Pacific Ocean, generating a year's worth of rainfall in just a few weeks. Considered a fifty-year flood, the 1938 event killed hundreds and inflicted the equivalent of one-point-five billion dollars in damage adjusted to today's dollars.

In the weeks leading up to Christmas, the flood basin had been filled with mud, rocks and burned trees following Station Fire II. The barren landscape was prone to landslides and erosion as rains began in late November. By the time the heavier rain events accompanying the atmospheric rivers came onshore, over two million cubic yards of sediment had been flushed into the reservoir.

As a result, Devil's Gate Dam was placed under tremendous pressure to hold back the silt buildup. Also, the reservoir itself was unable to maintain the same capacity as before the massive Station Fire II.

The heavy rains brought by El Niño conditions the year before had already raised concerns for county public works officials about the dam's structural integrity. In order to begin the project of removing silt following the prior rainy season, the Los Angeles County Flood Control District needed permission from a California environmental agency to destroy an endangered bird and its habitat.

The application, known as an *incidental take*, would directly impact the Bell's vireo, a rare songbird listed on both federal and state endangered species lists. In a two-hundred-page report accompanying the application, the county proposed waiting until the breeding season was over in late spring to begin the dredging operation, and assured officials the work would be done by November.

Environmentalists lost their collective minds. The project would use bulldozers and other heavy machinery to pull out debris, fallen trees, mud and sediment in the seventy-acre watershed where the Bell's vireo lived and bred.

The protests and rallies against the project accompanied multiple lawsuits filed by the Sierra Club and Earthjustice. Injunctions were filed and granted. The county was told to stand down until studies could be made by state and federal authorities. The litigation was costly to the county and lengthy. By December, as the heavy rains began to fill the reservoir, the lawyers were still fighting in court. Nothing had been done to remove the silt and debris.

Not unexpectedly, after the first atmospheric river struck the region, the water reached the top of the hundred-foot-tall Devil's Gate Dam. Built between the mountain and a rock outcropping that resembled the face of a devil, the dam was located in the narrowest spot on the Arroyo Seco's path toward Los Angeles. The geological formation created a funnel of sorts for the water flow from multiple lakes and rivers to its north.

It was necessary. It was also eerie. Almost spiritual.

Some said it contained a portal to Hell. Others

preferred highway to Hell. Songs referred to it as Devil's Gate Drive.

Officially, it was an outlet tunnel used by flood-control engineers to relieve the water flow during heavy storm operations. On one end, deep in the devilish rock formation, stood a sluice gate made of two solid steel doors designed to hold back water and debris. At Devil's Gate, the outlet tunnel was crucial to drain the reservoir when the dam reached its capacity.

At the end of the tunnel that opened up near the famed rock formation, the steel gates preventing entry into the flood tunnel had been repeatedly pulled off their hinges to the point that the county stopped repairing them. Anyone willing to make the hike up the side of the ridge could enter the portal to Hell.

If they knew the history, they'd be keenly aware of reports of L. Ron Hubbard and the occultist order known as *Ordo Templi Orientis* conducting *sex magick* withing the tunnel. Hubbard and his group hoped to spawn the prophesied anti-Christ, who would overthrow Christianity forever.

Satanic ritualists had performed dark magic there for decades. Pathological criminals had sacrificed animals. Once, four children entered the portal to Hell, never to be seen again. The deaths occurring within the chamber were countless.

There would be more.

FIFTEEN

Friday
Christmas
San Bernadino Mountains
Crestline, California

Pablo Sanchez and his family had looked forward to their Christmas vacation since they'd booked it ten months ago. It was the parents' fifteenth anniversary, and the week also corresponded with their twins' birthday. It was to be a momentous occasion.

They rented a cabin in the San Bernadino mountains near the small town of Crestline, northeast of Los Angeles. The recreation area was a favorite of LA and San Bernadino residents.

Nearby Lake Arrowhead featured boat rentals, kayaking, and fishing. There were numerous places to hike and ride mountain bikes. Campsites were abundant if you wanted a taste of the great outdoors beyond the expected comforts of your cabins or hotels.

The Sanchez family's visit to the area and stay in a cabin was anything but comfortable. Their first night, they ventured out to the Bear House, where locals enjoyed the atmosphere, generous portions, and scrumptious brownies for dessert. The snow that began to fall on their drive back to their rented cabin was exciting at first. It was certainly out of the ordinary for that time of year. Pablo, who'd never driven in snow, was careful to avoid sliding off the road as it accumulated.

Because of his concern, he envisioned several days in which the family was snowed in, as they say. To some, the concept was romantic. To Pablo, it meant all of his best-laid plans to keep the family entertained were thwarted.

Overnight, the National Weather Service had issued a blizzard warning. The ground was already covered with snow, and the NWS expected more than a foot of snow would be added to the existing accumulation. Moreover, state transportation crews might not be able to clear the roads, making travel hazardous and near impossible.

Pablo's concerns were correct, and the family was snowbound. They made the best of it for the first couple of days. Then additional snow accumulations up to seventy inches began to blow in even taller drifts due to the sixty-mile-per-hour winds. The blizzard raged, and the family became concerned about their food supplies.

Then the power went out. Already in an isolated area, Pablo could not get cell phone reception. The loss of electricity took away their way to store and cook their remaining food. They only had enough firewood for that morning, with nothing stored in a dry area.

Expecting the power to return, the family burned their firewood to stay warm. However, by evening, the darkness brought colder temperatures, and the fire began to burn out. They dragged mattresses into the living area near the fire and piled blankets on top to stay warm. The temperatures plummeted, and the howling winds made the conditions unbearable.

Pablo, like most of the locals and visitors, had only enough food to last them a few days. When the blizzard struck, the heavy snow piled onto the local grocery store's flat roof, causing it to cave in. Likewise, the large snowdrifts began to slide their way down the mountains, forming avalanche conditions that consumed homes in their path. Because of road conditions, Cal Trans crews were unable to deploy their heavy loaders.

His family became panicked, and Pablo felt compelled to do something. After the snowfall dissipated, Pablo dug his way out of the cabin and made a path to reach a storage shed. He found a snow shovel and then lumbered through the snow to a clearing near the tree line.

In the snow, he wrote the words *HELP US!!* The plea was easily seen from the sky if any rescue helicopters or small planes were in the area. The cabin was not visible due to the heavy snowfall remaining on the roof. The Sanchezes' car was buried.

So was Pablo.

He walked down the slope, thinking he could find his way to the winding road leading up to their cabin. He unknowingly stepped off a twenty-foot-high cliff into a ravine filled with snow. Pablo broke his right ankle and reinjured his left knee, which hadn't healed from a car accident several weeks prior. He tried to claw his way through the snow, dragging his battered lower body behind him. He dug deeper and deeper into the snowpack until he was exhausted.

He just needed a little rest, he thought to himself. *I'll try again*, he vowed. Then the cold overtook him until he died. Twelve others joined him that day, some of whom were trapped in their cars or homes.

For those living in the higher elevations of the San Bernadino Mountains, there was no escaping the blizzard. Yet their deaths were only the beginning of the death toll to come.

SIXTEEN

Thursday
New Year's Eve
Hendrick Residence
La Cañada, California

For the last week, the rain never stopped until the afternoon of New Year's Eve. The mood in Vons grocery store could best be described as jubilation as Sammy and the girls went shopping. Conversations ranged from the parties that evening to the Rose Bowl game the next day. Many said they were amazed the weather people got it right for a change. The next several days would be rainy, just like the last several. Sure, maybe a little windy. However, the shows, the partying and the Rose Bowl festivities would go on.

"What are we bringing to the New Year's party, Sammy?" asked Livvy, who was perusing the treats.

"Well, this is a British-themed party. I think it's gonna be kinda cool. We have a really neat clubhouse in our neighborhood. Some of our neighbors got together and came up with a New Year's Eve party as if we were in London."

The girls immediately began to sing the nursery rhyme. "London bridge is falling down, falling down. London bridge is falling down, my fair lady!"

They were getting a little boisterous, forcing Sammy to tamp down their enthusiasm. "Girls, take it easy. The party isn't until three o'clock."

Sophie seemed to have some understanding of time because she immediately recognized three o'clock as being a long way away from midnight.

"That's a long party," she mumbled as she kicked at invisible rocks on the tile floor.

"Not really," Sammy corrected her. "Here's the thing. London, England, is eight hours ahead of us. When it's midnight there, it will be four o'clock here. The people throwing the party are bringing big-screen TVs into the clubhouse and signed up for several British television networks. We'll get to see their fireworks and music and dancing, too!"

"We get to dress up, right?" asked Livvy.

"Absolutely. In fact, I bet your outfits are being delivered as we speak. I picked out some really cute stuff from Poshmark for all three of us."

"Will we be adorbs?" asked Livvy, who seemed obsessed with her appearance. She'd have the men wrapped around her finger, and they'd soon discover she was high maintenance.

"Yep. You two will have cute tweed skirts, and I'll have on a tweed puff-sleeve dress."

"What about Tyler?"

Sammy chuckled. When she told Tyler he needed to pick out an outfit, he'd suggested a pair of knickers and a sleeveless, plaid sweater like the golfers wear. Sammy had honored his request and found the ensemble.

At first, he'd said not a chance in hell. Then, rather than being the only person at the soiree without proper attire, he'd relented. Sammy wasn't sure if he'd go through with it, not that it mattered. She was thankful he could join them, considering the game was the next day.

Sammy got the ingredients to make shepherd's pie and picked up a couple of cans of Batchelors Beans in tomato sauce. The beans were located in the British cuisine section of the store although the brand was distinctly Irish. *Close enough*, she muttered to herself when she loaded them into the cart.

With the shopping complete, the three of them made their way to the house. While the girls planned a fashion show, Sammy prepared the food and got ready herself. It was approaching three, and she was beginning to get concerned that Tyler wouldn't make it.

She'd tried to call him; however, cell service had been spotty throughout the Crescenta Valley. The news reported the foundations of several cell towers had been compromised by the rain, causing them to fall over or move just enough not to function properly.

Sammy pulled out the shepherd's pie and the beans. After securing them in a container to stay warm, she enjoyed the girls playing runway models. She was laughing so hard at their goofiness she didn't notice Tyler slip in through the garage door. He snuck up from behind to grab her by the waist.

"Gotcha, lassie!" he exclaimed in his best, not-so-good British accent.

"Don't you lassie me, mister," she shot back. She'd apparently been practicing her English accent after watching another season of the Netflix program *Bridgerton*. "Come on. We need to get ready."

Twenty minutes later, they piled into Tyler's truck and drove in a light drizzle to the neighborhood clubhouse. They were astonished to find the parking lot full and several families making their way inside.

"I really didn't think this would be that popular," said Sammy while Tyler searched for a parking spot. "It's the middle of the day."

"Think about it, though," Tyler began. He surreptitiously pointed his thumb toward the girls in the back seat. "Parents have parties to go to. Kids are too young to stay up until midnight. Heck, I'll probably be asleep by ten."

"Sounds like me," Sammy said with a laugh. Tyler was the night owl of the family, frequently falling asleep while watching ESPN SportsCenter.

"Other kids didn't dress up," Sophie noticed. She pointed toward a family of five who were covered in rain gear.

"Maybe, but you guys will get all the attention."

"Yay!" exclaimed Livvy, not surprisingly.

Inside, the festivities were in full swing. On the perimeter walls, there were four large-screen televisions sitting atop heavy-duty easels. Each one was showing a different network. Music ranged from the Beatles to the Rolling Stones to Fleetwood Mac.

Part of the center of the room was dedicated to traditional British children's games like pin the tail on the donkey and the egg-and-spoon race using plastic eggs.

The adults gathered around the food tables, where everyone filled their plates as they worked their way through the buffet line. No alcohol was served, but tea was abundant.

Sammy and Tyler roamed the room in search of familiar faces. Their neighborhood had an equal mix of aging empty nesters and young families. They were an exception to that rule, as most young couples had children. Livvy and Sophie served as loaner kids.

Suddenly, the music stopped, and everyone was startled by the relative quiet. A man made his way to the center of the room with one hand raised. He began to speak.

"Good afternoon, neighbors. In case we haven't met, my name is Finn O'Brien. Now, for those of you with an ear for accents, you might notice I'm Irish. Well, the fire-red beard and the name might be a dead giveaway, too."

The group laughed. Finn came across as a lovable old codger, and he was certainly enjoying talking to the group.

He continued, "Since I'm the closest thing in our fair hamlet to a Brit, it seemed to make sense to join the folks from the neighborhood association to prepare for this special kind of New Year's party."

Everyone spontaneously applauded. Sammy leaned into Tyler. "Have you ever met him? He's such a nice guy and easily recognizable. But I don't think I've ever seen him around."

Sammy and Tyler ran three to five miles several days a week. They traversed the neighborhood and knew the streets like the back of their hands. Someone could show them a photograph of a home and they could easily identify its location.

Tyler shrugged. "I don't think I've seen him, either. Maybe he's new?"

Finn continued, "I've lived here for twenty years, and I really don't know why we haven't done this before."

"That answers that," said Sammy. "He must be a hermit or something."

Tyler laughed and then gave her hand a squeeze.

Finn looked at his watch. "I'm going to turn up the volume on the BBC network feed, and we've had someone much smarter than I patch the audio into the speakers overhead." Subconsciously, several people looked up at the ceiling as if to confirm he was telling the truth. Sammy, a student of human nature, found the reaction odd.

Finn pointed toward a man standing in front of a television near a gas fireplace, and he returned the gesture with a thumbs-up. BBC One was airing *The Big New Years & Years Eve Party* filmed near London in Hammersmith. An inset camera alternated between London landmarks like Big Ben, Buckingham Palace, and Trafalgar Square. Fireworks would fill the city's skies at the stroke of midnight, local time.

Everyone within the clubhouse was giddy with excitement. The girls left Sammy and Tyler to join other kids sitting in front of the televisions to get the best view of the show. This would be a rare opportunity to enjoy the feeling of ringing in a new year. Even the adults seemed to forget it was daylight outside, as the atmospheric conditions were more like London's fog than California's sunshine.

As they counted down in unison, Sammy

glanced around the crowd. She never thought she'd enjoy living in California. However, they'd found the right neighborhood in the perfect town. It gave her that feeling of permanency. Maybe even permanent enough to start a family.

SEVENTEEN

Thursday
New Year's Eve
Portland, Maine

Bekki LaMarre had a change of plans. Vacation plans, that is. She'd intended to visit family and friends in Portland, Oregon, where she was born and raised. However, knowing the chaos that would be created by the ARkStorm, she chose to travel cross-country to another Portland located in Maine. She begged forgiveness from her family and explained work required her to study a potential nor'easter. She didn't warn them about the coming ARkStorm, as it wouldn't impact them directly.

Instead, she opted for a room overlooking the ocean at the Canopy, a boutique hotel operated by Hilton.

She needed to be away from anyone she knew. She'd just murdered someone, and the reality had set in. She never disliked Entremont. Actually, she admired his work and valued his friendship while at Cal Berkeley.

Her spontaneous reaction to his intent to betray her was out of character for her and, as they say in legal circles, undertaken without malice aforethought. On the long flight to Boston, where she rented a car for the short drive up the coast, she considered the legal ramifications of her murdering Entremont. It was a rapid response to a threat without thinking of the consequences. If she had chosen the less violent option, she would've tried to talk Entremont off the cliff.

She had been triggered, so she killed him. Now, hopefully, the dead man's projections of the coming ARkStorm would wash away the evidence, and the investigators.

At midnight, she'd just finished her first bottle of wine when she stepped out onto the balcony to smoke a marijuana cigarette. She laughed to herself. She wanted to start the new year on a high note.

After burning one, she turned to her second bottle of wine and settled in to watch events unfold.

Ordinarily, weed made her relaxed and sleepy. Tonight, she planned on staying up to study the data from the NOAA and NASA weather feeds.

In the past week, heavy amounts of snow had fallen on top of already record snowpacks in the upper elevations. This, however, had been short-lived. The atmospheric river of the previous week had brought warmer weather with it. The El Niño effect did not simply disappear as a result of the powerful atmospheric rivers. The Pacific jet stream had moved to the south and spread farther toward the coast of Mexico. The warmer air had met the large band of moisture. Within days, the snowpack was melting and left mountain streams overflowing their banks as they rushed down to the valleys.

Throughout the evening, she'd compared the data at her disposal to Entremont's forecast model, making slight adjustments as conditions warranted. As expected, just after midnight in California, the first rainfall coming ashore would be light and misty. As Californians woke up on New Year's Day, they'd be greeted with gray skies and a light rain. There might be periods of clearing. However, the rains would begin again by morning, and then, by noon or shortly thereafter, the deluge would come.

In the first hour, twelve to eighteen inches of rain would fall, breaking the U.S. record of a foot in an hour that took place in 1948. Within the first three hours, more than fifty inches would have soaked the Central Valley, easily eclipsing the 2018 record of forty-nine inches in a twenty-four-hour period occurring in Hawaii. And it would continue.

LaMarre intently studied the flood warnings issued by the NWS from the last several days. As the last storm with milder air dropped heavy rain across the state, the snows began to melt. Flood warnings had been issued for much of Central and Southern California. Forecasters had warned of mudslides and very strong, gusty winds.

The NWS statement also warned of an additional storm in the offing. Their words would be repeated by weather forecasters throughout the morning hours.

"Californians are cleaning up from the previous storms, which means the next storm has the potential to become a disaster upon previous disasters, further compounding any impacts. The next atmospheric river event may also tap into a two-thousand-plus-mile feed of deep subtropical Pacific moisture, yielding heavy rain in the lower elevation and possibly the mountains as well. This moisture is expected to make its way onshore in the early morning hours of New Year's Day and continue for several days thereafter."

The USGS had created a storm-impact scale to determine the potential vulnerability of a particular stretch of coastline and the impact on its barrier islands, if any. Ranging from a Level 1, the least severe, to a Level 5, a severe storm that includes extreme flooding, impassable roads, and power outages for many days. The NWS went on to declare the coming atmospheric river to be a Level 3 storm.

So utterly benign, LaMarre thought to herself as she finished off the second bottle. She was drunk at this point but still capable of maintaining her faculties.

"They have no idea," she said aloud, emitting a maniacal laugh in the process. She continued talking to herself. "They've completely underestimated the timing of the rain event. It's coming, and when it does, it will happen all at once."

Insanely, she hoped she was right.

PART 2

NEW YEAR'S DAY

California Dreamin'
On such a winter's day

EIGHTEEN

**Friday, New Year's Day
Devil's Gate Dam
La Cañada, California**

"It's awwwn, man!"

"Paaarty!" his friend shouted back.

The guys had started their New Year's festivities at the Smell, a music venue in downtown LA. The music was blaring. The crowd was getting trashed. People were jumping on and off the stage. However, when the two friends became bored with the punk rock scene, they followed the advice of other party-goers and headed to Devil's Gate Dam.

They followed the directions to La Cañada

Verdugo Road toward the end of the cul-de-sac. They never made it that far.

There were dozens of cars lining both sides of the ordinarily quiet neighborhood. They pulled onto a dirt-covered shoulder just in front of a No Parking sign. For grins and giggles, the driver nudged the sign until his bumper threatened to bend it over. After exchanging high fives and a good laugh, they exited into the misty air to make the quarter-mile trek to the end of the street. That was the easy part.

Next, they had to wind their way, in the middle of the night, along a rocky, muddy trail. First, they went down the ridge, following the footsteps of dozens of revelers before them, until they reached the base of the dam. They marveled at the massive concrete spillway before looking upward at the Foothills Parkway, which appeared to rise a mile above them into the misty sky.

At the dam, they located the first tunnel on their left and followed it per the instructions they'd committed to their alcohol-muddled memories. The partiers at the Smell kept saying *see a tunnel and go through it*. So they did.

Then they made their way to the bottom of the ravine. There, the trek got messy. The ordinarily dry creek bed was knee-deep in water. They slogged through it to a duckweed-choked pond that reeked of sewage. On the other side, they found a rock to sit on. They needed to cop a squat.

The two were out of breath from a night of drinking and snorting cocaine. Yet they were determined to join the party taking place in the portal to Hell. During the daytime, if a hiker looked upward, they could make out the uncanny outcropping in the rock that resembled a demon, horns and all. However, they could only follow the muddy tracks of the partiers who'd arrived before them.

They started up the side of Flint Canyon, stopping frequently to rest or wipe off the mud from an inadvertent slip and fall. As they approached the tunnel, they heard music. And screams. They'd left a punk rock party for a full-blown rage. The guys could feel the energy of the alcohol and drug-induced dancing.

Like the Who-people scaling Mount Crumpit in search of the Grinch in the Dr. Suess classic, the two boys finally reached the summit, as evidenced by the graffiti-covered granite and the metal gates barely hanging on to rusty hinges.

The noise emanating from the portal to Hell would make the Devil himself blush. Just inside the opening, a group of people were passing around a crack pipe. Fires burned deeper inside the tunnel, filling the ceiling with smoke that billowed along the rock until it found its way outside. They passed people having sex under blankets while several feet away, others were dancing the night away. The smell of marijuana fought with the stench of the acrid smoke, not that any of the inhabitants of the portal to Hell noticed.

After a pass through the festivities toward the sluice gates, the two guys retreated toward the entrance, stopping to drink, toke, and snort along the way. More than once, they joked they'd found heaven and not hell.

They were wrong.

The Devil's Gate Dam had been showing its age of late, and the problem was not just the cracks in the concrete or the massive debris buildup exerting pressure beneath the water. Sixty percent of the employees responsible for dam operations were within five years of retirement. Because of the low pay, the county had been unsuccessful in recruiting and training skilled workers to monitor the last means of preventing the City of Los Angeles from flooding.

On New Year's Eve, a three-person team was supposed to be on hand to monitor water levels, conduct security rounds, and respond to a crisis. One of the three called out sick. The other two had gotten drunk, alternating sleeping it off before they began drinking again. One of them, Terry Jewell, had retired once already and had been begged to come back by the county. He was fifty-nine and the senior-most member of the dam's operations team.

Jewell drank black coffee in an attempt to counteract the vodka he'd consumed well before midnight. He was usually pretty good at holding his liquor, but tonight he and his cohort got carried away. It was, after all, New Year's Eve.

While his partner slept it off, Jewell stared across the dark waters of the Devil's Gate reservoir. The ordinarily dirt-covered void had been filled since the atmospheric rivers had begun weeks prior. As a result, dam operators were required to open the sluice gates on occasion to keep reservoir levels below the maximum recommended height.

Despite the cessation of heavy rainfall the day before, the waters seemed to inch higher. Earlier, he'd watched the weather report indicating the mountain snows were beginning to melt, causing streams and rivers to flow into the Crescenta Valley. Most of those floodwaters would arrive in the Arroyo Seco before making their way to Devil's Gate.

Jewell didn't know whether it was the strong, black coffee or the monitoring equipment's readings, but he was beginning to sober up. Every fifteen minutes, the water levels were rising by a half to a whole inch. If this continued unabated, the reservoir would threaten to reach the massive concrete spillover, an event that would require a lot of phone calls to public officials in the middle of the night as well as explanations for the miscalculation.

He woke up his coworker and explained the situation. Victor Garcia was a few years younger than Jewell and counting the days to retirement. He was hoping the county would offer him an exit package to retire early like they'd done in other departments. However, they didn't have a replacement for him yet. So he volunteered for the night shift and routinely drank his way through his eight-and-a-half-hour stint.

Garcia grumbled as he regained his bearings. He poured himself a mug of coffee and studied the readings with Jewell. As they did, an unexpected downpour occurred. The men were familiar with the forecast and knew intermittent rains would begin before dawn. Not this hard, however.

"Whadya think?" asked Jewell.

"No-brainer," replied Garcia. "We sure as hell can't let it reach the spillway. I say we open the sluice gates and let the tunnel drop the reservoir levels. It's nothing we'd have to report as long as we don't leave the gates open indefinitely."

Jewell nodded and then scowled. He leaned back in his chair, which almost toppled over from his weight. Both he and Garcia spent little time exercising as they got older.

"What?" asked Garcia.

"Phyllis called out. We're supposed to clear the tunnel before initiating flood-control measures."

"Call the LASD," suggested Garcia, making reference to the Los Angeles Sheriff's Department.

"We could try, but it's a nonemergency matter. Do you really think they'll hustle over here when I tell them they gotta climb down those ladder chutes in the rain?"

To enter the portal to Hell from above, employees were required to make their way down a flight of steel-mesh stairs to a pair of ladders that descended more than a hundred feet to the entrance. They were treacherous on a clear, sunny day. At night, with the rain pouring down and the wind picking up, they'd be very dangerous.

"I'm not going," Garcia said matter-of-factly. He stubbornly crossed his arms in front of his protruding belly.

"Me neither," said Jewell with a shrug. He glanced at the digital clock on the control panel. "Listen, it's three a.m. We have to make a decision. If we wait until daylight, the water level will reach the spillway. If it does, we're in a world of shit. Neither one of us needs that aggravation this close to retirement."

Garcia spread his arms wide as if there could be no other decision except this one. "Agreed. Open the gates, right?"

Jewell grimaced and began the process. Once everything was ready, he glanced out across the reservoir, caught Garcia's eyes, who returned the glance, and opened the sluice gates. Thousands of gallons of water mixed with all manner of debris rushed through the opening, carrying the force of a rocket.

Between the blaring music and their intoxicated minds, the dozens of partiers within the portal to Hell never heard the gates squeak as they opened. The roar of the water entering the tunnel sounded like the devil incarnate, roaring as it consumed the souls of the debauched partiers.

It was over in less than a minute as they were flushed through the concrete tunnel, down the ridge, to the rocky surface below. Those who survived the plunge were then crushed by the flow of water and debris that landed on top of them.

The thirty-three deaths and eleven critically injured with broken bones wouldn't be discovered until late morning, as the overfilled reservoir was continuously emptied via the tunnel. They would be the first of many thousands who'd die in the coming days.

NINETEEN

Friday
New Year's Day
Hendrick Residence
La Cañada, California

The day Tyler and the USC Trojans had been looking forward to had arrived. It would be easy to breathe a sigh of relief once the game was over. However, losing sucked, and winning meant advancing to the national championship game in New Orleans.

    He'd barely slept, tossing and turning throughout the night. Satisfied with ringing in the New Year with Londoners and their neighbors at the clubhouse, the couple turned in early at around ten. Sleep finally overtook him; however, his anxiety over the condition of the field forced him awake several times.

To avoid delay in case he overslept, he'd laid out his clothes the night before. His gameday uniform, so to speak, consisted of khaki pants with cargo pockets to hold all manner of essentials. He opted for a long-sleeve rugby shirt featuring cardinal and gold stripes, the official team colors. Their signature SC was embroidered on the left side near the heart.

Tyler had dreamed of joining the staff of his alma mater, Penn State. He couldn't believe he'd landed in LA with one of Penn State's longtime rivals. Maybe that was why he'd put in the extraordinary amount of time to prepare his players. Not only so they could compete and win. But, also, so he could impress the team he longed to play for. His contract with USC expired at the end of the season, and they'd put off negotiations until then. There was still time to get noticed by Penn State.

He eased out of bed and made his way to the bathroom. He took a quick shower. Afterwards, he took some time to trim his beard.

"Gonna look good for the camera?" asked Sammy, startling Tyler.

He chuckled as he replied, "I hope not."

Sammy was puzzled. "Why not?"

He got dressed as he spoke. "If I'm on camera, that means someone, like Malachi, got hurt, requiring me to go onto the field. That's not a good thing."

"So why trim the beard?"

"Just in case. You want me to look good, don't you?"

She patted the bed. "You always look good to me."

He laughed and eased into bed next to her. "No. You know, I've been overthinking everything about the game and what happens next. You know, after the season's over. It's complicated."

Sammy sat up and leaned against the upholstered headboard. "Weighty matters that can wait. Don't you agree?"

"I do."

"Ty, I'm so proud of you. The players will be ready. They'll play their hearts out. The band will play 'Fight On!' ad nauseam." "Fight On!" was the Trojans' iconic fight song for more than a century. The USC marching band was at the ready to jump to attention and enthusiastically play it when the Trojans made a big play.

"Thanks," he said humbly. He glanced at his watch. It was time to go. As he stood, he added, "I think you've done an amazing job with the girls. I've been zero help."

Sammy smiled. "Listen, I was a little scared at first. Truthfully, I consider my job to be a simple one. Keep them alive until their parents pick them up. This afternoon, I'll set a seventy-two-hour timer on my watch 'til your brother arrives at LAX."

Tyler bent over and kissed her. "I love you. And, um, if the game gets out of control, you don't have to watch it until the end."

She squeezed his hand. "Nothing can stop me from watching. I love you. Fight on!"

Tyler eased out of the bedroom and went downstairs without turning the light on. Sammy lay there for a moment, trying to decide if she wanted to get up at oh-dark-thirty or fall asleep. By the time she got through debating with herself, she chose to wake up and start her day with some exercise.

She rode her Peloton bike daily in addition to the evening runs with Tyler. Since the girls had arrived, she'd only had one opportunity to ride when Tyler was home to entertain them. She felt it would be rude to plop them in front of the television while she exercised. At this hour, they'd never notice.

She hit it hard, riding for nearly an hour at a feverish pace. She wasn't sure if she was making up for the lack of exercise, or perhaps it was working off the anxiety surrounding Tyler's big game. Regardless, she overexerted and quit before the hour was up, as her knee screamed in pain.

One of the most common injuries suffered by cyclists was known as cyclist's knee, one of four injuries causing pain around the kneecap. She'd injured her knee years ago, and she thought it had completely healed. She knew better than to make sudden changes in her training regime. Tyler was a physiologist and had cautioned her against doing too much too fast.

Normally, she'd reach out to Tyler, but she didn't want to bother him. Instead, she hobbled to the kitchen in search of a large Ziploc bag and some ice. She'd alternate icing her knee for twenty minutes on and twenty minutes off. Then she'd follow the self-care method every athlete learns at a young age—RICE. Rest. Ice. Compression. Elevation.

Before her knee ached too much, she set out a breakfast of cereal and milk for the girls. She'd also ordered several classic board games she'd enjoyed as a child. She hoped they'd keep the girls occupied so Sammy could focus on the game.

Lunch at game time would be easy to prepare. Hot dogs, tater tots and baked beans. Maybe, if her knee didn't complain too much, she'd make deviled eggs. As she prepared the ice pack, she wondered to herself how the term deviled eggs came about. She'd grown up in a Christian home in which anything having to do with the devil was serious business.

She just had to know why they were called deviled eggs, so she Googled it. After settling in on the sofa with her leg elevated and ice pack applied, she muttered aloud, "Okay. Eighteenth-century England. Highly seasoned and spicy. I still don't get it. What's the devil got to do with it?"

No longer interested in the answer after her search results were inundated with recipes, Sammy turned her attention to her neighborhood directory the homeowner's association published online. Sure, many residents opted out of the directory, as they deemed it an intrusion on their privacy. Frankly, she'd never bothered to look at it and couldn't remember whether she'd approved their address to be included. There was one name in particular she was searching for.

"There. Finn O'Brien. No wife. Retired. Lives farther down the valley toward the city."

Sammy wasn't one to stalk her neighbors on

Google. She didn't want people searching her name and digging around, although there was nothing to find. Still, it was creepy and a practice she wished people would quit. So she left it at that. Her curiosity about Mr. O'Brien had been satisfied. All she knew was that she liked him.

She cursed herself under her breath because she forgot to take Advil. That required her to get up, and that, she was certain, would hurt like hell.

TWENTY

Friday
New Year's Day
Prado Dam
Riverside County, California

East of Los Angeles, in Riverside County, the bedroom community of Corona's residents enjoyed beautiful views of the Santa Ana Mountains. The nearby canyons were a favorite of those who enjoyed the outdoor activities. Others enjoyed fishing in the reservoir holding the Santa Ana River above the Prado Dam.

The earth-filled dam had been authorized to be built in 1936, and as it turned out, it was completed just before the Los Angeles flood of 1938, when two atmospheric rivers roared onshore in February and March. The Prado was credited with preventing the fifty-year flood from being far worse.

Now, almost ninety years later, the dam was in dire need of repair and restoration. Federal engineers had issued their warnings that a significant flood event, as they called it, could potentially swamp Orange County communities from Disneyland to Newport Beach. In fact, the U.S. Army Corps of Engineers had raised the Prado Dam's risk category from moderate to high urgency.

Federal engineers were discovering that the dams built in California as part of their flood-control systems were not as resilient as they thought they were. By contrast, the extensive dam system built as part of the Tennessee Valley Authority rarely required repairs of this magnitude.

Located between Corona and Anaheim, the dam protected one and a half million residents from dangerous floodwaters resulting from torrential downpours. At first, a minimal amount of funds had been allocated to the Prado Dam project, mainly used for cosmetic repairs. The underlying structural integrity of the dam required significantly more financial resources of just under a billion dollars.

The state and federal governments found other more pressing matters to spend the taxpayers' dollars on, leaving the Prado dam repairs for another budgetary cycle.

As the three prior atmospheric rivers brought heavy snows to the San Bernadino Mountains and corresponding rainfall to Riverside, the Prado Dam was being tested. The dam's operation team began to open the spillway gates just after Christmas to alleviate the pressure. Because of the rain events, inspectors were unable to access the water piping through the foundation of the dam. As a result, they were unaware of the significant erosion taking place there.

As a gravity dam, the overall forces creating the dam's structure include the weight of the concrete pushing downward and the uplifting pressure from water forcing upward. If the weight of the reservoir water is too great, then the massive concrete structure could be lifted upward and overturned.

It would be considered a worst-case scenario. Engineers understood the potential force water can exert on any structure, both man-made and natural. They frequently point to the Grand Canyon as their exhibit A.

At the start of the week, the dam engineers' opening of the spillway gates out of concern for the dam's viability resulted in downstream flooding in the Anaheim Hills, much to the chagrin of business owners and residents. However, had they not taken the pressure-relieving measures, the dam most likely would've failed five days ago.

The failure to open the spillways would've created a significant flood event that would kill hundreds and destroyed buildings throughout Anaheim. Many would later argue that the early warning signs resulting from the dam's potential failure would've prompted evacuation warnings in advance of the New Year's Day ARkStorm.

There were no evacuation warnings, and the Prado Dam was failing anyway. A muddy wall of water over two hundred feet high was exerting tremendous pressure on the aging dam. In the next several hours, the amount of water accumulated in the dam's reservoir would claw its way through the concrete like a monster in a Godzilla movie.

The millions of gallons of water would carve a sixty-mile path through Anaheim toward the Pacific Ocean near Long Beach. The massive flood would take with it the iconic structures of Disneyland and its visitors. As well as anything else in its path.

The failure of the Prado Dam would occur near simultaneously with the breakdown of the Mojave

River Dam to the northeast of Prado and the smaller, but just as important, Whittier Narrows Dam in downtown LA.

That day, however, Prado was not the first dam to suffer a catastrophic failure.

TWENTY-ONE

Friday
New Year's Day
John McKay Center
University of Southern California
Los Angeles, California

USC's John McKay Center was abuzz that morning as Tyler entered the spacious main floor. He glanced up at the two-story-high video wall equivalent to three hundred flat-screen monitors. The content team had created a continuous loop of videos featuring great USC games at the Rose Bowl dating back to the Trojans' first appearance in 1923 when they beat Penn State 14–3. The two teams met in the Rose Bowl again in 2009 and 2017, with USC winning both games. The Nittany Lions hoped to turn the tide today.

"Not on my watch," mumbled Tyler as he made light conversation with members of his staff. Each of them was assigned duties and specific players to work with. Their job was both physiological and psychological.

Before any big football game, each player had their own routine to prepare themselves physically and mentally to maintain a level of high energy. During the week, they studied game film and met with their assistant coaches. The training staff worked on any physical issues they might have.

Cramps and heat-related injuries were typical in late summer or early fall. As winter came, even in temperate climates like LA, these elite athletes were prone to muscle injuries and pains in their lower extremities.

Tyler knew the strengths and weaknesses of every player. He worked in concert with the medical team to assess and treat injuries. He'd instruct his staff to respect the players' mental preparation that often occurred during the pregame taping of specific injuries. Players liked the feeling of tape on their injuries, as it gave them the support they needed to play.

He was also actively involved in their pregame meal and hydration. Carb-loading was the nutrition strategy of eating appropriate foods filled with carbohydrates to maximize the storage of glycogen in the muscles and liver. Tyler didn't want his players sluggish during the game. The timing of the meal was just as important as the menu. It was indicative of the pregame regimen that Tyler had perfected.

He ascended the stairwell, taking them two steps at a time. His energy was off the charts. The upper level was devoted to coaches' offices, team meeting rooms, and a team auditorium for meetings. Because he'd arrived early, only a few members of the coaching staff were present. They were already at work. Some studied last minute notes and game film. Others grabbed players for one-on-one conversations.

That morning was hectic. Everyone in the facility had a job to do, and they strived for perfection. The preparation was taken to another level because of the importance of the game. Everyone, including Tyler, had forgotten about the prospect of inclement weather as they went about their duties. It wasn't until they boarded the buses to make the twenty-minute drive to Rose Bowl Stadium that they noticed the skies had opened up with rain.

    Again.

TWENTY-TWO

Friday
New Year's Day
Hendrick Residence
La Cañada, California

The alternating ice packs helped Sammy relieve some of the swelling and pain of her knee. Just as the girls were emerging from their slumber, she managed to make her way to the kitchen to swallow four Advil. The relief was not immediate, but within the hour, she was able to flex her knee. It was still painful, yet manageable. She was relieved she hadn't hurt herself more seriously.

The morning went well. She allowed the kids

and dogs to play with one another in the backyard until the rain and wind suddenly picked up. She'd expected another weather system to move in, although the forecast was for it to hit hours later.

The girls were dressed in their tweed skirts and white tee shirts from the day before. They'd enjoyed the party so much and the attention they got for their outfits that they vowed to wear them until their parents picked them up on Monday. After breakfast, they settled in front of the television. The chatty duo used the oak coffee table to play Jenga, the classic block-stacking, stack-crashing game from her childhood. She played a round with them first until they understood the concept. Then Sammy wondered if the girls were enjoying the game simply to stack the blocks high only to intentionally knock them down.

"Earthquake!" shouted Sophie as the blocks crashed onto the sturdy oak coffee table. "Run for your lives!"

Both girls grabbed their sides, as they thought this was beyond hilarious. They had no idea California was prone to tremors, including the Big One, as they called a fracture along the San Andreas fault system. When she and Tyler had moved there, she studied the fault lines in relation to their home. She was surprised to learn the San Andreas fault, the longest in California, sliced through Los Angeles County not that far from where they lived near the San Gabriel Mountains.

While they continued to play, she turned on ESPN to watch coverage of the day's bowl games. She expected the announcers to talk about the Rose Bowl and the availability of Malachi Nelson to play quarterback. Regardless of his being able to perform, she knew Tyler would be glad when the day was over. He'd been so stressed out. He had to be exhausted although he never let on.

Sammy had enjoyed the party as much as the girls had. Several of the neighbors with kids had invited them over to watch the game. She had to explain what Tyler's job was and how she'd be pacing the floor during the game as nervous energy likely consumed her. This was an important day for the USC program, and all eyes would be on the conditioning of the players. If they weren't ready, fingers would unfairly be pointed at Tyler. She was content to stay home and fix the girls a game-time meal, which included her planned menu of hot dogs, tater tots, and baked beans. Plus deviled eggs.

As noon approached, Sammy had recovered somewhat from her knee injury. She took more Advil even though it had only been a few hours. This time, it was for a headache developing from stress. The rain was coming down in sheets, which meant the field would be soggy and treacherous. This was Tyler's biggest nightmare. The USC quarterback had barely recovered from his injury. He'd be at risk of pulling the injured hamstring again.

With a sigh, she exited the kitchen and set the girls' plates on the breakfast room table. They scampered over and immediately dug into their hot dogs. She moseyed around the house in an attempt to keep her leg from stiffening up. As she did, she glanced out each window.

At the back doors, her eyes were drawn up the hill, where small streams were forming in the otherwise hard-packed dirt. The water grew in volume, splashing hard against the rocks before finding its way back to the muddy waters in the newly created streams. She surmised that this was occurring throughout the Crescenta Valley except on a much larger scale. Sammy furrowed her brow and placed her hands on her hips. She leaned against the glass and looked toward the sky. The sheets of heavy rain were being thrust toward the earth by the strong winds.

"How much of this can we take?" she asked herself under her breath.

TWENTY-THREE

Friday
New Year's Eve
Crescenta Valley
Central California

The rain fell in torrents as it came onshore. If the worst part of a hurricane was defined by its twenty-to-sixty-mile-wide eye and the path it followed, one could imagine the swath a two-to-three-hundred-mile-wide ARkStorm would carve. From Catalina Island, just south of LA, to San Luis Obispo, west of Bakersfield, the ARkStorm roared into California with hurricane-force winds and rains to match.

Initially, in the first two hours, the amount of rainfall wasn't all that different from what Californians had experienced from the three prior atmospheric rivers. The downpours were heavy, and the soggy ground was unable to handle any more. As the deluge continued, coupled with the strong wind gusts, ridges and mountains began to lose the battle.

The sparse vegetation following the wildfire season allowed mudslides to occur through Central California. Trees toppled. Cell towers were destroyed. Electric grids darkened. Initially, the power grid failures were beginning to be felt on a localized basis at the higher elevations and along the Pacific coast. As the day continued and the ARkStorm exerted its pressure on the state's infrastructure, a cascading failure of the entire Pacific Gas and Electric Company grid was imminent.

Along the ridges, landslides blocked the Pacific Coast Highway. The magnificent homes overlooking the beaches found themselves teetering on the brink of crashing into the ocean. Mudslides carried dirt, trees, and any small structures in their paths downward, roaring toward the valley below and the swollen rivers and reservoirs.

ARKSTORM

To the south, the ARkStorm reached the Los Angeles Basin, where it slammed into the San Gabriel and San Bernadino Mountains. The unique formations of those mountain ranges in terms of elevation and steepness resulted in the air rising quickly, followed by a sudden cooling. As the atmospheric pressure dropped, the water vapor produced a deluge like nothing else the region had seen, including the storm of 1862.

Southern California was known for its semi-desert-type climate and shallow soil. The already saturated ground couldn't take any more. The unprecedented runoff immediately flooded much of downtown LA. The geological formations became the perfect flood-generation machine that performed with swiftness and deadly accuracy.

All of this water moved toward the LA River, the concrete flood-control channel made famous by so many Hollywood movies. The channels were designed to hold water not debris. A single shopping cart could create a jam anywhere along its fifty-mile course. It was certainly no match for the rubble and debris resulting from the ARkStorm.

By the time inhabitants of LA realized the magnitude of the event, it was too late to escape.

Roads were clogged with vehicles. Many were impassable, as the mudslides and accompanying debris flows washed them away.

The fight for survival was one between man and nature. Nature clearly had the upper hand.

TWENTY-FOUR

Friday
New Year's Day
The Rose Bowl
Pasadena, California

The world-famous Rose Bowl Stadium in Pasadena had hosted five Super Bowls, the Summer Olympics, soccer's World Cup Finals, and countless concerts featuring iconic performers. However, the annual Rose Bowl game, for which it was named, landed the stadium on *Sports Illustrated*'s list as the number one game venue in college sports. They went so far as to name it the Greatest Stadium in College Football history.

Built in 1922, it was recognized as a U.S. National Historic landmark. Its storied history included many firsts, such as the first transcontinental radio broadcast of a sporting event in 1927 as well as the first national telecast of a college football game in 1952. Both accomplishments were befitting a city world renowned as an entertainment mecca.

As the busses arrived that morning despite the rain, Tyler recalled his first visit to Rose Bowl stadium when USC officials had invited the couple to tour the facility. Tyler had given her a double take when her initial reaction to the massive structure was saying it was beautiful. Over time, he'd understood. The stadium might be old; however, its beauty was timeless.

Walking onto the field, you could feel the energy left behind by the great football players who'd battled on the field. The collegiate warriors whose desire to win was fueled by their passion for the game and their school pride. Tyler was a throwback in that he firmly believed the players gave it their all because they wanted to win for USC and their throng of fans. It was not about money, despite certain players cashing in on name, image, and likeness contracts. For Tyler and the players, when the game started, it was about honoring the others who'd worn the cardinal and gold uniforms.

After getting organized in the locker room, Tyler and several assistant coaches made their way onto the field. Their assessment of the conditions was spot-on. This field was beautiful now with its artistic paint and pristine sod. As the rain continued, it would turn to a muddy mess that would make conditions for the players difficult as well as dangerous. They agreed to outfit the players with Nike Anti-Clog Traction shoes to avoid their wet cleats from clogging with the muddy turf. They were bulkier than some of the players liked. When first introduced, the receiver corps complained the Nikes slowed them down. However, after practicing in them, they learned their ability to make cuts on their routes gave then a distinct advantage over their defenders.

While in the bowels of the stadium prior to the one o'clock kickoff, the rain came down harder, and the winds picked up. The NWS had revised their forecast to show the latest atmospheric river moving across central and southern California throughout the duration. It was expected to grow in intensity by late afternoon into the night.

The coaches had been informed of this development. They were also told that, because no lightning was associated with the storm, the game would be played.

It was time.

Led by Head Coach Lincoln Riley, the Trojans took the field through the end zone portal near the student section. Their fans were boisterously chanting U-S-C, U-S-C, U-S-C. Then the band got into the action and began playing "Fight On!" much to the delight of the sixty-some thousand Trojans fans who braved the weather to cheer for what was essentially a home game for them.

Tyler ran out of the portal to the side of the excited players, but just behind the team's star quarterback, Malachi Nelson. He studied every stride the young man made. With each plant of his foot on the soggy turf, Tyler looked for a change in his gait.

He'd told Coach Riley several weeks ago that Nelson would be ready to heal, work, and compete in the game. Just before the coach gave his team its final pep talk, he stopped Tyler in the locker room and asked if his quarterback would be one hundred percent. Tyler gave him the good news the coach needed to hear.

Aloud, his response was yes. Inwardly, he withheld a caveat.

Pending weather.

TWENTY-FIVE

Friday
New Year's Day
Hendrick Residence
La Cañada, California

The game was about to start; however, Sammy's focus had been on the coming storm. She'd just hustled about the backyard, securing lawn furniture and umbrellas. Despite being in the valley at the base of a ridge, the winds were pummeling their home from the north, forcing her to go outside in the driving rain. She noticed her immediate neighbor to the right was doing the same. They waved to one another as Sammy joked how she'd left Florida to avoid this kind of weather.

She'd changed the large-screen television to display the game on the right half. On the left side, ABC7 carried live, continuous news and weather reports. She covered her mouth and gasped as the reporter stood just half a mile away from their home, discussing the dead and mangled bodies below Devil's Gate. She kept the volume turned down so the children weren't distracted, and blocked their view from the closed-captioning scrolling across the screen. This was not something they should be exposed to.

Minutes before kickoff, at the top of the hour, the weather was the lead story. She increased the volume so she could hear the details. The chyron read *Intense storm claims first lives.*

The meteorologist appeared grim as he spoke. "The term rapid intensification is not something we often use in California when discussing rain events. It is most often associated with warnings issued by the National Hurricane Center when maximum sustained winds of a tropical cyclone increase by thirty-five miles per hour in a twenty-four-hour period.

"Well, we have those types of conditions and then some. For weeks, we have been reporting on the series of atmospheric rivers that have come ashore in the central part of the state. We expected this one to be no different. However, it is.

"As the atmospheric river approached, it has strengthened due to multiple environmental factors, including warmer ocean waters, light winds throughout the vertical layers of the atmosphere, and large amounts of moisture-filled air within the storm itself.

"Typically, especially in the western U.S., these factors don't always align, which typically slows the strengthening process and makes rapid intensification a rare event. That said, we are experiencing that very thing this morning."

Sammy would've stomped around the room if her knee hadn't begun swelling again. She thrust her hands on her hips and glared at the meteorologist.

"Why didn't you tell us earlier?"

"What's wrong, Sammy?" asked Sophie, who was studying her aunt's face.

Sammy took a deep breath and rolled her neck on her shoulders to relieve some tension. "I'm sorry, girls. I'm just mad at the weather guy."

"Because it's raining?" asked Livvy. "I'm mad at him, too."

She approached her adorable nieces and gently rubbed the backs of their heads. "Well, you know what? There's not a whole lot we can do about the weather, is there? Maybe I should ignore this stuff and watch the game." This was an attempt to convince herself as much as relieve the girls' apprehension.

She switched the volume back to the game although she continued to focus on the weather being reported. A graphic filled the screen, indicating some of the wind damage along the coast. The station was reporting winds reaching 125 miles per hour. Widespread structural damage had already been reported. The Golden Gate bridge had been closed as soon as the winds hit sixty.

Then they began to show video feeds shared with the network of beach erosion, flooding, and cliff failures. This immediately drew Sammy to the back doors again to study the rain washing down the ridge. She wondered if the cliff far above their house could fall apart, as the news was reporting.

"Not here, right?" she said barely above a whisper.

Her eyes grew wide as videos of homes sliding

down the sides of a mountain were shown. This had occurred last week near San Luis Obispo. *That's a long way from here*, she thought to herself. *It's a coastal town. We aren't.*

She tried to convince herself this couldn't happen to her. It wasn't working.

TWENTY-SIX

Friday
New Year's Day
Devil's Gate Dam
La Cañada, California

An hour earlier, a couple running through the rain glanced over the Foothills Parkway Bridge adjacent to the Devil's Gate Dam. They caught a glimpse of a man holding onto a toppled tree, gripping a branch as the water released through the sluice gates pummeled his body. The sheriff's department was called, and a massive rescue operation began. Also, investigators were on the scene to question the operations team on duty and the one who worked last night.

While brave fire and rescue personnel rappelled down the rocks above the portal to Hell in an attempt to reach the numerous bodies they'd now discovered, rescue choppers fought the high winds and blowing rain to assist in pulling out any survivors. The entire scene drew crowds onto the top of the bridge despite the inclement weather. Camera crews soon arrived to turn the deadly disaster into a full-blown three-ring circus.

All of this served to distract the dam operators from the task at hand, which was to closely monitor the water levels threatening to overflow Devil's Gate. Because visibility was limited, they were unable to see all manner of debris flowing toward the dam, driven by a fierce wind rushing through the Crescenta Valley. While they were fielding investigators' questions or commiserating in tucked-away offices, Devil's Gate was on the brink.

Finally, a fresh set of eyes in the form of a supervisor for LA County Flood Control arrived on the scene. While most everyone at the dam was consumed with the rescue operation and how it had happened, she studied the reservoir and the data points generated by electronic sensors.

ARKSTORM

Without consulting those preoccupied by the investigation, she contacted her boss, who in turn reached out to emergency management personnel. It was agreed that the relief tunnels were insufficient to relieve the buildup of water and debris at the dam. They would have to open the spillways to allow large amounts of water to flow over.

This decision, however, would have to be delayed until the mayor approved it and adequate notice was given to the residents and businesses below the dam throughout La Cañada Flintridge all the way down to Pasadena, where the Rose Bowl was being played. LA County Emergency Management had developed a text message warning system to advise local residents of flash flooding, earthquakes, and wildfires. These text messages were rarely sent and were generally adhered to. However, not everyone had subscribed to them.

As the ARkStorm hit, its ferocity increased every hour. As it slowly inched onshore, it gained strength, pulling moisture from the coastal waters.

The warmer rains pummeled the barren ridges of the mountains. Muddy ground became more saturated. The seventy-mile-an-hour winds uprooted the already compromised root systems of trees that had survived the Station Fire II. The fallen trees swept up boulders and millions of cubic yards of silt as the Earth's gravity won the tug-of-war with the ridges that once held the debris.

Snow-packed areas were treated to the same warm rainfall, causing a rapid melt and corresponding runoff. The creeks and streams overflowed their banks, washing out roads. The water found any way available to head towards the Crescenta Valley.

This massive volume of water made its way toward the Arroyo Seco River basin, which began to form a massive lake. It was relatively shallow at first, maybe ten feet in depth. However, there was more rain to come.

Over sixty inches in the next four hours.

The Flood Control supervisor rudely kicked out everyone who wasn't employed by her department or the dam. One investigator objected. She angrily dragged him by the arm outside onto an observation platform. She shouted at him and pointed at the reservoir. "More people will die if you don't let us do our jobs," she shouted. She shoved him back toward the control room, to several astonished faces.

By the time the investigators left, deep under water at the base of the Devil's Gate Dam, a stitch in the concrete had developed. A three-inch crack ran fifty feet from the bottom toward the top. Pieces of concrete began to break away, causing the crack to grow wider and longer.

The fallen trees, aided by the high winds, acted like battering rams against the dam. The ARkStorm grew stronger, howling like a demon throughout the valley. The battering rams smelled blood as they continued to pummel Devil's Gate.

And then the Devil himself burst through the dam designed to hold him in Hell.

TWENTY-SEVEN

Friday
New Year's Day
Hendrick Residence
La Cañada, California

She stood in front of the television, transfixed on the videos of homes disappearing over cliffs. The game was no longer on the screen after she'd moved the girls into the dining room to eat their lunch. She was astonished by the destruction. Questioned how it was even possible. Yet she knew there were homes above and below the ridge overlooking the lush, green golf course below.

Suddenly, an explosion rocked the house,

knocking her backwards onto the sofa. She immediately looked at the flower vase to determine if the water inside was rippling like when the tremors started for an earthquake.

The girls shrieked and came running into the family room, tears flowing down their cheeks from the sudden blast. She stood up, forgetting about the pain searing through her knee, and opened her arms to embrace them. She tried to offer them words of comfort, not dissimilar to the ones she'd love to hear from her husband.

"Come here. We're good. I'm sure there is an explanation for this."

They held each other for a moment, and when no additional explosions were felt, Sammy thought it was over. "See, girls? It's just fine."

Then the power went out. The television screen was blank. No lights were on. The ambient noises generated by the refrigerator and ceiling fans stopped. Even the girls stopped breathing momentarily out of fright.

Sammy's eyes darted around the room and toward every window. *What the hell is happening?* She shouted the question inside her brain. She had to gather her composure.

"Girls, please stay right here for a moment.

Okay?" She gently nudged them toward the sofa. They were crying now. It broke Sammy's heart to see their little bottom lips pucker and their beautiful eyes well up with moisture before they opened up the floodgates. Children were so innocent. Pure. Deserving of protection from all threats. Their young minds were unable to discern the dangers resulting from circumstances they were unable to comprehend.

"I'm going to step outside and take a look," she said in her best motherly voice.

"Nooo, Sammy! Don't leave us!" begged Livvy.

"Can't we come with you?" asked Sophie.

Sammy took a deep breath and looked through the windows. Other than the heavy rains and winds obliterating her view beyond a hundred feet of their home, she couldn't see how the weather could be the cause of the explosion. She was beginning to think that a nearby transformer was the culprit; however, she wanted to make sure.

"Okay, under one condition. Stay just inside the doorway. I promise not to leave your sight."

The girls jumped off the sofa in unison. "Okay," said Sophie, the leader of the two, anointed simply by being older.

Sammy led them to the back of the house first.

She wanted to get a look at the power pole up the ridge from their home. The streetlight had been a source of annoyance since they moved in, as it shined directly into their bedroom. Above the streetlight was a transformer.

With the girls standing just inside the doors, Sammy walked into the backyard toward the back of their bedroom. Not only did she want to determine if the transformer was intact, but she also wanted to get a better look at the water runoff she'd noticed earlier.

The tiny creeks had expanded to streams, and now muddy water flowing down the hill covered the entire hill behind their house. It was splashing against their wood fence and then being diverted away from the house in a swale built for that purpose when the home was constructed. However, the sheer volume of water was now spilling over the swale and seeping under their fence. Before long, it would threaten to flood their backyard and the patio doors. She suddenly wished their garage were full of sandbags.

The transformer was still in place, and there was no evidence it had been damaged, so Sammy turned her attention to the front of the house. The girls had retrieved a bath towel for her to dry off, earning them both hugs, kisses, and smiles.

The front of the couple's hacienda-style home featured a portico entry with a rounded header. It jutted out from the house into the yard, blocking their view up and down the street. Sammy made her way outside, and the girls entered the portico. Within seconds of stepping into the yard, Sammy's eyes opened wide with astonishment. She covered her mouth with her hand as she gasped. She couldn't see the golf course.

Not just because of the wind and rain obscuring a clear view of it. But because it had been turned into a massive river stretching as far as she could see toward Pasadena. Its width measured from the ridge where the 210 Freeway was located all the way to North Arroyo where she lived.

From her viewpoint, she was unable to see the Devil's Gate Dam. On a sunny day, she could walk directly down the hill in front of her house, past the homes overlooking the golf course, to the cart path in order to catch a glimpse of the massive structure. However, by the volume of water she was seeing, it was clear the dam operators had opened up all their available spillways.

"What was the explosion?" she mumbled under her breath. She cursed herself for not having a better understanding of how the dam worked. But why should she? There was barely any water being held in the reservoir. Well, at least until this December.

"Sammy, what do you see?" asked Sophie.

Her question dragged Sammy out of her musings. She glanced back toward the golf course. She lowered her brow to focus on the waves created by the wind. She wasn't sure, but she swore to herself that the water had risen in the quick few minutes she'd been observing it.

"Just some flooding, girls. Let's get back inside so I can try to get a cell signal."

For the next five minutes, Sammy paced the floor, trying to place a call or send a text to Tyler. She knew it was the middle of the game; however, she was concerned about the volume of water heading toward the Rose Bowl.

After her attempts to call and text, she opened Safari on her iPhone and tried to connect to the internet. It wasn't allowing her to, so she threw the phone on the sofa out of frustration. "Stupid 5G. It doesn't work on a good day." She lamented the highly touted 5G network coverage that seemed to make accessing cell towers more difficult rather than easier.

Sammy began to pace again, alternating between the back windows and those looking toward the front. The girls had calmed down and were now playing Sorry!, although less enthusiastically than in the past several days. With them distracted, she decided to put on her rain gear she wore when running with Tyler. She had to get a closer look at the river that was now flowing across the Brookside Golf Club.

A few minutes later, with the girls preoccupied, she eased out the front door and into the rain. Another minute later, she was standing on the street, peering between the two homes directly across from them. She was amazed at the raging waters flowing toward LA. However, it was what happened next that completely shocked Sammy.

TWENTY-EIGHT

Friday
New Year's Day
The Rose Bowl
Pasadena, California

The game had been hard fought with both teams struggling to get their offense hitting on all cylinders. The defensive struggle resulted in the special teams' play being integral to USC taking an early 3–0 lead. At the end of the first quarter, Tyler was able to catch his breath. He took in the spectacle of the fans throughout the stadium. Penn State's team colors were on display on one side, and the USC colors were more predominant on the other. There weren't very many seats filled by casual fans, as the rain seemed to keep people away. Only the hardcore fanatics braved the elements and remained for the game.

Penn State had just recovered a fumble caused when Nelson was blindsided while attempting a pass. He seemed to hobble off the field although it was difficult to determine because none of the players seemed to enjoy the terrible field conditions.

The USC quarterback coach summoned Nelson to the bench and spoke to him about the play. Tyler stopped being a spectator for the moment despite the fact Penn State was moving the ball closer to the goal line. He joined the coach with the star player and listened in on the conversation. While he did, he glanced into the stands.

What he saw at first was odd. Most of the fans were stressfully watching the field as Penn State drew closer to scoring again. However, others were gathering themselves up to exit the stadium. They weren't leaving to hit the refreshment stands or go to the restroom. They were taking stadium seats, cushions, and rain gear to leave. As they climbed the concrete steps toward the stadium exits, some would stop from time to time and speak to their fellow fans. A few of those fans suddenly gathered their belongings and joined the dozens of people leaving.

Tyler looked toward the dark gray sky. The rain pelted his face, stinging the exposed skin his beard didn't protect. The quarterback coach patted him on the back to get his attention just as a loud groan spread through the USC fans' assigned seating. A much louder cheer arose from the Penn State fans and players. They'd scored a go-ahead touchdown.

Nelson hopped off the bench and began toward the sideline to take the field following the kickoff. Tyler stopped him briefly to ask about his leg. His quarterback was curt in his response, most likely hiding the truth from his trainer. Ordinarily, Tyler might've pressed him. However, the unusual activity in the stands puzzled him.

What do they know that we don't?

He wanted to shrug it off; however, the odd behavior continued to nag him. He spent an equal amount of time watching the plays on the field and the exiting of the fans in the stadium. His obsession with the fan activity caused him to miss an injury to one of the Trojans' players.

When he noticed the medical team rush onto the field, he hustled to catch up. He pulled his cap down over his brow to avoid the pelting rain. Oddly, he chuckled to himself; he wondered if Sammy had noticed him coming onto the field. His doting over his beard that morning had been a waste of time. Now it was simply holding water as he knelt over the injured player.

After he assisted the young man off the field, the game continued. USC took advantage of any complacency on the part of the Penn State defense during the long break in the action. On the first play from scrimmage, Nelson dropped back to pass, eyed his favorite receiver on a crossing route, and hit him right in the numbers. The race was on as several defenders chased after the receiver, who ran untouched down the middle of the field for a touchdown.

The USC fans exploded with a roar of approval. The band played as loud as humanly possible. The spontaneous eruption of cheers and music muted the sound of the Devil's Gate Dam exploding from the massive force caused by the water.

Tyler didn't hear it. Some might have but disregarded it in their exuberance.

The dam that was holding back millions of gallons of water and countless tons of debris was barely two miles from the Rose Bowl.

They had no idea what was coming because

during the on-field celebration of the touchdown, the power grid collapsed. Somewhere in the universe, Don Meredith, the famous Dallas Cowboys quarterback turned *Monday Night Football* announcer was singing *turn out the lights, the party's over*.

TWENTY-NINE

Friday
New Year's Day
Hendrick Residence
La Cañada, California

Through the howling wind and the rain pounding everything around her, she heard a high-pitched squeaking sound. It was piercing at first, and then it was replaced by a low rumble that resulted in a crash. Sammy started walking toward the source coming from the direction of Devil's Gate.

She'd momentarily lost focus as she walked down the middle of the street. An electric pickup truck came racing by her, waiting to honk until just before it arrived by her side. Although she drove a Tesla, she'd always complained about how the vehicles could sneak up on a pedestrian without warning. Naturally, she knew better than to stand out in the road. However, she was mesmerized by the storm and the need to know what was happening beyond her home.

She walked a quarter of a mile toward the three large estate homes sitting on a point overlooking the golf course. She and Tyler ran down this road every night, oftentimes admiring the half-dozen properties lining the street. They were valued around ten million dollars, and several Hollywood stars were rumored to live there.

Sammy got the nerve to walk down one of the driveways in the direction of the golf course. She knew the distance across the course to the park was narrowest at this point.

Well, it used to be, anyway.

She made her way down the winding driveway surrounded by trees and heavy vegetation. She questioned whether she should continue to the end, not fearful she'd be arrested for trespassing but simply not wanting to further intrude upon someone's private property. Still, her curiosity to get a better look at the newly created river encouraged her to continue.

She heard the squeaking sound again, followed by a groan. The noises were foreign to her.

She reached the bottom of the driveway and looked across the backyard toward the water. She focused all her senses to block out the wind and the incessant rain. Sammy tilted her head, trying to make sense of what she saw. Then the visuals from the weather report earlier gave her a point of reference.

It was a roof. The roof of a house was floating down the river. There were all kinds of debris from a house that had been swept away by the raging waters.

Crash!

Sammy jumped, startled by the sudden noise to her left. She leaned over a wrought-iron railing at the massive home's parking pad. Two houses down, she could see the water crashing against the backyard landscaping and into the pool. With each crushing wave caused by the wind, large chunks of the yard disappeared. Within seconds, the shell of the swimming pool was visible. Then, a moment later, it was gone, floating for a moment before capsizing.

Instinctively, Sammy looked up at the three-story home she stood next to. Soon, it would be under attack. With a new sense of urgency, she turned and raced up the concrete driveway, slipping twice on the mud-filled water rushing down it from the ridge above.

Momentarily disoriented, she turned right at the top of the drive, allowing her memory of their running route to overtake her logic. She ran a hundred yards before realizing she was going the wrong way, in more ways than one.

In front of the house that had already succumbed to the deluge, the road was beginning to break away in chunks. The side of the asphalt was exposed down to the gravel base. The once firmly packed soil beneath it was no match for the turbulent waters below.

Sammy stared in wonderment for a minute, amazed at how quickly a house and its beautifully landscaped yard could disappear. She looked over her shoulder back toward her own home, which was just out of sight. Then she whipped her head back towards Devil's Gate. She came to a realization.

One by one, this new river would consume their homes.

Sammy froze. Her mind was in disbelief at what her eyes revealed to her. What was unfolding in her neighborhood was no different than the reporting on the news. Tears streamed down her face. She cried for the people who lost their homes. She cried for anyone who got swept up in the water. She cried as she thought about Tyler being in peril. Did he even know what was coming toward him?

And then she panicked. The girls. Her beloved dogs. They were all in danger.

She gathered herself and ran like the wind, allowing the gusts to push her forward while avoiding landing face-first on the asphalt. When she reached her front yard, she saw Sophie and Livvy standing just inside the covered entry to the house. They were wet from rain spray and tears. She should've told them where she was going.

"You left us!" said Livvy as she sobbed.

Sammy, breathless from racing back to the house, knelt down in front of the sisters. "I'm so sorry. I didn't want to concern you. I just wanted to check on something."

"What's happening, Aunt Sammy?" Sophie referred to her as aunt. They locked eyes. Then Sammy knew why. She was no longer Sammy the playmate or meal-maker. She wasn't necessarily Aunt Sammy. She was family and now must assume the role of their mother. They had given up their youthful independence and turned their lives over to their protector—Aunt Sammy.

She took a deep breath and gathered her thoughts. She managed a smile. "Girls, we need to leave."

"Where are we going?" asked Livvy.

Great question, kiddo. "Well, I'm not really sure. Maybe we'll head toward the Rose Bowl and pick up your uncle. Or he and I always enjoyed walking at Cherry Canyon Park. It's just north of here. The top of the mountains gives us a great view of the ocean. Whadya think?"

"How will he find us?" asked Sophie.

Sammy stroked the child's face with the back of her hand. She didn't want to say out loud that he'd have to fend for himself. That they couldn't wait at home because she didn't want to get sucked into the floodwaters.

"I'm gonna leave him a note, and then we'll touch base by cell phone as soon as the storm passes."

That was Sammy's plan. Not a great one, but the only one she could come up with. Unfortunately, Tyler would never see the note she wrote, and Sammy never made it to Cherry Canyon with the kids.

THIRTY

**Friday
New Year's Day
The Rose Bowl
Pasadena, California**

The fans sitting in the upper rows of the north end of the stadium heard the commotion and were the first to view the deluge. Despite the two-mile distance, they had an unobstructed view across the Brookside Golf Course toward the 210 Freeway. They couldn't see the dam itself, or what was now left of it. Those who'd brought binoculars to watch plays in the far end of the field from their seats described the scene to others. Their excited voices shocked their fellow fans.

"A wall of water!"

"It's crushing houses."

"And trees!"

"It's coming right for us!"

"Run!"

On a normal day, the man-made concrete trough, measuring forty feet wide and eighteen feet deep, would contain barely a trickle of water. Plants and weeds grew out of the cracks where the sloped walls met the concrete floor. Lately, with the heavy rains, the water flowed downhill, first in tiny rivulets and then making its way into larger creeks. The creeks flowed into rivers before the Arroyo Seco flood-control channel carried it past Rose Bowl Stadium.

Onlookers with binoculars reported they couldn't see the concrete. Most of the golf course was under water, which was rapidly rising. Faster than anything they could imagine. The lush green grasses of the country club were covered. Trees were being toppled as other trees tumbled along the rollicking waves created by the suddenly strong winds.

In the distance, one brave observer who hadn't joined the others in the mad dash to the exit swore they saw houses on the ridge disappear. One man said that was impossible. He had to be wrong. Then another exclaimed that the water was rushing over Washington Boulevard, which crossed the golf course. Carloads of people trying to flee the area were unexpectedly swept up by the rushing water.

Inside the stadium, fans crushed one another in an attempt to exit the stadium. Two of the largest parking lots were bisected by the Arroyo Seco channel. Television trucks covering the big game were parked nose-to-tail perilously close to where the water would normally funnel past.

Screams filled the air, coupled with cries of pain as people pushed and shoved their way past their fellow fans. Some who assessed the water's rapid rise opted for a higher ground—the top rows of the stadium. They gambled that the massive concrete structure would survive the onslaught of water and debris. At one hundred feet tall, their gamble would pay off. For a while, at least.

As the chaos in the stands unfolded, players and coaches on the field were caught in a confused state. The public address system in the stadium was inoperable due to the power outage. Law enforcement personnel on the field had been cut off from dispatch due to the collapsing communications towers. The warnings from those who'd observed the massive volume of water coming toward them hadn't made their way to the field yet.

Unable to discern what was happening, most of the participants began jogging back to their locker rooms to await further word regarding the status of the power outage and to learn when the game would resume.

Tyler stood a few feet onto the playing field and slowly turned around to observe the fans' reactions. It had been years since he'd recalled a power outage during a football game. Usually, everyone waits for the power to be restored. This was different. People were in a panic. Some forced their way through the portals into the concourse. Others, inexplicably, ran over one another toward the highest rows of the stadium. None of it made any sense, so despite being soaked and cold, he stood his ground until he could make sense of it all.

Very few people joined him, which instinctively told Tyler he was in the wrong place. As a strong wind gust threatened to knock him off his feet, he thought some crazy weather event like a tornado or hurricane was headed toward him. Still, if that was the case, why were people pushing and shoving to get to the top rows of the stadium.

He walked briskly down the tunnel leading into the locker room. Just as he arrived at the bottom, he heard the sounds of feet sloshing and people shouting. In the pitch darkness, he moved closer to the lower-level concourse leading to the locker room.

People were shouting.

"Get out!"

"Everybody, get out!"

Whatever they were fleeing, it was too late. Water rushed along the concourse, knocking down frantic fans trying to find their way out of the stadium. A couple of players who had difficulty maintaining their balance on the concrete while wearing cleats slipped. They struggled to regain their footing and got caught up in the rushing water.

They tumbled past Tyler, who remained inside the tunnel, watching the rapid flowing water in astonishment. More bodies and football equipment washed past him, urging him to back up several steps in order to retreat to the field. He debated trying to help but became concerned the frantic victims might cause him to be injured.

His mind switched to survival mode although he remained concerned for Sammy and the kids. The water levels were rising, confirming the obvious—the stadium was flooding. If it was flooding like this in Pasadena, what it was it like two miles away where they lived?

How am I gonna get back to Sammy?

THIRTY-ONE

2010
Board of Supervisors Special Closed Session Meeting
USGS Presentation
Los Angeles County, California

Dale Cox was the program manager for the SAFRR Project, a multiagency collaboration designed to apply scientific evidence to reduce the risks and repercussions of natural disasters. He'd been invited by the Los Angeles County Board of Supervisors to brief them on the potential threat of atmospheric rivers on the county, with a particular emphasis on the ARkStorm scenario.

"Mr. Cox, we appreciate you providing us these three-hundred-plus pages describing this major storm event. However, to be honest, with our busy schedules, most of us haven't read the report in its entirety, much less absorbed the scientific details. Would you mind addressing the scenario in simple terms?"

Cox was not surprised at the request by Michael Antonovich, the supervisor from the fifth district, which included some of the Crescenta Valley communities most likely to be impacted by flooding. He'd requested Cox appear to make the presentation at the special closed-session meeting and was certain he was the only member of the board to have read the USGS study in its entirety. His initial foray into the subject was intended to avoid the other four members of the board being embarrassed by their lack of preparation.

"Certainly, with pleasure," replied Cox as the two men exchanged knowing glances. He expected as much.

"Let's start with the CliffsNotes, shall we?" asked the supervisor from the south end of the county.

Cox spent a moment explaining how atmospheric rivers form and the circumstances under which the thousand-year flood event would materialize. After several questions regarding the science, the obvious question was asked—when?

"Without being evasive, no one knows when it'll happen. It could begin this winter or a dozen winters from now. The last ARkStorm event occurred in the winter of 1861 into 1862. One can't say it's overdue or not yet due to hit the state. It could happen every year for a decade."

"If it's that unpredictable, how are we supposed to prepare? I mean, how do we have our emergency response teams at the ready as well as federal assets like FEMA?"

Cox nodded. "The short answer is always. Every single winter, the potential is there. I might add, as the planet's surface temperatures rise, the potential for stronger and more frequent atmospheric rivers should be taken into account."

"Why do they call it the Other Big One?"

"The computer models indicate the ARkStorm will continue for weeks, and the destruction could dwarf California's wildfires, droughts, and even earthquakes in terms of overall economic damages. The loss of life could potentially be in the hundreds of thousands."

"Come on, Mr. Cox!" exclaimed the supervisor from South LA. "From a rainstorm? That's a little overdramatic, don't you think?"

Cox bristled. He wasn't trying to sell a disaster-movie script. He was trying to raise their awareness of the threat. Nonetheless, he'd been warned to watch out for her pushback. This particular supervisor was known to oppose any potential expenditures except for the pet projects in her district.

"As the report indicates, and keep in mind, this is based on historic precedent, an ARkStorm will dump over one hundred inches of rain in a very short period of time into the Central Valley. Let me add, although we don't address the issue of snowfall in Southern California very often, when the ARkStorm hits the mountain ranges, for every inch of rainfall, ten inches of snow accumulates. If the continuous flow of moisture brings warmer temperatures at the tail end, as is most likely, the snow will melt, bringing the water toward the valley."

"A major flood event, I take it?" asked another supervisor.

"That's correct. Unprecedented. This would be worse than anything Southern California has experienced in more than a century. With the region's dense population, there's no historical analogy for a storm of this magnitude. Only the USGS study."

A couple of supervisors glanced at each other and raised their eyebrows. Cox surmised they regretted not reading the entire report. One of them asked, "Lay it out for me. You know, what do the damages look like?"

"The astonishing amount of rainfall coupled with the snow melt will create incomprehensible flooding, triggering mudslides and washing debris from the ridges bordering the valley. Trees, structures, animals, just about anything that depends on stable ground to remain upright.

"Cell towers will be toppled, taking out the ability to notify residents or for first responders to communicate with one another. The power grid will collapse, thrusting the entire region into the nineteenth century. Roads and highways will be impassable as they're washed away. Entire areas, including much of Los Angeles County, will be under water."

"Okay," began the South LA supervisor in a sarcastic tone of voice. "This does sound like a novel or movie script. However, the fact of the matter is our citizens will be provided adequate notice, right? I mean, our advanced weather forecasting capabilities will give them plenty of time to evacuate, limiting loss of life. I'm sure the insurance companies will suffer as they pay out the damage claims, but they can afford it."

Cox paused before responding. He really wanted to point out that thousands of residents in New Orleans had ignored the mandatory evacuation notifications when Hurricane Katrina came onshore. The news had been filled with images of people standing on their rooftops, waving for help. Many lives could've been saved during that storm event had residents simply left as instructed. The Katrina response had become a political football that he didn't want to cloud the issue at hand.

"Well, that's one of the reasons I assume I was asked to address the board today. The county needs to consider evacuation measures for an event like this. Notice is part of that. So are appropriate routes out of the region, similar to hurricane evacuation measures in the southeastern United States. In addition, there is the matter of human nature."

All of the supervisors were puzzled by his last statement.

"Please explain," said Antonovich.

"Every year, we experience atmospheric river

storm events in December through March. Some seasons are worse than others. The ARs, as we call them, can come in rapid succession. Citizens may become desensitized to the threat. They may see the heavy rain as an annoyance and inconvenience rather than a matter of life and death. The first time the county declares an evacuation and it becomes a false alarm, residents may never heed the warning again or delay their evacuation until the last minute.

"Even if the highways headed away from the valley aren't destroyed by mudslides and flooding, they'll be packed with vehicles. Residents in Malibu, Oxnard, and Ventura will be isolated for months. Residents in the Hollywood Hills and upward through the Crescenta Valley would see their homes sliding down ridges.

"Emergency vehicles would be rendered obsolete, so fleets of boats and helicopters would need to mobilize to rescue stranded residents. That is, assuming boats and helicopters could operate during the heavy rain events coupled with the hurricane-force winds."

The stunned supervisors whispered amongst themselves while Cox remained ready to field more questions. He was prepared to advise them on the aftermath of the ARkStorm. However, they'd heard enough and ended the session.

He shrugged and closed his binder. He wondered if they'd call him back to discuss the recovery effort. He really intended to provide more suggestions on how to prepare. Even if it meant gathering the animals, two by two, onto a massive boat.

THIRTY-TWO

Friday
New Year's Day
Rose Bowl Stadium
Pasadena, California

Consumed with worry, Tyler knew he had to get home. He ran back toward the tunnel leading to the locker room and the lower concourse. He was greeted head-on by a throng of stadium personnel and players shoving their way out of the lowest level of the stadium. They were chased by fast-flowing water nipping at their heels.

"Out of the way," yelled one burly guy, a defense lineman on the Trojans' squad. He forced his way past Tyler, who spun around like a top. He was struck in the side by a food vendor and then shoved in the back by a fellow member of the coaching staff.

The crazed mixture of people fleeing the floodwaters had little regard for their fellow man as they sought higher ground. From the shouts and screams emanating from the concourse, Tyler realized some people were being trampled as the human stampede attempted to evade drowning.

He found his footing and forced himself against the wall of the tunnel. Any attempt to get out of the stadium toward higher ground would be thwarted by the panicked people rushing through the low-lying concourse. He turned and rushed up the ramp onto the field again. He needed to get an assessment of what was happening outside the stadium.

He joined several others running toward the north end zone, where they scaled the short wall to enter the stands. Then the long climb up the concrete steps threatened to take all the oxygen out of his lungs. His routine of running, which included participating in half-marathons, paled in comparison to the effort he exerted to climb the stairs in a driving rain when his chest was heavy with apprehension.

As well as regret. He couldn't believe Sammy was home alone with his nieces. They were probably justifiably panicked. He should be with them. Yet here he was, confused and feeling worthless.

Tyler had to shove his way past several fans who were craning their necks to view the valley leading to Devil's Gate. Despite being cursed at, he persevered and reached the railing. He was shaken emotionally and battled to maintain some semblance of composure.

A half-mile-wide river was flowing where the Brookside Golf Club had been since 1932. The water was rushing toward the stadium with a vengeance, picking up parked vehicles to join the remnants of homes and tree trunks that flowed atop its tumultuous waves.

Tyler leaned forward to see directly below the stadium. The wreckage of destroyed homes had obliterated the fencing near the stadium and was now pounding away at the concrete walls. Trees and other rubble from mudslides acted to clog the exits to the stadium, which was helping to divert the water around the sides. However, the newly formed river was rising and soon would be near field level.

Tyler had to make a decision. The torrential downpour gave no indication of letting up. The howling wind was reminiscent of the hurricanes that made their annual appearances in Florida. However, it was the flooding that left him awestruck. He'd never seen this much water seemingly appear out of thin air. Furthermore, as it continued to rain, he imagined it would get worse.

He looked west toward the ridge that bordered the golf course where their home was located. It was impossible to locate Linda Vista Avenue, a scenic road he and Sammy used to jog toward the parks surrounding the stadium. The wind-blown rain obscured his vision.

Logically, the floodwaters would be at their worst along the Arroyo Seco flood-control channel that led from his neighborhood to the stadium and beyond into LA.

Then he had an idea.

He pushed his way back through the hundreds of people trying to get a look at the floodwaters. He ran along the bleacher-style seats until he reached the northeastern corner of the stadium. Visibility was somewhat better, as the winds were blowing from the northwest.

He squinted his eyes and pulled the bill of his cap lower on his forehead. He searched for a point of reference east of the stadium. Rosemont Avenue, which ran parallel to the river along the golf course, was flooded. However, as the ridge climbed, he could make out houses and streets. He knew the 210 Freeway was at the top of the ridge.

If he could make it to there, he could run across the bridge overlooking Devil's Gate Dam and take the exit leading to NASA's Jet Propulsion Laboratory. Tyler set his jaw, and a determined look came over his face. If he couldn't cross the wild water blasting its way toward the Rose Bowl, he'd try to go around it.

THIRTY-THREE

Friday
New Year's Day
Hendrick Residence
La Cañada, California

Sammy's four-door Tesla S was a roomy sedan. The girls were small enough to share the front seat. The front and rear trunk compartments included a back seat that folded flat. This enabled her to include her mountain bike for alternate transportation in case the all-electric vehicle drained its batteries. She would at least have some means of travel to search for help.

The girls packed all their clothes, including the winter gear they'd worn on the flight to LAX.

Sammy packed the couple's camping gear as well as warm clothing. Every nook and cranny of the Tesla was jam-packed with necessities, including food, water, and basic medical supplies.

She double-checked the *Find* settings on her Apple Watch and iPhone to confirm that Tyler would be able to locate them when the cell service was restored. In the event there was a prolonged outage, she wrote him a lengthy note. Or it was more like a letter. She got the business side of their evacuation out of the way first.

She reported what she'd observed and heard as it related to the breached dam. She provided him a list of the things she'd packed in the car, including her bike, assuming he might need it to reach her. She also told him where they were headed, identifying the precise location where they frequently picnicked.

Then she poured her heart out to him. She wrote about how much she loved their life together. To ease any guilt the couple might have held inside about leaving Florida, she added how grateful she was for the life they'd made in California despite the present circumstances.

She provided him words of encouragement that, after he read this note, he could make it to the top of Cherry Canyon Park. Then, as part of their inside joke, she wrote, *You've got this, babe!* She kissed the letter and smiled. She was certain he'd get a chuckle out of that last part.

She set it on the kitchen island along with a bottle of Coco5, a premade electrolyte drink. Despite the rain, she was reminding him he needed to stay hydrated in case he had to make his way to them without a car.

She got the girls settled in the white sedan, with Carly and Fenway seated behind them. The group was packed in like the proverbial sardines. She was beginning to doubt herself. Perhaps she'd overreacted. Maybe the waters would recede as they found their way toward downtown LA. Regardless, she wanted them to be prepared for staying on higher ground for several days, just in case.

Sammy had to pull the string on the garage door opener to pop the track open. Within seconds after she tugged the door upward, the wind-blown rain soaked the garage and her. She considered a change of clothes until she glanced toward the golf course, or at least where it used to be. There was no doubt the water had risen substantially in the time it took them to pack and prepare to leave.

With a new sense of urgency, she pulled out of the garage. Oddly, fearful of looting, she rushed out of the car into the rain to pull the garage door down. It bounced off the concrete and rose a few inches. She used her foot to push it all the way closed, but it rebounded slightly.

"Dammit! Stay closed, you stupid thing!" She cursed the door, which stubbornly rose back up to leave a three-inch gap every time. With the bottom of her fist, she gave the door a good slam and then stormed back into the car.

"Sammy, are you okay?" asked Sophie, who had a better viewpoint of the confrontation than her sister, who'd slumped down in the seat.

"Um, yeah. Sorry. Just frustrated."

In an innocent voice in a joking way, Sammy was certain, Sophie asked, "Maybe you need a time-out?"

Sammy burst out in nervous laughter. She hadn't bothered to check her pulse rate on her watch until now. In addition to her resting heart rate being low ordinarily, her doctor recommended she wear the Apple device at night to emit a warning signal when her rate dove near the forties. The medical condition known as bradycardia had been an issue for her since high school. Bradycardia was a condition that resulted in a resting heart rate during sleep near a dangerously low forty beats per minute. When awake, the condition had caused her to feel faint, short of breath and experience chest pain.

She glanced at her watch to check the time. Her rate was well over one hundred, highly unusual for her except when on the final leg of a long run. She took a deep breath to calm her nerves before pulling out of the driveway. They faced a lot of potential danger ahead, and she didn't need to make a stupid mistake because of anxiety.

She backed the Tesla out of the driveway and headed away from the dam because she knew the road had washed away in part. As she drove off, she glanced in the rearview mirror. She scowled and tilted her head, certain that something appeared to be out of place.

Sammy shrugged and continued, looking for the first opportunity to turn right in search of higher ground to avoid the raging river. Above her home was a series of winding streets snaking upward along the ridge. Tyler loved the steep incline and the sharp turns when running, as he considered the neighborhood streets along the ridge to be the ultimate test of their endurance. Sammy hated them, although she never let Tyler know that. She thought running downhill was a much wiser choice.

She drove carefully, as the streets held a couple

of inches of water. She was fully aware that it didn't take much to cause a vehicle to hydroplane. She took some comfort in knowing her Tesla was heavier than most cars of its size due to the weighty batteries required to power electric vehicles.

As she navigated through several three-to-five-foot-wide boulders that had rolled down the steep slopes, she noticed most vehicles were still parked in their driveways. Many residents stood under covered porches or entryways. Some braved the winds to commiserate with their neighbors while holding umbrellas that could any moment carry them away like Mary Poppins. Apparently, they were unaware of what the force of the rushing water was doing to the homes down the street from her.

There was one thing for certain, they were wholly unaware of the threat that loomed from above them, as Sammy would soon discover.

THIRTY-FOUR

**Friday
New Year's Day
North Arroyo Neighborhood
La Cañada, California**

The residents of North Arroyo loved their neighborhood. They appreciated the older, classic homes, many of which dated back to the middle of the last century. Homes that had fallen in disrepair had been immediately snatched up by enterprising house flippers, who made a decent profit after renovations. Others were passed down to family members in estate settlements. All would agree that the properties were beautifully maintained, and the neighborhood was considered safe.

It was not unusual for the couple to run through the streets at night to stay in top physical condition. As Sammy steered the car around the curvy streets, she mentally checked off the familiar names. Devon. Braemer. Normandy. Inverness.

Higher and higher up the ridge she drove, beginning to feel a sense of relief the farther away they were from the raging river. She'd just made a sharp turn on Normandy toward Inverness Drive, the street that would carry them to the top, when she drove up on stalled traffic.

Certainly, traffic jams on LA roads and highways were considered the norm rather than the exception. However, she didn't expect it to be like this in her neighborhood. Especially under these conditions. She'd gotten the impression that most of the residents had remained sheltered in place, as local emergency management organizations always implored them to do.

With cars parked two abreast heading toward Inverness, Sammy settled in to wait. While she explained to the fidgety girls and her bored pups that this was just temporary, she craned her neck to determine the cause of the delay.

Out of frustration, she instructed the girls to remain in the car while she walked ahead to find out what was happening. After exiting, she glanced behind her. She noticed, in just a matter of minutes, six cars had lined up behind her, and several more were slowly driving around a hairpin curve toward them.

Sammy debated whether she should leave the car running with the girls and dogs inside. She looked back and forth several times before starting to jog up the hill toward the next street. She reached the point where Inverness and Edgehill, an appropriately named street, intersected. The sandbags that once sufficed to hold off silt and mud runoff during a rare rain event had been washed away. The road was muddy and treacherous. And full of cars trying to reach the top of the ridge.

The multimillion-dollar homes perched two hundred feet above her on the ridge had been admired from afar by the couple as they exercised. The massive structures stood on the edge of a manmade cliff of rubble, rock, and soil. Many were owned by A-list celebrities like Angela Bassett, Meryl Streep, and Shia LaBeouf. Even a member of the Gambino crime family was rumored to have retired to the ridge above North Arroyo.

Sammy stood for a moment in the driving rain, allowing the muddy water to rush over her feet up to the middle of her calves. Dozens of cars were sitting still, inching forward, brake lights flashing on and off as they made limited progress.

Then, without warning, drivers laid on their horns. Not a polite beep-beep or even a legitimate honking to warn another driver to be careful. This was a cacophony of blaring, perhaps out of anger or sheer panic.

Confused, Sammy looked in all directions to determine what was causing the drivers' angst. Then she heard it. A crumbling sound followed by a deluge of mud and rock sliding into the cars only a hundred feet up the hill. She shielded her eyes from the rain, using her hand as if she were trying to avoid the brightness of the sun. She squinted. She didn't want to believe what was happening, but her eyes didn't deceive her.

One of the homes, a massive three-story stucco structure, was sliding down the ridge toward Inverness Drive. Some cars tried to bull their way upward, crashing into the vehicles in front of them. Others threw their transmissions into reverse, using the rear bumper like a bulldozer blade to push the car behind them out of the way. Tires fought to get a grip on the muddy pavement. Brakes struggled to keep vehicles from being pushed out of the way as the fourteen-thousand-square-foot mansion followed rock and mud down the ridge.

Sammy turned to run, only to be knocked down face-first into the mudslide by stampeding motorists fleeing the house that was now breaking apart.

"Here comes another one," a man shouted as Sammy tried to regain her footing, only to slip on the mud-covered asphalt. A woman helped her to her feet and bolted off before Sammy could thank her.

She, too, ran down the street, glancing behind her as the avalanche of homes picked up speed. The earth's gravity was going to get its pound of flesh by sucking the magnificent properties into the rushing waters below. That was when Sammy realized her car might be in the path of the stucco house. She became frenzied, now running with reckless abandon without regard for her own safety or those she shoved out of the way to get by.

She crashed hard into a car, reinjuring the cyclist's knee she'd barely begun to heal. Hobbled, she tried to rush back to the car; her awkward gait resembled a member of a two-person sack race, only the partner had disappeared.

She slipped down the hill and fell on her backside, causing her to slide thirty feet down the steep, rain-soaked slope until she reached Normandy. It was a painful fall; however, it allowed her to save precious seconds. Seconds she needed to protect the girls and her dogs. Seconds that only enabled her to accomplish one thing.

Watch as the massive house crashed into her Tesla and carried it down the slope along with a dozen other vehicles.

THIRTY-FIVE

Friday
New Year's Day
Rose Bowl
Pasadena, California

The bodies fell like dominoes. Little toy soldiers lined up in rows, only to be knocked backwards by an invisible hand without regard for the consequences.

As Tyler turned and made his way across the seating toward the stairs, a massive gust of wind swept over the Rose Bowl. That preceded the structure to shaking violently, causing him to lose his footing. He waved his arms to catch his balance. The hundreds of people lined up along the railing of sections nine through thirteen of the north end of the stadium were not so lucky.

The force of the wind coupled with something breaking loose at the base of the stadium caused the structure to shudder just enough for people to lose their balance. Packed in, side by side, they grabbed onto one another for stability. This only served to drag their fellow fans backwards, toppling over in near unison.

They were mercilessly thrown against the bench seats. The sounds of broken bones preceded the groans of pain overtaking their bodies. Others fell on top of them, rolling farther down the stands until their limbs and skulls made contact with concrete and steel.

Tyler watched in horror as the faces, full of agony, screamed, only to be muted by the howling wind. It was as if a mighty demon had inhabited the clouds in search of the weak and vulnerable. Like his pups and young nieces and his wife, a thought he couldn't shake from his mind.

Tyler started down the concrete steps toward the field when he heard an older woman's voice call out, "Please help me."

To be sure, all of the fallen were crying in pain,

calling for help, begging for it to end. However, her voice spoke to him. As if she knew only he could help her. Tyler stopped his downward momentum, losing his footing in the process. He landed hard on his side and hit his shoulder on the end of the bleachers. The stinger, as athletic trainers call them, occurred when there was a severe collision around the upper body. Tyler knew it immediately. The stinging and burning sensation shot down his left arm into his hand. It was if someone had stuck a cattle prod in his shoulder and turned up the power.

He sat upright and gingerly tried to raise his left arm, to no avail. Then the pain hit his shoulder. He hurled a series of expletives, as he knew this type of injury could take weeks to heal. *If*, he emphasized in his mind, he rested it.

"No time for that," he muttered as he forced himself to stand. He walked quickly up the concrete steps toward the pile of bodies, who were trying to extricate themselves from one another. Once he reached the last several rows of the stadium, he found an older woman dressed in Penn State colors lying on the concrete below a bleacher seat. She was crying.

"Nobody will help me," she said in between sobbing fits as Tyler reached her.

She was breathing rapidly, and his first concern, due to her age, was that she might hyperventilate or even suffer a cardiac event. He subconsciously tried to reach out to her with his left hand. The jolt of pain through his arm reminded him that wasn't possible.

Tyler fought back. He shook his arm despite the pain, demanding the nerve injury cooperate, at least for the moment. He thought he could suppress the effects of the stinger long enough to help the woman.

It didn't work. His attempt to shake his arm only made it worse. His antics only served to cause the woman additional consternation.

Tyler forced a man who was sitting on the bench next to her to scoot over. He was dazed and was bleeding from the side of his head. He was then able to assist the woman off the concrete with his good arm. He made direct eye contact with her and spoke in a calm voice just loud enough to be heard over the injured people around them.

"I'm Tyler. What's your name?"

"Charlotte. Charlotte Snyder. I think I broke my arm."

Tyler glanced around. As people extricated themselves from the pile, they stumbled and slipped on the bench seating. Several fell in the process, causing a mini avalanche of bodies once again.

"Can you stand, Charlotte?"

She nodded and pushed off the bench with her right arm. She held her left arm closely tucked against her body so it wouldn't be jostled.

Tyler led her down the row to the steps, and they began to slowly make their way toward the field before she stopped.

"My husband," she said before beginning to cry. "We got separated, and I don't know where he is."

Tyler looked toward the top of the stadium, assuming that he'd be there somewhere. She corrected him.

"No. He went to get us drinks when it all happened. He's near the concessions stand, I hope." Tears streamed down her face. In that moment, her broken arm became the least of her worries. Her breathing became more rapid again, and she became pale.

Tyler tried to calm her down.

"Wayne! Wayne!" she began shouting. Her voice was weak.

"Okay, Charlotte. Hang on. We'll find him. First, let me ask you about your arm."

She still frantically looked around, but eventually allowed Tyler to examine her. He didn't want to hurt her, but he had to determine how the severe the fracture was, if any.

"I'm going to gently touch your arm, okay?"

She nodded, easing it away from her body.

Tyler lovingly felt the woman's forehead and cheek for signs of fever. It was wet and clammy, a good thing and not unusual considering they were in a cold, driving rain. Then he gently examined her forearm up to her elbow.

"Does it hurt higher up?" he asked.

"No, underneath the lower part of my arm."

Tyler leaned down to check her forearm again. There was no sign of deformity and certainly nothing protruding through the skin. He surmised she had a hairline fracture. Painful but not a break.

He pulled off his USC windbreaker and smiled. "Charlotte, this may hurt more than the fall."

Her eyes grew wide. "Why? Maybe we should find a doctor."

Tyler laughed. "No, nothing like that. I'm gonna use my windbreaker to create a sling. Your team colors are gonna clash. Hold still."

She was beginning to calm down as Tyler tied the sleeves of his windbreaker into a loose knot and draped it over her head. He gently inserted her injured arm into the loop he'd created. He placed her arm in a comfortable position and then strengthened the knot. The sling worked perfectly.

"How's that?" he asked.

She smiled for the first time. "Not bad for a USC guy. My husband may not approve, but I do."

She gently stroked his cheek with the palm of her hand. It was reminiscent of how his grandmother would comfort him as a boy.

Tyler assisted her onto her feet and allowed her to drape her arm through his as they made their way down the steps. Leaving the mayhem at the top of the stadium behind, he made small talk with her.

"Can I tell you a secret?"

"Sure."

"I'm a Penn State alum. Now I'm the head athletic trainer for USC."

"Oh my," she began with a hearty laugh that caused her to wince. "And here you are consorting with the enemy."

Tyler asked, "Are you guys from around here?"

"No, actually. Well, you've probably never heard of it. But we just sold our business. It's a restaurant and bar called Hotel Wayne in McVeytown, Pennsylvania."

Tyler burst out laughing, a spontaneous reaction that threatened to knock them both over. "I know it well. It's less than an hour from State College. I used to visit it when I was young to see my uncle. Everybody knew him as Farmer Joe."

Now Charlotte was laughing. She and Tyler compared notes and realized they could have very well crossed paths in the past. Just as they reached the tunnel, her husband appeared out of nowhere. He was hugging the wall to avoid being knocked over by fans running in all directions. He was battered and bruised but elated to reunite with his wife.

The two shared a joyful reunion and exchanged a few words with Tyler as they entered the concourse near the concession stands. Tyler glanced through the openings at the back of the stadium. In just that short period of time, the waters had risen by nearly ten feet.

THIRTY-SIX

Friday
New Year's Day
North Arroyo Neighborhood
La Cañada, California

Psychologists called it acute shock disorder. Many terms were used for the psychological response to a terrifying experience. There were several warning signs to indicate you were suffering from emotional shock. Fear was one. Brain freeze, or the feeling you'd become disconnected and were floating outside your body, was another. Physical effects included nausea, racing heartbeat, and muscles tensing up.

For Sammy, her initial reaction was to freeze, staring in disbelief as she saw the mudslide consume the Tesla with the innocent girls and dogs inside. Her brain told her what she was experiencing was illogical. Surreal. Fictional. Like, it could only happen in a novel or on the big screen.

Yet as the rain pelted her body and the mudslide expanded to almost knock her off her feet, Sammy was able to return herself to reality. As she struggled to make sense of the situation, her brain was filled with all the different scenarios that could result from the house debris sweeping her car down the ridge toward the river.

She ran toward the remains of the structure as it slid down the hill. Then she turned to see if anyone else had observed what she had, hoping someone might help her. Nobody else cared. They had their own problems, her brain told her without feeling. She looked down the ridge, wondering if she should chase after the flow of debris.

She freed her feet from the mud that had slid around them, stepping closer to where the cars were once parked. Hers was not the only one that had disappeared as the two homes came tumbling down. She decided chasing the landslide downward would only get her killed.

She turned back up the hill and slogged through the water and silt. She found a driveway to a home that was still standing and immediately made her way toward their backyard. The heavily wooded lot hindered her view of the landslide, not that it mattered. She could hear it.

Not just the rush of mud and debris. But, also, the screams of those desperate to escape a certain death.

Sammy raced through the backyard and stopped momentarily when a voice called out to her. "Hey! What's happening?" It was a man wearing a USC sweatshirt, standing on his sun deck.

"Landslide!" Sammy shouted back and pointed towards the man's neighbors' homes. "Get out! Now!"

She didn't waste any more precious time as the man stood dumbfounded, trying to get a look at what was happening. She hopped over a rail and carefully found a way down the rocky slope toward a side street that branched off Braemer Road.

Over the initial shock, Sammy had found remarkable clarity and calmness. Then her adrenaline kicked in. She moved down the slope faster now. Her knee screamed at her in agony with each misstep or every time it hyperextended. At one point, she yelled at it aloud. "Just do your job!"

By the time she approached Putney Road below, she moved with a noticeable limp. She didn't have to reach down to confirm that her knee was swelling and would restrict her mobility.

Once she reached the street, her visibility was obstructed by mature landscape and trees. Homes used six-by-six landscape timbers to hold up a variety of plant material. The timbers had washed away, carrying the plants into the street. Sammy plodded through the mess downward until she reached Braemar.

This was when she had her first close-up of the river that had flooded the valley. It was much higher than when they'd left the house what seemed like an eternity ago. In reality, it had been less than an hour. In that short a period, the river had consumed more houses, including the two directly in front of hers. She wondered if the road would stop the floodwaters' ravenous need to eat the earth.

She glanced up Braemar. The scene was not surprising to her. In fact, it had raised her hopes. As the two mansions broke loose and began to surf the mudslide, they fell apart. The weight of the homes was still there, just not compacted like the footprint of the house. After they crossed the road above her and met the stopped vehicles, they rode the downward slope until they rammed into the existing homes on Braemar. Those homes had worked to slow the landslide before it reached the floodwaters raging through the valley.

She briskly jogged toward the mud-covered ruins of the houses, forcing the pain of her knee into the recesses of her mind. Like before, she met cars stalled on the street. This time, however, they were abandoned, their doors left open, with some still running.

Sammy tried to make her way toward the point of impact where the mansions met the still-standing homes on Braemar. Her panicked neighbors were rushing toward her, carrying armloads of clothing. One couple even dragged their rolling, carry-on luggage behind them. She could visualize them stuffing their family photos and the wife's jewelry inside before running for their lives.

Sammy ran toward danger. She was going to find her car and rescue the girls, Carly, and Fenway. There simply was no other result that she was mentally prepared to accept.

THIRTY-SEVEN

Friday
New Year's Day
North Arroyo Neighborhood
La Cañada, California

Sammy paused to catch her breath. To relax. To pull her soaking wet hair out of her face as she assessed the situation. She couldn't just run into the wreckage half-cocked, as they say.

She moved closer, careful of her footing and keenly aware that the entire debris field continued to slide toward the river. As she did, the house on Braemar succumbed to the weight crushing it from up the slope and slowly became detached from its foundation. It eerily slid across the road until it crashed into a much larger home. Behind it, Sammy saw several vehicles sticking through the hundreds of cubic feet of mud that accompanied the landslide.

She strained to make out their color. Despite the muddy mess, she hoped her white Tesla would stand out. Unfortunately, the most popular car color in California, as was the case in most states, was white. She saw the roofs, fenders and hoods of several white cars in the deluge.

Sammy moved deeper into the debris, opting to inspect one car at a time until she could identify whether it was her Tesla. Once again, the state with the most Tesla owners was California.

Her heart leapt for a moment as she noticed the damaged front end of a white Tesla. It bore the unmistakable "T" logo of the car brand. She crawled over a palm tree's trunk as it slid past her. She landed waist-deep in a combination of plants and mud. Keeping her eye on the Tesla, she pushed forward, calling for the kids as she did.

"Livvy! Sophie! Can you hear me?"

She struggled to get closer. Another car was being pushed behind the Tesla, causing it to turn on its side. Sammy picked up the pace the best she could. She used her arms to move the debris out of her path to make her way to the vehicle, which now presented its sleek undercarriage to her.

Just as she fought past more plant material, the Tesla began to slide again. It twisted slightly just as she reached it, threatening to crush her against the back of an SUV.

"Girls!" she shouted. She slammed her fist on the bottom of the car, certain it would garner their attention.

Nothing.

Sammy stood on a piece of house in order to peer inside the vehicle. She used her sleeves to clear the mud off the windows. It didn't take her long to realize this wasn't her car. It was empty except for a Yeti cooler in the back seat.

"Dammit!" she shouted in frustration. She pounded the door of the car repeatedly until the bottom of her fist was bruised. Then she cursed herself for causing harm to another part of her body. It was the car moving again that forced her to overcome the emotional fit she was having.

Sammy held onto the side of the car as it slowly moved downward. The stucco piece of house she'd used to boost herself had moved on, leaving her legs dangling just above the mud flow. She used all her strength to pull herself upward until she was lying prone on the side of the Tesla. It was rocking back and forth, so she didn't dare stand to look around. Not to mention the incessant rain continued to make treacherous any place she tried to gain her footing.

There was another white car thirty feet away from her. A portion of a tile roof was now wedged in between the Braemar house and the empty Tesla. Sammy grimaced as she surveyed her surroundings. Her only hope of moving quickly was to use the debris to walk across. The pull of the mudslide was getting stronger as it crossed the street and headed toward the floodwaters. She was running out of time as gravity joined the battle against her.

She crawled on all fours toward the hood of the Tesla. The dovetail joint of the roof truss was within reaching distance. Sammy lay flat and grabbed it with her right hand, pulling herself off the Tesla back into the mudslide. Then once she could get a grip on the roof truss with both hands, she pulled herself on top.

The next white vehicle was only forty feet away. The roof truss, floating on the mud, almost reached the other car. Hand over hand, Sammy dragged herself across the length of the truss. She winced as splinters dug into her exposed skin. She gritted her teeth as the truss hit hard into standing trees that had not yet been toppled. Her eyes grew wide as the truss suddenly turned upright when the mudslide found its way across the street toward the river.

For a brief moment, she lost sight of the white car. Panic set in as the truss picked up speed. She had to hurry, as she could now feel the power of the water rushing by, eating away at the ridge. Then, inexplicably, a horn began honking. Long bursts, followed by several short bursts. In her mind, it sounded intentional. Was it meant to represent 9-1-1?

There! she shouted to herself. She saw the white vehicle turning in a circle. It rose out of the mudslide as a tree pushed its way underneath.

Whoever was inside the car was still honking, and she also heard barking.

THIRTY-EIGHT

Friday
New Year's Day
North Arroyo Neighborhood
La Cañada, California

"Sophie! Livvy!" She shouted their names as she got closer to the car. The honking turned into a solid blare. In an electric car, the horn is powered by the twelve-volt battery, same as the lights. The Tesla she discovered was not running. Like the last car she inspected, it had been partially turned on its side. It was also sinking into the mud.

Sam had reached the undercarriage. It was similar to the Tesla she'd just inspected. Just feet away, she reached out to grab any part of the car to pull herself over without falling into the steady flow of mud and debris.

She took a chance and prepared to jump. Like a surfer rising to a crouch from a prone position, she hopped up and kept her center of gravity low by bending her knees. She walked along the truss made of two-by-six lumber. It was stable. She steadied her nerves and eyed the part of the car where she wanted to land. Suddenly, everything changed.

The side of a house bumped into the Tesla, turning it upright. A sharp corner where a door was once located broke through the rear hatch's glass and also the rear passenger door's glass. The clapboard siding was still attached to the stud walls, floating on top of the mudslide like a boat dock released from its pilings.

The dogs barked loudly and then suddenly emerged through the broken glass. It was Carly and Fenway.

"Carly! Fen!"

They barked in response. However, the excited pups didn't come to her. Carly spun around quickly, as the sometimes overenthusiastic dog was prone to do. She ran away from Sammy, leaping from one piece of house debris to another. Fenway stood for a moment, barking at Sammy, as if to say, "Follow us. We know what to do."

Sammy always believed animals had an inner instinct on when it was appropriate to fight or flee in a dangerous situation. That animal instinct could be trusted to find their way to safety.

However, she couldn't. There were lives to save first.

"Go! Be careful!" she shouted at them, giving encouragement to the two pups, who were the closest thing the couple had to children.

As they disappeared from sight, Sammy turned her attention to the girls. They were unable to roll down the front seat windows, so they were frantically beating on the glass. The car was suddenly jolted as two large pieces of debris crashed into one another. The chain reaction of the collision found its way to Sammy's Tesla.

Sammy was at the rear trunk lid. "Come this way!" she shouted over the sound of the raging river, which was drawing ever closer to them. As the car joined the heavier debris in its descent down the ridge, Sammy began emptying the rear compartment to give the kids room to crawl out.

They were crying and calling out her name as they inched forward, uncertain of which was safer, the vehicle they'd been riding in down the ridge or being out in the elements with their aunt.

Livvy shimmied across the bicycle and through the camping gear. She stretched her hand out to Sammy, who quickly grasped it. She was cold and shivering, but her hand was remarkably warm, a comforting feeling for Sammy. After Livvy was pulled free, she wrapped her arms around Sammy's waist. The car lurched forward and down the slope. Sophie hustled through the back, making her way out with Sammy's assistance.

With both girls free of the banged-up car, Sammy looked around to get her bearings. She spotted the tennis courts of a retired neighbor she and Tyler had befriended after they moved in. She had frequently been invited to play on the courts, until the home was sold.

The three of them held onto the back of the Tesla as it continued downward. The home with the tennis courts was four houses away from hers. She looked to her left. The mudslide was gaining in size and weight as more homes were consumed by the unstoppable flow of debris.

The water now covered all of Linda Vista Street where her home was located. She knew it would be lost, although that was the least of her concerns at the moment.

"Girls, can you be strong for me?"

Initially, neither responded. Then Livvy's innocent voice asked, "Can't we just go back to your house?"

The truthful answer would've been, "No, because my home is about to be washed away." Instead, Sammy needed to tell a white lie.

"Yes, but we have to go this way first. After the rain stops, we can go back."

"To that house?" asked Sophie, pointing past Sammy.

The debris flow had shifted, placing them closer to the tennis courts. Sammy considered it a great stroke of luck.

"Yes. We're gonna try to make it to the tennis courts. Then we can get to the street leading to the Rose Bowl where Ty is."

"I can make it," said a confident Sophie.

"Me too," added Livvy, who was trying to put on her best *big girl* impersonation.

Sammy took a deep breath and grabbed the girls by the hands. She made eye contact with them both.

"No matter what, never let go of your sister's hand. Understood?"

They nodded and took each other's hand as they let go of the Tesla trunk. Sammy led the way through the mud, which was thinning due to the terrain. The girls still struggled, but they were able to keep pace. Both sides of Linda Vista Avenue were relatively flat, resulting in the mudslide slowing as gravity lost its grip. The mostly one-story block homes were more solid than their newer two-story neighbors up the ridge. The tree-lined street helped Sammy with her plan to reach safety.

They trudged along together, climbing over the occasional piece of debris or a tree trunk. The tennis court, although covered with mud, was clearly defined. She identified the opening in the chain-link fence, which was somehow still intact. Once they were within the fenced area, they stopped to rest. The girls stood by the net, shivering, as the soaking rain lowered their body temperatures.

Sammy couldn't see very far. However, she knew this part of her neighborhood very well. If she could guide the girls just a quarter of a mile toward Pasadena, they should be clear of this mudslide and closer to Tyler.

"Ready?" she shouted from the other side of the tennis court. She waved for the girls to join her.

They remained still like their feet were stuck in

concrete. Their faces revealed the fear inside them. Sophie pointed toward Sammy. She shouted, "Behind you!"

The red tile roof of the Mediterranean-style house across the street was collapsing into the structure. Then it disappeared.

THIRTY-NINE

Friday
New Year's Day
North Arroyo Neighborhood
La Cañada, California

"Seriously?" Sammy shouted her question as she looked to the heavens for answers. They were being sandwiched between the floodwaters below and the landslides coming from above. There was no escaping the dual threats. The rain pelted her face, forcing her to cover her eyes. It was Sophie who gave Sammy a new sense of urgency.

"Can we go up there?" she asked, pointing up the steep slope toward a house on Devon Road.

Sammy gauged the threats of the mudslide versus the raging floodwaters. They'd never survive if they got sucked into the river. Their bodies would be swept all the way down the Los Angeles River. The mudslide was not an option either. It was pushing its way toward the river and would eventually add to the remains of her neighborhood rushing downstream.

Their only option was to move along the terrain of the ridge, staying high enough above the river and cognizant of the landslides that were sure to occur. She turned to study the steep backyard of the homes hovering above them. She recalled the street and where it led. It might help them escape. However, they had to hurry.

She led the girls up the slope. Using small trees and landscape rocks, they climbed upward toward the back of the house. Despite the saturated ground, the root systems held as the trio pulled their way up the hill. Only once did Sophie slip and fall. She'd quickly grasped a small tree to avoid sliding down to the street. After a brief respite, they started their climb again.

Sammy nervously changed her attention from the task of ascending the difficult terrain to the status of the mudslide. She kept a wary eye on the floodwaters, which seemed to be rising at a rapid rate. As it consumed more of the newly created shoreline, houses fell into the water in rapid succession.

They neared the home's backyard. It was fenced like so many others, making it impossible for the young girls to climb over. Instead, they grabbed the wrought-iron pickets and inched their way around to the home's driveway. There, they found the garage door open. It appeared the family who lived there had made a hasty exit, even leaving the door leading inside wide open.

Sammy led the girls into the garage. All three of them had been close to being badly injured or even killed throughout the ordeal. Standing in the garage provided them the opportunity to relax, at least for the moment.

"Hello? Is anybody home?" Sophie wandered over to the entry door and took the brave step of calling out to the owners. "Knock! Knock!"

Sammy managed a smile at the child's innocence. She reached for Livvy's hand. "Come on. I don't think these nice people would mind if we sat down for a little while, do you?"

Once inside, Sophie entered the great room, which was filled with glass doors overlooking the valley. She pressed her face against the glass and looked around.

"Wow!" Sometimes an often-used expression of astonishment said it all.

Sammy and Livvy joined her side, where they had a bird's-eye view of the catastrophe. They stared out at the half-mile-wide river that flowed rapidly across the submerged golf course. The water was muddy and full of all kinds of debris.

While the girls watched in wonderment, Sammy studied the damage the river was doing to the homes on her street. Almost all of them had been gobbled up, with the ones below their location still standing, as the torrent seemed to flow around the point. She suddenly felt safe in the abandoned home and wondered if they should stay put until the storm passed.

With the girls mesmerized at the window, Sammy went into the kitchen. The refrigerator was still cold. It was filled with party foods like small sandwiches, cubed cheese, and several dips. Apparently, the owners had had a gathering on New Year's or for the game and took the time to clean up before bugging out in a rush.

Regardless, there was enough food and drinks to

sustain them for a couple of days until she could figure out a way to find Tyler.

"Girls, who wants a snack?" Sammy had pulled out the plate full of sandwiches and set them on the counter. She looked into the cupboards and found a large bag of Cheetos to eat. While the girls ate and drank milk, Sammy found her way to the bar and made herself a well-deserved margarita. She needed a drink to clear her head.

The girls found their way onto the spacious sectional in the family room and stretched out. Sammy sipped her drink and stared out across the valley. It was hard to make out any details from their location due to the heavy rain and the wind, which continued to blow the precipitation sideways. It was an ugly, ornery scene. One that convinced Sammy the best thing to do was stay put.

She was worried about Tyler but confident in his ability to stay safe. When the storm passed, she'd get as close to her home as she deemed safe and wait. She felt the instincts of her pups would also draw them back home. Even if their house was gone, dragged away by the landslide, it would be the expected rallying point for all of her family.

Sammy finished her drink and contemplated another. The longer she stayed in the home, the more convinced she became to remain there until the sun was shining again. Or at least until the rain and wind calmed down.

She set her glass down and slid into a leather recliner near the fireplace. It wasn't all that comfortable although it had a familiar feel. It was very similar to Tyler's. In a way, snuggling into it was almost as good as her husband holding her. Within minutes, her eyelids grew heavy, and she drifted off to sleep, blissfully unaware of what would be coming her way.

PART 3

"... on that day, all the springs of the great deep burst forth, and the floodgates of the heavens were opened. And rain fell on the Earth forty days and forty nights."

FORTY

**Friday
New Year's Day
Port of Los Angeles, California**

The river had reached the ocean. Or perhaps it was the other way around. Not that it mattered. As the ARkStorm roared onshore, it generated massive waves unlike anything the California coastal areas had seen since the middle of the nineteenth century. The gray skies and the hundred-mile-per-hour winds drove the rain and surf directly towards Los Angeles with a force of a Category 5 tropical cyclone. Nothing was immune from its destructive forces, including LA's Gateway to the World—the Port of Los Angeles.

For months, bottlenecks continued to delay cargo deliveries from the massive container ships moored around the Port of Los Angeles. A longshoremen's strike had crippled the port's operations, causing hundreds of vessels to remain just offshore, awaiting a resolution to the standoff.

The massive waves caused by the ARkStorm pummeled the ships for hours, accompanied by winds that broke records. The Beaufort Wind Force Scale, first referenced by an Irish seaman of the same name, had recognized winds in excess of seventy-three miles per hour as being a Beaufort Scale 12. Under these conditions, the ocean was completely white with driving spray. Visibility was near zero, as the horizon was filled with foam and sea spray.

Such was the case that afternoon when the *Xiang Chi*, a twenty-eight-thousand-ton vessel, broke loose from its cable lines. Its sheer size and the height of the vessel's superstructure created an attractive sail area for the wind to beat against. The ship's captain was unable to gain control of the massive ship as it was forced toward the port. It collided with another smaller ship, the fourteen-thousand-ton *Yawei*. They floated alongside each other until the massive vessels collided with other moored ships, slowing the vessels' progress toward the port somewhat.

In the span of an hour, eleven ships broke loose and were forced into the port. Some crashed into docked vessels and remained there as their steel hulls beat against one another. The *Yawei*, however, snaked its way past the wreckage and entered the mouth of the Los Angeles River.

Guests at the Crowne Plaza Harbor Hotel were astonished to see the enormous vessel rocking uncontrollably as the wind pushed it toward the city. Once it entered the main channel of the river, it sideswiped the USS *Iowa* battleship, which had been converted into a museum.

It battered smaller vessels as it continued into populated areas now under twenty feet of water due to the rain brought by the ARkStorm and the Pacific's tidal surge coupled with the breach of the Prado and Carbon Canyon Dams.

Soon, in a sadistic, devilish game of pinball, the *Yawei* began to crash into empty containers awaiting a ship to carry them to the Far East. The containers had joined the invasion of large, floating debris forcing its way inland toward residential areas.

The heavily populated areas of Compton,

Carson, and Gardena were no match for the steel structures as they crashed into high-rise apartment buildings and homes situated high enough above the floodwaters to protect dozens of residents.

As the depth of the water rose, the larger ships that required a deeper draft to navigate were forced inland. The invasion of wayward vessels grew in numbers. Their buoyancy protected them from capsizing.

Their girth, weight, and the speed generated by the hurricane-force winds made them the perfect weapons to destroy tall buildings deemed safe by many Southern Californians. Battering the high-rises with such great force compromised the structural integrity of the buildings, causing them to collapse with all inside. Built to earthquake standards was the norm. Protecting against the monstrous ARkStorm had never been contemplated by building authorities.

This attack would last for days before the massive vessels would eventually find resting places throughout California's Central Valley.

FORTY-ONE

Friday
New Year's Day
Rose Bowl Stadium
Pasadena, California

Tyler didn't regret helping the woman from Central Pennsylvania. The joyful tears the couple shared warmed his heart. He wanted that same feeling when he reunited with Sammy. He did, however, lament the loss of time. Nearly an hour, according to his watch, that resulted in the water rising at a much faster rate than he could've imagined.

Earlier, when he'd made the decision to hike up

the nearly one hundred rows to the top of the north end zone seating, the floodwaters had been confined to the lower concourse of the stadium. Now the field was waist-deep.

Tyler sloshed through the people milling about, oddly calm under the circumstances. As he made his way toward the east side of the stadium, he heard conversations ranging from stealing food from the concession stands to whether the game would be called in favor of USC, who had been winning when all hell broke loose.

He shook his head in disbelief as these fans, mostly men, seemed oblivious to the threat they faced. By Tyler's calculations, the water had risen ten to fifteen feet in an hour. With the rain coming down harder than ever, he imagined it would continue to rise at a rapid rate.

As he reached the lowest point of the stadium near gate C, he was able to catch his first glimpse of the river that had suddenly appeared in the valley. It was muddy, flowing at a whitewater pace, and full of debris, including vehicles and parts of buildings.

And bodies. The first battered corpse had been crushed between the chain-link fence and a transportation bus just inside gate C. The mangled face was unrecognizable as the rushing waters continued to force the bus, which was wedged between a tree and a lamp post, to crush the corpse.

Tyler tried to control the urge to retch but could not. With water up to his chest, he threw up repeatedly into it, much to the consternation of people fleeing the stadium just downstream of the current. Just as he emptied his stomach, a hot dog vendor's cart crashed hard into his back, knocking him under the water momentarily.

Between the violent vomiting and getting hit in the back, Tyler briefly lost his breath. He needed to steady himself, so he made his way to the chain-link fence to get a grip, literally and figuratively speaking.

He found himself face-to-face with the corpse. His body's reaction was immediate. Devoid of contents, all his stomach could do was convulse repeatedly. Nothing came out but bile, which left an awful taste in his mouth. He was desperate to wash it out but didn't dare use the muddy floodwater. He simply had to deal with the vile taste.

He held onto the fence until he reached the gate. As soon as he did, he realized the task of making his way to higher ground where Rosemont Street was once located was going to be near impossible.

Others had tried and failed. The rushing water was so powerful that anyone attempting to cross was quickly knocked off their feet and washed away toward the city. He remained in place for a moment, studying the raging water and what his potential options were. He decided to take it one step at a time.

He used floating cars as a means to move point to point until he reached the block wall that separated the parking areas from the stadium grounds. The State Farm-sponsored gate had a series of steel-fenced gates that were open. He shoved his way through the water, avoiding trees and debris riding the torrent as it sped past. Within minutes, he managed to make it to the exit of the stadium, where he joined a group of thirty or so fans.

All of them were pointing across the parking lots toward the ridge of magnificent homes overlooking the stadium and the golf course. The raging floodwaters had swept away most of the vehicles except a couple of motorhomes parked on the side nearest the ridge. A smattering of trees and the occasional lamp post was all that remained in the parking lot.

Tyler realized it would be impossible to take the shortest route to the ridge above Rosemont. He'd have to go point to point based on his success in fighting the rapid flow of the river. Resigned to the fact that he could be washed downstream several thousand feet, if not farther, he psyched himself up for the task. The rain wasn't letting up, which meant the river wasn't gonna dry up in anytime soon, if ever.

With trepidation, he pushed through a group who was hesitant to move through the river. He identified a storage building on the other side of Rose Bowl Drive as his first stop. Standing against the block wall by the gate, he shoved off with his feet like one might do in a swimming pool. He swam fifteen feet across the utility road when he got swept up in the current. It quickly overwhelmed him.

Tyler was being carried uncontrollably down the river. He didn't panic. Panic meant death. This was not his day to die. He took a deep breath and strengthened his resolve.

He fought to establish some kind of swimming stroke in attempt to move at a ninety-degree angle from the flow of the water. When he was able to identify a fixed obstacle in the form of another utility building downriver from his location, he relaxed and allowed the water to carry him toward it.

He was floating faster than he'd ever swum in his life when the water thrust him against the concrete block building. Because he was prepared for the impact, he didn't suffer like he had after the unexpected hot dog cart smacked him earlier.

Now Tyler found himself pressed against the side of the building as the river tried to flatten him against it. He kept a wary eye on debris headed his way. He didn't want to end up like the guy crushed against the chain-link fence by the bus.

Slowly, to avoid being swept away, he inched toward the edge of the building to find his next possible stopping point. There was a large span of cleared area that included a parking lot and an open green space used for public tailgating and corporate hospitality tents. All of the pregame festivities had been washed away by the river. The vehicles in lot B had been forced downriver, where they piled up inside the Jackie Robinson Baseball Stadium south of the Rose Bowl.

A fenced queue to funnel fans into the stadium still remained in part of lot B. He ran the risk of getting caught up in it, so he couldn't make any attempt to swim toward the ridge. He had no choice but to allow the river to carry him south toward Jackie Robinson Stadium while he swam toward higher ground. He recalled from jogging the Rose Bowl Loop with Sammy that a middle school was on the hill just past the tailgating grounds. If he could make it to there, then he could find his way up to the 210 Freeway.

It was his best shot at avoiding a much longer run home.

FORTY-TWO

Friday
New Year's Day
Rose Bowl Loop
Pasadena, California

Tyler had never surfed although he'd attended a few surf competitions at Mavericks Beach south of San Francisco. The surfers rode those waves at fifteen to twenty miles per hour, an incredible rate of speed when trying to stand on a board. The river's eight-to-ten-mile-per-hour flow rate he was enduring felt like he was being dragged behind a tractor trailer rig on the interstate. His body was twisted and turned, bashed against slower-moving debris like trees and cars, and frequently submerged in the muddy abyss.

It seemed like an eternity for him to exit the parking areas and cross into the grassy tailgating space. Tyler fought to keep his upper body high enough above the rollicking floodwaters to see the direction he was headed. If he perceived a moment of a calm, he tried swimming toward land, only to be caught up in debris and forced farther downstream.

The pileup of vehicles that were trying to break free from the trees and fencing surrounding the baseball field was looming large in his field of vision. He feared getting caught up in the middle of it, only to be battered mercilessly until his body was crushed.

He gritted his teeth and tried to swim across the current. In his mind, every few yards of progress toward shore would help avoid the pileup of vehicles growing larger in his field of vision.

Up ahead, the lamp posts surrounding the four-way stop next to the stadium swayed back and forth, gradually losing their grip on the bolts fastening them to the concrete. Tyler struggled. If he could just manage another twenty yards, he'd miss the scrum of vehicles. The worst case would be getting sucked toward LA.

He mustered all his energy and swam like his life

depended on it. Because it did. He was clear of the intersection and swimming toward a stand of trees in front of a white stucco house. The trees were bending against the force of the river but were holding their ground.

He swam harder and faster. The current had picked up. If he couldn't get caught up in the evergreen's branches, he'd be pulled much farther downstream. He swam, arm over arm, ignoring the two dead bodies that bumped his legs as the river carried them away.

"Harder!" he urged himself on. His chest was getting tight, and his muscles were burning. Tyler prided himself on his stamina, but running was his thing. Swimming was Sammy's.

Inexplicably, the water began swirling just before he reached the trees. The sudden change in movement startled him, and he lost his focus. He wanted to stop and look down to learn the cause of the small whirlpool.

He didn't. He couldn't.

He continued swimming, and seconds later, he was hugging the tree like a bear cub hoping his mama grizzly would soon rescue him. The tree was swaying, leaning over from the force of the water and the wind. However, like Tyler, it was holding on for dear life.

He looked in all directions to assess his options. He even took a moment to see where he'd come from. Even with the limited visibility, he was able to make out the bodies of fans dressed in USC's cardinal and gold team colors floating swiftly toward the baseball stadium. The lifeless corpses were stopped temporarily, hung up at the baseball stadium's vehicle pileup before being swept around the facility and past his position.

Tyler shook his head in disappointment. He wondered how many of these people had followed his lead and attempted to enter the raging flood. Were they physically capable of swimming and battling the torrent? Sadly, many underestimated the daunting task.

Now that he was across the most ferocious part of the floodwaters, he had to devise a path across the water that was bashing the homes at the base of the ridge. The two-story homes were still peeking above the water's surface, while the one-story rooflines were barely visible. Tyler estimated the river to be twenty to thirty feet deep at this point.

He reluctantly let go of the evergreen's trunk and swam to the stucco house nearby. From there, he hopscotched to the next property, a one-story that was on a slightly higher elevation. He was now able to see the ground within reach. He eagerly entered the water again, swimming to the finish line, as his mind considered it.

The terraced backyard of the next home was remarkably intact, as the ridge was not that steep in that part of the Pasadena neighborhood surrounding the Rose Bowl grounds. He was less than a mile from the intersection of the 210 Freeway and Ventura Freeway, a massive spiderweb of concrete overpasses and ramps that carried hundreds of thousands of cars on a given day. Through the wind and rain, he could make out the sound of horns honking, angrily it seemed, as people tried to flee the city. If the traffic helicopters were on duty that day, they'd be hovering in circles like vultures over the interchange.

Tyler made landfall. Spontaneously, like sailors of old, he crawled onto the soggy grass and kissed the ground. Then he collapsed from exhaustion.

FORTY-THREE

Friday
New Year's Day
Devil's Gate Dam
La Cañada, California

A stitch became a crack. The crack extended from the bottom of the Devil's Gate Dam to near the top. At that point, the concrete structure was compromised but not destroyed. The dam might've held except for the constant battering of debris both above and below the water's surface. As the wind speed increased and the mudslides caused more than just trees to fall into the reservoir, the dam was no longer viable as a means to withhold the millions of gallons of water and tons of debris from forcing the crack to become a gaping hole.

Yet it still took more than an hour for the dam to fall apart completely. When it did, the entirety of its concrete fell downward, crashing at the feet of the bridge carrying Oak Grove Drive across the ravine.

The pressure of the water and the tumbling concrete from the dam began to beat against the piles making up the foundation of the bridge. When the power of the floodwaters joined in, the aging roadway gave up the fight. The piles were knocked free from their caps at the center of the bridge, causing the piers above them to sway. The pavement twisted and tilted, causing the motorists attempting to flee the destructive force of the ARkStorm to lose control of their vehicles.

They crashed into one another. Those who weren't injured immediately ran to safety. Those who were injured or trapped in their vehicles rode the bridge downward as its substructure failed.

The destruction of the bridge was not as efficient as the work of demolition engineers when they intentionally collapse an obsolete building. However, the ARkStorm didn't need to get permits or use a large number of explosives. The storm was akin to the big bad wolf of "Little Red Riding Hood" fame. The storm was far more powerful than dynamite.

When the bridge at Oak Grove Drive fell, it was forced into the pilings holding up the 210 Freeway. The foundation of the eight-lane interstate bridge was more complex and sturdier than the Oak Grove bridge. However, it had been built to earthquake specifications. The ARkStorm was a far different kind of beast.

The water was rushing through huge openings in the rocks left by the destruction of Devil's Gate. The debris swept through, pushing the concrete and boulders ever closer to the 210 Freeway. Then like a massive underwater jackhammer, every bit of rubble and debris at the base of the interstate's piles began to pound away.

To those in the vehicles above, or the pedestrians fleeing on foot, they might not have noticed the constant barrage pummeling the bridge's foundation. Between the force of the wind and the volume of rain, there were plenty of distractions to draw their attention away from what was happening a hundred feet below them. Especially since it was below the surface of the raging muddy floodwaters.

While people were unaware, the foundation of the much larger bridge at the 210 Freeway was being chipped away continuously, little by little, until it would surrender to the forces unleashed by Devil's Gate.

FORTY-FOUR

Friday
New Year's Day
North Arroyo
La Cañada, California

"Sammy!" Sophie's shouting her name, accompanied by Livvy's shriek, jolted her nerves and caused her to leap out of the chair until she stumbled over the coffee table. She'd been in a deep sleep, exhausted by the travails of the day and barely coherent to determine what caused their screams. Then she saw it.

The home they occupied, ostensibly a safe place far enough from the floodwaters and a measurable distance from the landslide, was suddenly at risk.

The architect had designed the house to provide light into the living area via large sliding glass doors at the rear and a series of floor-to-ceiling windows in front that afforded her an immediate view of the girls' concern.

The block wall across the street, holding up the house perched above it, was falling apart. The solid concrete sculpted blocks had developed a series of cracks as the mortared joints became compromised. Water seeped around the blocks, and they were flying out as if a massive fist were under the ground, attempting to punch its way through.

She rushed to the front of the house and burst through the entry door to get a better look. The rain had not dissipated in the hour she'd been sleeping. If anything, the flooding had worsened, and the street was now a river of mud-filled water.

She shielded her eyes to look upward. The blocks were dislodging from the wall at a steady pace, falling downward and splashing into the rushing water. However, what concerned her most was she could now see the roofline of a house. Earlier, after she'd located some food for them to eat, she'd walked around the home and checked its potential safety by looking out of all the windows.

She never saw the house above them on the ridge. Not even a glimpse.

It was sliding as the compacted soil beneath it began to erode. The strength and stiffness of the soil had been liquified by the water finding its way into the rock formation making up the ridge.

They had to leave.

"Now!" Sammy unintentionally verbalized her thoughts, startling the girls.

She ran past the girls, who huddled together in the foyer, crying. She'd calm their nerves after she had a plan. She thrust open the sliding glass doors without bothering to close them behind her despite the wind-blown rain. Most likely, the Devon Road home wouldn't be there very long anyway.

She leaned over the deck railing, which afforded her a clear view up and down Linda Vista Avenue, her old street. The floodwaters, which had risen at least ten feet or more since she last looked, had taken most of the homes to her left, including her own. To the right, Linda Vista was farther away from the valley where the golf course once stood. The houses were still in place.

Sammy stopped to think. The ridge was continuing to collapse. The heavy rains might have compromised the soil, but it was the weight of the homes that was hastening the landslides. Her only option was to continue toward Pasadena and the Rose Bowl.

"Girls! Let's go!" she shouted from the deck. Soaking wet, she ran back inside and found them standing in the middle of the open space. They were shivering uncontrollably and sobbing. With a quick glance toward the house that was looming large above them, she knelt down next to her nieces. She forced herself to remain calm. After taking a deep breath, she gently took their hands.

"Guys, I'm sorry we have to go through this. I really am. But I need you both to be big girls right now. We're gonna have to walk quickly, but carefully. Okay. The street's muddy and will be very slippery. But I promise, we can do this together because we're a great team. Right?"

She let go of their hands and shook them to shed the rain droplets. She gently touched their faces, a loving gesture that immediately stopped their crying. Then she took their hands again and squeezed them. She whispered to them as their crying came to an end.

"I love you both. So does Tyler. We will not let anything happen to you."

Sophie managed a smile. "We can be big girls, right, Livvy?"

Livvy nodded. Sammy sincerely thought she meant it.

"Okay, let's do this. Hold my hands. We're gonna walk together. I won't make you go faster than you can handle. Deal?"

They each took one of Sammy's hands and squeezed. "Deal," they replied in unison.

The trio briskly walked out of the house and onto the street, mindful of the blocks being shoved out of the wall. Sammy led them downward toward the bend in the road. From her recollection, this part of Devon Road was steep and contained a series of winding turns until it connected with Linda Vista at the bottom.

The tree-lined stretch of road was bordered with an eight-inch-tall concrete curb to prevent motorists from inadvertently driving off the edge into the landscape on one side, and the ridge overlooking where the golf course once was.

They'd rounded the second turn when an enormous crash shook the ground, knocking the three of them off their feet. From behind, rocks, blocks and other debris came tumbling down the street, bouncing high into the air as the landslide picked up steam.

Sammy brusquely jerked the girls off the pavement and rushed them along to get away from the tumbling rubble. They made another turn just as the rock and blocks making up the destroyed retaining wall rushed past them and into the hedgerow of another home. Confident they were out of the reach of the landslide, Sammy slowed their pace to give the girls a chance to recuperate from the near miss.

As she looked upward toward the steep slope and the vegetation at the top, she knelt in front of the girls. She decided to give them a pep talk, as the phrase *are you okay* had clearly worn out its welcome.

"You did sooo good, girls. I mean it. When the time came to run, you were awesome."

"Yeah, we were fast goers, right?" asked Livvy.

Sophie was about to weigh in when another explosion frightened them. All three of them dropped to their knees on the mud-soaked street.

"Sammy! Look out!" shouted Sophie.

She was downhill from the girls, just a few feet away. She instinctively rushed toward the children to protect them. Her quick reaction saved her from serious injury.

The water had completely filled the storm drains. Something must have caused the stormwater to be shoved through with so much force it caused a two-hundred-fifty-pound manhole cover to blow upward. The cast-iron disk was in the middle of the street only a few feet from where Sammy crouched, slowly wobbling until it was submerged below the running water. Sophie's warning and her quick reaction had prevented it from landing on top of her.

"God, please," she begged the Almighty. "Please give us a break!"

Just as she shouted, an evergreen toppled over along the high ground just behind them. Its root system was fully exposed as it slowly slid down the bank. Another one closer to the trio was teetering on the brink of being dislodged, prompting Sammy to lead the girls down the steep roadway again.

They managed to make two hairpin turns before the road leveled off at the bottom of the ridge. Sammy was in more familiar territory now. She urged the girls to pick up the pace, stopping once to avoid a green, ten-yard dumpster that came floating by them. The floodwaters on Linda Vista had accumulated to being waist-deep on the six-year-olds. Their mobility was greatly hampered, and their weight, at forty to forty-five pounds, made them too heavy for Sammy to carry, even if her busted-up knee would allow it.

Sammy urged them on. They sloshed through the flooded street, using a herculean effort for the young girls to fight the resistance of the water. For the first time since the deluge had brought the apocalypse to them, Sammy saw some familiar faces. This stretch of Linda Vista had smaller, mostly one-story homes on both sides of the street. She and Tyler had become friendly with many of her neighbors during their runs or casual walks.

The floodwater was four feet deep in most of the homes. Many people had left their front doors left open, a sign they'd given up any hope of saving their belongings. Others were trying to walk through the water toward Pasadena with their luggage floating alongside them. It was a tragic scene of refugees abandoning their homes and heading into the unknown.

Sammy spoke to a few as they walked along the street, telling them of the landslides behind them. Many began to cry as they thought about friends who lived in that part of the neighborhood.

The population was denser the closer they got to the Rose Bowl. More people were seen moving toward LA and away from the landslides. Their faces were pale and expressionless except for those who wept. The tears flowed, mixing with the rain. They didn't bother to wipe them away.

She and the girls moved steadily along Linda Vista while her neighbors turned towards higher ground. Being alone, parallel to the river, gave her pause. Was she doing the right thing, potentially putting the kids in danger in order to find Tyler? As she inwardly debated her decision, Sammy suddenly stopped when a building caught her eye.

Sitting high enough to avoid being flooded was Pasadena Fire Station #38. She imagined it was empty, as, at least thus far, the possibility of a structure fire wasn't the problem in North Arroyo. Nevertheless, she felt compelled to go inside to see if she could find a brace for her knee and first aid for the everyone's cuts.

The roll-up door holding the fire trucks was closed. However, the plate-glass entry door had been propped open with, ironically, a sizable river rock. She took the girls by the hand and led them toward the fire station. All of them were appreciative of getting out of the two-foot-deep water.

"Girls, wait here for a moment," she said in a whisper. "I wanna make sure it's safe to go inside."

She slowly entered, her eyes struggling to see in

the darkened space. She listened for any sign of life. The station hadn't been damaged and was remarkably neat considering the catastrophe unfolding around it. She decided to call out.

"Hello? Is there anybody here?"

She waited for a couple of seconds that seemed like an eternity.

"Hello?"

A man's voice responded. It sounded oddly familiar. She saw his dark silhouette standing in front of a wall of windows on the other side of the spacious room.

"I am still here."

FORTY-FIVE

Friday
New Year's Day
Pasadena Fire Station 38
Pasadena, California

Finn O'Brien had retired on Christmas Eve. A ceremony had taken place at the county's fire department headquarters and had been attended by several local government dignitaries. Finn had been credited with saving countless lives during his career and was hailed for his heroic efforts during both Station Fires.

Like many people who retire from a job they loved, the thought of *having plenty of free time* looked good on paper. However, in practice, after just a few days of *doing all the things I haven't been able to do*, the reality set in. Regret was followed by boredom, which was followed by the question of whether unretiring was an option.

Finn had experienced all of those emotions. Despite the fact he hadn't been assigned to Pasadena Fire Station 38 on Linda Vista Road since he'd been promoted years ago, he found himself strolling down there daily despite the heavy rains. He missed the comradery. The trading of stories. The ribbing of rookie firefighters as they were given menial tasks around the fire hall.

Finn had come to Station 38 just after midnight. He'd been paying close attention to both national and local news broadcasts as they reported on the series of atmospheric rivers that had soaked California. He'd even gone to social media to view opinions on the potential damage these storms could bring. That was when he first heard about the ARkStorm scenario.

He studied everything he could, from USGS reports to weather blogs. He even dug into the history behind prior major flood events in California. He was beginning to get the sense this winter's storms were far different than those in the past.

Just before noon, he printed out the most relevant research he'd found and carried it with him as he walked to the Station 38. There was a skeleton crew on duty that day because of the holiday. Some were required to work the Rose Bowl game. Since 9/11, enhanced security measures at major sporting events not only required a beefed-up law enforcement presence but also a large contingent of firefighters and their equipment. Improvised or incendiary bombs were the greatest threats to a large gathering, so firefighters would play an important role in limiting deaths.

Fifteen minutes before kickoff, and just as the heavy downpours began to pummel the valley, Station 38 got a call. There had been a multi-vehicle accident with injuries several miles away in the nearby San Rafael Hills. Two stations were called to respond, as the vehicles were leaking fuel, and despite the rain, dispatch was concerned about the risk of fire.

Finn was left behind, manning the fort, as they say. An honorary firefighter who'd unofficially been pulled out of retirement. His only job was to enjoy the snacks and monitor the game to give reports to the firefighters and paramedics dispatched to the accident scene.

Finn never heard from them, nor did they return.

The first responders' communications capabilities had gone down throughout the area. Cell phones weren't working. Sudden mudslides most likely prevented them from driving back to the station.

For his part, the moment Devil's Gate broke open, he'd known what had happened and what it meant. When he had been a member of the search and rescue teams, they'd trained for mass flooding events. Dams like Devil's Gate, Prado, and Oroville were frequently used as examples, as they affected different parts of the county.

A total breach of the Devil's Gate Dam had never been contemplated during their training workshops. However, after the research he'd stayed up all night accumulating, it was clear that emergency planners should have. To Finn, the failure of Devil's Gate was not only possible, it was probable when a major rain event like an ARkStorm came along.

The first thing Finn did was find any way possible to make contact with emergency communications for the county. He even drove to the Rose Bowl as floodwaters began to rush past the back of the fire hall. He warned them about the amount of water to expect. At the time, the concrete trough of the Arroyo Seco was filling rapidly but had not yet spilled over onto the grass of the golf course. He was thanked for his efforts and patted on the back as if he were a retiree trying to remain relevant.

Despite the brush-off, Finn still wanted to help anyone who was willing to accept it. By the time he returned to the station, the avalanches were beginning in the parts of his neighborhood closest to Devil's Gate. Water was rushing off the ridge and filling the streets with debris.

He walked up and down Linda Vista with a bullhorn, urging people to evacuate immediately. Some heeded his warning; others thanked him and shut the door. He knew what they were thinking. Catastrophes happen all the time, just not to them. Their house had been perched atop this hill overlooking the pristine golf course for eighty years. The earthquakes that frequently happened throughout the area hadn't knocked their home down. Surely, a rainstorm wouldn't.

Finn wasn't exactly sure what kind of response he expected or deserved. It would've been easy for him to shrug and return to the station or even home. However, he persevered.

He continued warning residents all the way up to the point when the first massive landslide took nearly two dozen homes down the ridge into the raging river below. At that point, he had to focus on protecting himself and anyone else who reached out for help.

So for the next several hours after Devil's Gate was torn open, he pulled people from their flooded homes. He rescued a couple whose car had been swept down the ridge on Inverness. He even managed to help a dog swim to safety.

Now he was exhausted and somewhat defeated. He helped those he could. He prayed for those he couldn't. He watched his beloved home get swept down the ridge. And at that very moment, he was following his home's roof floating downriver until it crashed into another house and broke apart. The home he'd shared with his beloved, deceased wife.

"Hello?" He heard a woman's voice, which brought him back into the present. Maybe it was someone who needed help? He abruptly turned and moved quickly through the dark fire hall. Earlier, he'd moved all the furniture against the walls to avoid tripping over it as he moved around.

"I am still here." He slowly walked toward the front door, the only means of entry. As he got closer, he noticed a woman standing near the entrance, along with two children.

"Miss, do you need some help? I'm Deputy, um, Finn O'Brien. I recently retired—"

"Hey, I know you," said Sammy excitedly. "My name is Sammy Hendrick. We met at the party yesterday."

"Sammy, Sammy. Wait, your husband is a coach, right?"

"Head athletic trainer," she replied and turned toward the girls. "Sophie, Livvy, come inside. I know this nice man. He was at the party yesterday."

Finn drew closer so that they could all see one another. He shook Sammy's hand and bent over to address the girls. "I remember you two lasses," he said with his Irish accent. "Weren't you wearing these skirts yesterday?"

"Yes, sir," answered Sophie. "Um, we planned on wearing them until our parents came home, but, um ..." Her voice trailed off as she began to cry. She looked down and wiped her hands on her tweed skirt, which was covered in mud.

Finn rose and addressed Sammy. "Okay, I know it isn't much, but we have some clothes in a storage room that were donated over the holidays for families in need. You're welcome to find something dry for the girls. And, well, yourself, if you'd like."

Sammy looked down to the kids, who looked like the proverbial wet rats. "That would be nice, Finn."

"We also have some snacks on the table over there," he offered.

Sammy glanced toward the window and looked at the landscape beyond. The last place they'd eaten had disappeared an hour later.

"We're okay, thanks though," she said before turning to the girls. "Let's find you something, and then we should get out of this nice man's way."

Finn led the way with a flashlight he retrieved from his cargo pants. The high-lumen light brightened up the fire hall as if the fluorescent lights were operating again. He spoke as they found the girls some apparel better suited for an apocalyptic flood.

"Where do you live?" he asked casually.

Sammy's eyes welled up in tears. Finn noticed her reaction and quickly apologized. "Oh, darn. I'm so sorry."

She gathered herself and nodded. She briefly summarized what the three of them had been through thus far. Finn was impressed with their tenacity and resolve. These were the kinds of neighbors he wanted to help.

He continued, "Well, from what you've told me, it won't be long before this whole block is at risk. We need to consider a better place to wait out the storm and load up some supplies to take with us."

Sammy said, "I don't think a car will make it through the streets. The water's three feet deep. Probably more now."

"Okay, we'll improvise, then. I have an idea."

Sammy smiled. For the first time, she was seeing a glimmer of hope that they'd make it through this.

FORTY-SIX

Friday
New Year's Day
210 Freeway
Pasadena, California

Once Tyler reached the 210 Freeway, he was exhausted; however, his adrenaline fueled his desire to get home to Sammy. He tried running along the shoulder, dodging vehicles that were inching along, completely disregarding the lane markers. In fact, both sides of the highway were blocked with traffic as residents attempted to escape the flooding.

It was only two miles to the exit that would lead to his neighborhood. As he approached

Devil's Gate Dam, the freeway turned toward the North Arroyo neighborhood. His excitement grew, as he expected to see Linda Vista Drive from the center of the bridge crossing at Devil's Gate.

His chest heaved, as a lot of miniscule dirt particles sucked into his lungs as he ran. He tried to force himself to breathe through his nose; however, the high humidity brought by the ARkStorm made that near impossible.

He slowed his pace to a brisk walk as he approached the bridge. Vehicles on both sides had stopped. The drivers were suddenly exiting their cars and trucks, frantically running in his direction. He pressed himself against the solid concrete barrier protecting him from dropping hundreds of feet to his death.

As people ran past, he felt a slight quiver running through the barrier. Since their move to California, they'd become accustomed to the many tremors associated with seismic activity. This felt different.

"Run!" a man shouted at him as he brushed past Tyler.

"What's wrong?" Tyler asked.

"The damn bridge is gonna collapse, that's

what's wrong!" he shouted in reply as he shoved a woman onto the hood of a car to get past her.

Tyler leaned over the barrier. The water rushing through the narrow pass was unlike anything he'd ever seen before except in movies, and that type of flooding was usually computer-generated imagery. This was very real.

His proximity to where his house once stood allowed him to see the destruction the water had brought to their neighborhood. Their street was gone. The magnificent homes on the ridge had been swept downward into the river, or they'd created a jumbled mess of debris along the way.

Tyler, usually stoic in the face of adversity, couldn't contain his emotions. Tears streamed down his cheeks, mixing with the rainwater in his beard, a rarity for him. He couldn't shake the thought of Sammy, his nieces, and their beloved dogs being crushed under the weight of the landslide or swept away in the floodwaters.

He began to breathe heavily the more his concern grew. Then he inwardly cursed himself. His wife was the smartest person he knew. She had always shown remarkable common sense. She wouldn't have waited too long to evacuate. He was sure of it. They were there, somewhere. Either at the top of the ridge or closer to Pasadena.

"Where I just came from, of course," he mumbled to himself as he physically shook his body, intending to relieve his mind of any negativity.

He had to get to them. Save them. Protect them.

He took a deep breath. The number of people rushing toward him had dissipated to just a few elderly residents who calmly walked away from the bridge. He needed to see whether it was still possible.

A strong gust of wind greeted him as he reached the last of the vehicles parked on the bridge. He immediately saw the reason for people fleeing. A five-foot-wide crack had formed in the center of the concrete. It stretched from the south side of the eight-lane bridge to the north, where Devil's Gate was in plain view. It was too small for any cars to fall through but too wide to attempt to drive over.

The scene was the same on both sides of the freeway. Some motorists were standing with their hands on their hips, daring to stare over the edge into the abyss. Others had gathered their belongings and retreated in the rain to solid ground. Nobody, at least thus far, had attempted to cross the crack by jumping.

Tyler was not only well-versed in physiology, he was also a student of athleticism. He prepared all the athletes at USC to attend the National Football League Scouting Combine, referred to as the NFL Combines. It's a weeklong opportunity for college football players to perform physical and mental tests in front of NFL general managers and scouts. Some of the physical tests include the forty-yard dash, vertical jumps and the broad jump. The broad jump, or standing long jump, exhibits lower-body power and explosiveness. It's important for linemen, in particular, to show their flexibility to anchor in the trenches.

Tyler knew the average person could broad jump around seven feet. He gauged this jump would be about five. *Piece of cake,* he thought to himself, until he considered the weather conditions he was battling and the ramifications of failure. At the NFL Combines, if a player had a bad jump, he fell backwards and was the subject of jokes and laughter. On the 210 Freeway bridge, falling backwards meant death.

As he walked the length of the opening, he looked for the narrowest width of the crack that also allowed him to get a running start. He paced back and forth, analyzing his options until the bridge began to shake.

People shrieked and screamed in panic. Tyler lost his balance as the massive structure seemed to be under attack by a mysterious battering ram below. Large chunks of concrete broke loose from its steel rebar and plunged downward towards the raging floodwaters. He didn't have time to overanalyze it. He had to do it or turn around and find another way across.

Tyler cleared the area where he planned to jump. Because of the amount of water on the bridge, he couldn't get a running start without slipping. He had to stand firm, crouch and leap.

His palms were sweaty, and his heart raced. He begged for the wind to die down. The jump was difficult enough without a headwind. He took a deep breath, told his wife he loved her, and asked God to give him a boost.

Tyler jumped. He didn't dare look down, focusing instead on the front bumper of a pickup truck outfitted with a steel grille guard. His feet made a solid landing although they were perilously close to the edge. Concrete crumbled under his heels, falling into the dark water below. Tyler waved his arms to maintain his balance. He reached out for the grille guard, but it was just beyond his outstretched hand.

Suddenly, a man appeared and grabbed Tyler's wrist. The stranger jerked him toward the pickup, where Tyler met the grille guard with his chest, knocking the wind out of him for a moment.

"You're nuts, young man," said the Good Samaritan. "I hope wherever you're goin' is worth that dang fool effort."

Tyler smiled and nodded, wondering if he was too young for a heart attack, as the most vital organ in his body demanded to exit the *dang fool*.

"My wife is over there," he said breathlessly as he pointed his arm toward North Arroyo.

"Son, I hope she's all right, but I gotta tell ya, there ain't many houses left on that ridge. I live on the other side in Emerald Isle. We were driving along Highland when we saw the houses start to slide down. That's been hours ago. We've been stuck on this dang freeway, tryin' to get across to the San Gabriels."

Tyler had recovered. He and the man shook his hands while Tyler thanked him for the assistance. Without taking any more time, he made his way off the 210 Freeway bridge before it collapsed completely.

FORTY-SEVEN

Friday
New Year's Day
Pasadena Fire Station 38
Pasadena, California

Finn gathered several duffel bags and a trauma medical kit. They filled the bright orange duffels with blankets, clothing, food, and bottled water, with equal amounts in each. They were somewhat heavy and certainly more than Finn and Sammy could carry. However, he intended to use the floodwater to their advantage.

He retrieved a basket stretcher from the storage room in the fire station's garage as well as two Styrofoam tubes used to respond to rapid flood events. Prior to today, Finn doubted Station 38 ever had a need for the floatation attachments. They were mainly used in the recreational areas where lakes were located. The county, however, insisted upon each fire hall having the same equipment in the event a large-scale emergency required other stations to respond.

He strapped the contraption together and tested it in the water that had begun to approach the fire station's entry. Sammy tried to gauge the rate of increase in comparison to the girls' height. It was not over their heads but would certainly make moving very difficult.

Satisfied that the floating basket stretcher would work, Finn and Sammy carefully loaded their gear inside the basket while being mindful of weight distribution. The plan was for Finn to take the front, and Sammy would stabilize the rear. The girls would walk on each side of the stretcher using it to hold onto in case of a sudden change in the water's depth or ferocity.

"Okay, ladies. Are you ready?"

Sammy gauged the girls' reaction to his question. They just wanted this to be over, and she doubted they were ready for anything. They sheepishly nodded, and she gave each of them a reassuring smile.

"We're ready, Finn," she replied before asking, "Where are we headed?"

"I don't think going towards Pasadena is a good idea. We're too close to the river. Plus, depending how bad it is at the Rose Bowl, we may run into people who would cause us, um, well. Not that way."

Sammy understood where he was going with the statement. She didn't elaborate when she added, "I agree. My first thought is to climb the ridge, but I'm afraid it might be unstable."

"I haven't seen any evidence of landslides toward the west. I think we can use the water to haul our supplies through the base of the ridges and then choose our most valued supplies before beginning the climb up."

"To where?" asked Sammy. She was a goal-oriented person. Having a destination enabled her to psych herself up for the most difficult of tasks.

Finn paused. "Honestly, any stable ground we can find. We'll just head down a quarter mile or so and then choose a route up the hill."

He was interrupted by the sound of the earth groaning. An enormous volume of mud and rock crashed into the water behind them, followed by a house, or at least what was left of it. The noise was deafening, much louder than what Sammy and the girls had experienced earlier. That partial landslide had been slow, steady, and methodical as it carried earth, homes, and people toward the valley.

This time, the ground seemed to give way all at once as if it had exploded. The rubble fell so fast and hard that when it reached the three-foot-deep water on the street, it sent a series of waves toward the group.

When the first wave hit, it knocked the girls forward, causing them to lose their grip on the floating stretcher. Before Sammy or Finn could reach for their arms, another wave hit and pulled them under water.

The makeshift raft flipped over and capsized. Their duffel bags were scattered about, barely floating atop the rapidly increasing flow of water.

Sammy became hysterical when the girls did not reappear from under the water. "Sophie! Livvy! Where are you?"

She was turning in all directions, trying to catch a glimpse of the girls. She even went under water and opened her eyes in an attempt to find them in the silt-filled flood. That proved to be a mistake. She quickly rose back up and struggled to clear her eyes of the scratchy particles.

"There!" shouted Finn, who pointed downstream toward a bus stop forty feet away. Livvy had grabbed the steel pole and wrapped her arms around it. She tried to shimmy higher out of the water but kept sliding down beneath the surface.

Sammy began swimming, using the flowing water to propel her toward the child. Within seconds, she was standing next to Livvy, barely keeping her head and shoulders above the waves. She frantically searched for Sophie, who was several inches taller and weighed slightly more.

Finn was running through the floodwater as fast as he could, battling with his arms to push against the resistance.

"I see Sophie!" yelled Sammy. She glanced back at Finn and waved her free arm down the street.

"Go! I've got her!" He lumbered through the water toward Livvy, whose face immediately revealed fear for her older sister's safety.

As Finn arrived to hold Livvy, Sammy was off, stroke after stroke, racing diagonally to the current where she saw Sophie last. She stopped to look around and then saw a willow tree suddenly bend over. She took a chance and swam toward the spot. Fortunately, she was right.

Just before Sammy reached the tree, she'd popped her head above water and gasped for breath. The child was holding onto the thin branches, her little arms struggling against the raging water as it picked up speed.

Sammy found her footing and wrapped Sophie in her arms, a bear hug that she hoped would comfort the child more than it squeezed her. Sophie burst into tears before burying her face in Sammy's neck.

"Hey!" Finn shouted over the roar of the landslide carrying more houses toward the river. "Can you make it across the street towards that driveway? Up the hill is a house they donated to some kind of museum. Maybe we can ride it out there?"

Sammy whispered to Sophie, "I'm gonna carry you across, okay. Just hold on tight and trust me."

Sophie had stopped crying and nodded imperceptibly. Sammy was beginning to wonder if the child had gone into shock. She wouldn't know until they could get her settled down in a safe place.

If there was one.

FORTY-EIGHT

New Year's Day
Crescenta Valley
La Cañada Flintridge, California

Every aspect of life was impacted in California's Central Valley as the atmospheric rivers continuously pounded the state. In addition to the landslides destroying homes in populated areas, wildlife found their homes washed away as well.

Caught up in the torrents were nests, young animals, and mature wildlife of all types. Ordinarily, wild animals will adapt to unusual weather patterns by moving to higher ground. However, the ARkStorm brought a once-in-a-thousand-years rain event. Some creatures, both mammal and reptile, unwillingly found themselves riding the rapids downstream.

The animal kingdom preferred to stick to themselves. Deer and bears don't want to run the risk of death by approaching human populations. Snakes don't like their habitats or feeding grounds disturbed by human traffic. Rats carrying diseases like hantavirus or bubonic plague would rather live in the woods, not the residential streets of La Cañada Flintridge.

Yet the massive flooding changed everything.

The black bears of the Crescenta Valley were not very deep sleepers during their hibernation, unlike their counterparts in much colder climates. Although they were not true hibernators, they did experience what scientists called carnivorous lethargy, or denning. It was more of a period of reduced activity than the long periods of hibernation most people associate with the beasts.

However, as was the case with hibernation, a denning bear can come out of its relaxed state or slumber if disturbed. The ARkStorm disturbed the black bear population of the Crescenta Valley—all seven thousand of them.

Still fresh in the minds of Las Crescenta Valley

residents was the story of Meatball, the black bear that had roamed the area for years. He'd found his way into the hearts, garages, and backyards of valley residents a little over ten years ago. He had been photographed eating meatballs out of a freezer in a resident's garage. The videos had made the rounds on social media, and Meatball became an overnight sensation.

However, state wildlife officials reminded residents, Meatball, like all black bears, was extremely dangerous. Their powerful sharp-clawed paws could kill a person with a single swipe. Their jaws could crush bones and skulls. If provoked or angry, then tragic outcomes could occur if humans didn't heed these warnings.

Meatball had been captured, relocated, yet he'd returned to the area every time. Finally, he had been placed in a *wildlife refuge exhibit*, also known as a zoo, to be viewed by the public for a nominal charge.

The rest of the black bear population roamed the rural hills and ridges of the Crescenta Valley. Many made their way to higher ground to avoid the deluge. Others got caught up in the floodwaters and washed away with the current.

There was also a little-known fact that eluded most residents. Black bears were notoriously good swimmers, readily entering water in search of food. According to the North American Bear Center, there was even one that swam nine miles, or possibly longer, along the Gulf of Mexico despite the waves impeding his awkward movements.

Thousand-year flood events brought change to the lives of all living creatures in the Central Valley, including their habitats and feeding grounds. The common idiom *every man for himself* applied to the animal kingdom as well.

PART 4

He who has crossed the flood knows how deep it is.
~ American Proverb

FORTY-NINE

Friday
New Year's Day
North Arroyo Neighborhood
La Cañada, California

California was known for its incredible sunsets. The most idyllic views across the Pacific Ocean as the sun dropped over the horizon was when clouds were present to change the light into various shades ranging from pink to yellow to bright orange. Unfortunately, as darkness swept over the valley, ominous, black clouds accompanying the ARkStorm foreshadowed doom for those who'd survived the storm's wrath thus far.

Finn led Sammy and the girls to the mansion-sized residence turned museum just as the last of the day's light disappeared. Despite venturing into the unknown, Sammy was relieved to be out of the soaking rain. The girls needed time to mentally regroup. Finn needed to clear his head in a place he thought would be secure from the elements.

He'd managed to grab one of the large duffel bags that floated atop the water after their makeshift raft capsized. He loosened one end of its shoulder strap and tied it off to the belt loop of his khaki pants. As he carried Livvy, he pulled the tote through the water until they reached the driveway of the museum. He quickly did an inventory and was glad to find the flashlights, food, and fresh water inside had remained dry.

To the human mind, darkness is unsettling. It could create a darkened mood within us. Depression can set in. The illumination of a flashlight was more than enough to counteract the psychological impact being forced on the young children whom he'd be asking to endure a strange building, in a driving rainstorm, coupled with wind making strange noises in the night.

The door was locked, so Finn used the back of the watchman-style flashlight to break open a pane of glass next to the door handle. He was relieved it was not a double-deadbolt-style lock. Within seconds, they were inside the two-story-tall foyer. He slowly shined the light in all directions to get a look at their surroundings.

"This is a fancy house," said Livvy. It was an astute observation.

Marble floors. Ornate moldings. Elaborate artwork on the walls and a variety of exquisite sculptures on pedestals throughout.

Finn set the duffel on the floor and located another flashlight. It was smaller, designed to be held in a firefighter's tool belt. He handed Sammy the larger model.

"Gimme a moment to look around. I wanna make sure we don't have any surprises."

"Like?" she asked.

Finn chuckled as he used a term often associated with sailing vessels, as it seemed appropriate under the conditions. "Stowaways."

Sammy smiled as she got the reference. She hoped this would be their ark to ride out the storm.

While Finn roamed the lower floor before heading upstairs, Sammy encouraged the girls to take a seat on one of the two velvet settees that faced one another in the foyer. After they got settled, their legs dangling in the air because they were too short to reach the floor, Sammy moseyed across the foyer to sit on the other one. Within seconds, both girls scooted off the settee and rushed to join her. They crammed themselves onto the piece of furniture. Sammy adjusted her seat and wrapped her arms around the children. She realized they'd be clingy for a while.

Finn checked on them before ascending the stairs, careful not to slip. The extraordinary amount of moisture and the lack of ventilation had created a humid environment inside the building. The wetness on the marble floor made for slippery conditions. He was gone several minutes before emerging at the top landing of the sweeping staircase.

"It's all clear. From what I can tell, the museum was probably locked up for the long weekend. The curators must not be concerned about damage to the artwork."

Sammy added, "I wouldn't blame them for being more concerned about themselves." In a way, she hadn't stopped chastising herself for not leaving their home sooner. If she had focused more on the unusual weather and the ramifications, she wouldn't be in this predicament. More importantly, she wouldn't have put these innocent kids at risk.

Finn carefully came down the stairs to join them at the settees. He sat for a moment and looked around before rendering his assessment.

"It used to be a house, but now, obviously, it isn't. That means there are no bedrooms or many places to sit other than these loveseats."

Sammy snickered at the reference. She never was much for interior design. Tyler believed in functionality. For example, a sofa should have matching recliners on each end to watch television. Early on in their marriage, Sammy had struggled with learning the difference between a couch and a sofa. For her, it was a cushy place to cop a squat at the end of a long day. Then, thanks to a friend, she discovered there was a difference between a settee, for example, and a loveseat. A vase was a flower holder valued at under ten or twenty bucks. A *vaz*, she'd say with her best elitist accent, was valued much higher. People didn't call a bedspread a bedspread anymore. In today's vernacular, a bedspread was called a duvet or a coverlet or a comforter.

Then she let out a laugh that only nervous tension could conjure up. She was beginning to appreciate what was important in the scheme of things. It didn't matter whether you used the most generally accepted term for something. It didn't matter what kind of furniture you had or how much.

What mattered was not dying.

"Is it safe for us to stay here?" she asked.

"I think so. Yes. I know this area. Behind the house, it's relatively flat. At least we're not at the base of a ridge where landslides might be an issue. Sure, I'd like to be at a higher elevation. With higher ground, we run the risk of landslides. Damned if we do, damned if we don't."

"Language, Mr. O'Brien!" admonished Livvy.

Sammy and Finn burst out laughing as he attempted to apologize. After some playful banter, Finn pointed his flashlight in the direction of Sophie. He made eye contact with Sammy and scowled. She grimaced and nodded. The child hadn't spoken since she'd been scooped up out of the floodwater.

FIFTY

Friday
New Year's Day
North Arroyo Neighborhood
La Cañada, California

By the time a weary Tyler reached the top of the ridge at Highland Drive, night had set in, and his visibility was greatly restricted. On top of the ridge, the winds were very strong, blowing the rain sideways and carrying with it salty sea spray off the Pacific.

Tyler knew the streets of their neighborhood from running and riding his bike. He enjoyed the challenges of the sudden turns and steep inclines. He and Sammy could take a different route every day of the week and never get bored with their exercise regimen.

Upon exiting the freeway, he immediately turned toward Linda Vista Drive, which led directly to their home. He only had to walk a thousand feet down the slope before he realized it was gone. All of it. Their home. The road. Everything else around it, including most of the streets.

Tyler retreated to the exit ramp, marching up the hill with trepidation on his face. Once again, he was fearful that something had happened to Sammy. He had to believe she got out of the house safely. He wanted to trust that was what had happened. But to where? He tried to put himself in her shoes.

Would she instinctively go to higher ground? Maybe she was parked at the top of the ridge. He began jogging up the hill to where Linda Vista turned to the appropriately named Highland Drive. She wouldn't go far from home, knowing that he'd come looking for her.

A stream of water several inches deep hampered his effort. Cars abandoned on the street did as well. Many residents had attempted to turn toward the freeway to escape the landslide and were stymied when the bridge broke apart.

As Tyler jogged up the hill, he passed a few of the refugees who were walking to his right. He glanced at their faces. They were exhausted. Defeated. Scared. You could count on two hands the number of people who'd experienced a catastrophe of this magnitude. While living in Florida, the couple had seen the worst of what a hurricane had to offer. However, it was nothing like this.

Tyler slowed his pace to catch his breath. He began searching driveways and potential parking areas for Sammy's Tesla. He resisted the urge to walk down the driveway of the large homes that once had a pristine view of the valley below and the San Gabriel mountains. Now they teetered on the brink of collapsing and joining the graveyard of homes crashing toward the river.

He stopped for a moment to gather his thoughts. He bent over and rested his hands on top of his knees, looking at the pavement. He had to limit his search to the streets. If she'd found her way into one of the homes, she might be safe. If he tried to enter the homes searching for her, he might face the barrel of a gun.

Tyler arched his back and worked out the kinks.

It had been a long, stressful day. He was still sore from falling down in the stadium. He needed to rest, but he was too hyped up. He gathered the strength to continue, searching for any sign of her car. He wound his way through the streets, viewing the destruction, but not giving up hope.

He made his way to the walking trail along the ridgeline that connected one side of the neighborhood to the other. Sometimes, they'd load Carly and Fenway in his truck and drive to the top to watch the sunset. The memories filled him with emotion, and he began to cry once again. Everything he loved was missing. How would he ever find them? When would this end?

He sat in silence, resting on a flat rock overlooking a massive landslide that had wiped out dozens of homes before they piled up against another hill. Half an hour passed, and he stared at the dark landscape without thinking. He'd become numb inside. Completely out of sorts. Struggling to know what to do.

Then, nearby, he heard a dog barking. It was an insolent yapping that was somehow familiar. It continued until another dog, somewhat farther away, barked back. It was a single yet excited bark reminiscent of Carly's when it was time to go outside for a walk. She was a high-spirited pup who had difficulty containing herself, much to the chagrin of her veterinarian. Tyler admired her enthusiasm, and besides, vets were a dime a dozen. There was only one Carly, and she just crashed into him, knocking him off his perch.

FIFTY-ONE

Friday
New Year's Day
North Arroyo Neighborhood
La Cañada, California

"Guys! You're here. Safe!" Tyler fell to the ground and rolled around on the rocky soil. He got mud on his clothes, but it didn't matter. He had the couple's kids back.

Carly smothered him with kisses, then took a break to run in circles before coming back for more. Fenway did the same without the circling around. He simply stood over his best friend and yapped repeatedly, likely screaming at Tyler to take him home. Fenway was a homebody. Carly was more free-spirited and liked the great outdoors.

After the joyful reunion, reality set in. Were the dogs alone?

"Sammy! Are you here? Sammy!" he shouted as loud as his lungs would allow. Yet he sensed the howling wind and pounding rain muted his voice.

He noticed his dogs were still excited, so he gently rubbed their backs and faces to calm them down. They were soaked to the bone, the rain having a greater effect on Carly's long hair compared to her much shorter companion.

"Where is your mommy?" he asked, hoping that somehow the pups would lead him to her. They just stood there, panting and smiling. Tyler looked down the slight slope toward an adjacent street. He recognized the dead-end street and the chain-link fence that surrounded the green space around the landfill just past where the street turned toward the bottom of the ridge.

He began to wonder if she'd driven up that way, toward the landfill, thinking it would be safer than the large houses that were collapsing around her. He looked down toward Carly and Fenway. They appeared to be up for anything.

"Come on. Let's go find your mommy."

Tyler brushed off his clothes and began walking briskly down the trail toward the gate. He felt like his luck was turning for the better after he found his dogs. He didn't want to injure himself because he was anxious to see her.

In the late eighties, the City of Glendale had created a *defined waste shed area*, California-speak for a landfill, to dispose of the area's garbage. The facility was built on top of the ridge just above the neighborhood filled with multimillion-dollar homes. It had been dug into the ridge, so the county assured the residents that they'd never worry about the refuse washing downward into their lawns. When they made those promises at the county commission hearings, they didn't envision an ARkStorm's effects on the earthen surround of the landfill.

Tyler and the pups reached the trail that traversed the ridge alongside a chain-link fence. The large parking area where hikers and exercise buffs parked was an area familiar to Sammy. Because the dogs had approached him from that direction, he presumed she'd parked the car there. There were a couple of abandoned vehicles in the parking area, but not Sammy's.

Tyler buried his face in his hands and dragged them down his beard, pulling the moisture with them. The rain quickly soaked him again, drawing a heavy sigh.

He backtracked a hundred yards and tried another street leading up the ridge. It ended in a cul-de-sac near a large tower holding up high-voltage power lines delivering electricity to Pasadena. As he walked up the slope, he looked for Sammy's car and also for any of the residents. He thought about quizzing them, asking if they'd seen her and the kids. The homes seemed to be empty.

Tyler began to think he was wasting his time and energy searching for them in the dark. He thought allowing some time to pass overnight would allow the storm to move through and the sun to peek out again like it had done the day before.

Fenway started barking again. This time, the subject of their attention was not Tyler. He couldn't see the animal that drew their ire, but he could hear it. The low growl was not a dog. It was more vicious. Much larger. It was a bear.

Tyler looked around for a means of escape. In the bad weather, an animal would have the upper hand because they were used to inclement conditions.

Come. Sit. Stay. These were basic commands he'd hoped to teach his pups when the couple took them in as rescues. They were a little too old to learn new tricks, or parental requests, for that matter.

"Carly! Fen! Come here!"

Apparently, his voice was full of apprehension because they didn't ignore him like they usually would. They came running back to him, their paws sloshing in the water covering the street.

"This way," he ordered them. He turned toward a single-story rancher, the closest to them. It had a wrought-iron gate protecting the courtyard entrance. Even if he couldn't break into the front door, they could separate themselves from the bear with the iron gate.

The dogs barked the entire time, which seemed to annoy the black bear. He pounded his paws on the wet grass where he stood. Then there was another growl. Louder and deeper. Two bears had found their way into that part of the neighborhood in search of food. Tyler knew black bears could be aggressive when agitated and were not to be trifled with.

The ARkStorm had a way of causing agitation in everyone. And fear.

The dogs yelped at the sound of the second bear and ran to Tyler's side. The three of them scurried across the driveway and sidewalk leading to the gate.

The bears entered the street, smacking the two inches of running water on the concrete. They growled again as they gave chase.

Tyler fumbled with the gate's latch. He reached through the bars and managed to gain entry from inside the gate. With it securely locked, he turned his attention to the front door. It was locked with two deadbolts.

"Crap!" he hollered before covering his mouth with his hand.

The bears were at the gate, pawing at Carly and Fenway, who continued barking at the ferocious animals. Frustrated, the bears beat their bodies against the wrought-iron posts in an attempt to push the gate over. Tyler couldn't imagine they would be so aggressive. Yet here they were, trapped behind a gate that hopefully would hold back the three-hundred-pound creatures.

Tyler grabbed the dogs by the collar and pulled them into a corner of the courtyard as far away from the gate as possible. He calmed the excited pups, who eventually stopped barking. It took fifteen minutes of growling, pawing, and pounding the gate for the bears to lose interest. They wandered off toward the landfill, disappearing into the rainy darkness.

Tyler finally relaxed. He let go of his dogs and rested his back against the stucco wall of the house, where his head was protected by the roof overhang. He couldn't believe it. Didn't he have enough to deal with trying to find Sammy and the kids without dealing with pissed-off bears?

As he processed everything, the dogs fell asleep, and so did he until the earth shook hours later.

FIFTY-TWO

Late Friday Night
New Year's Day
American Modern Museum
Pasadena, California

The group had gathered in the kitchen of the former residence, an extravagant place to fix fancy finger foods and cocktails when hosting soirees at the gallery. The full-size Sub-Zero refrigerator had a glass-door front, allowing the refugees to peruse the many food options. Finn estimated the contents had been without power for ten hours. In that length of time, especially considering the quality of the appliance, he was confident the food was not spoiled.

Before opening it and removing the contents, he had another idea. It was somewhat risky, but worth the effort. "I've seen this brand of gas range and cooktop before. Wolf is pretty high-end, and I believe I can light it without power. Sammy, would you mind looking through the drawers for a lighter. Um, preferably the stick kind."

Sammy began her search while the girls watched. She needed Sophie to engage with the group. She shined the flashlight on the ceiling to get a good look at the child's face without blinding her.

"Hey, Sophie. This is a pretty big kitchen. Would you mind helping me find a lighter? You know, the kind to light candles."

Although she didn't verbalize her response, she nodded her head unenthusiastically. She slowly went through the drawers of the kitchen island. Sammy would've loved more, but she was glad to see Sophie was no longer in a near catatonic state.

After a minute during which everyone assisted in the search, it was Livvy who wandered into a walk-in pantry. She came out with a lighter and a candle.

"Well done, young missy!" exclaimed Finn. "We now have light and maybe fire. Stand back, everyone. Professional fire maker and fire putter-outer at work."

Finn adjusted the knobs on the front of the range and allowed gas to enter the largest burner. He flicked the Bic lighter, and the gas burner roared to life. Sophie gasped. Livvy applauded. Sammy's stomach immediately began to growl. She was ready to cook.

As it turned out, most of the food in the refrigerator consisted of packaged sandwich meats and cheeses. There were bagels and cream cheese as well. The pantry had a loaf of bread, a variety of crackers, and an abundance of mixed nuts.

She made the girls grilled cheese sandwiches with a side of potato chips. She and Finn ate bagels with cream cheese. Using a method her mom taught her, Sammy even made coffee, much to Finn's delight. She poured water and the coffee grounds into a tea kettle and brought it to a near boil. Then she strained out the coffee grounds using a filter for the drip coffee maker she'd found in the pantry. A few grounds slipped through, but Finn guzzled it down like there was no tomorrow.

He led the girls upstairs, and they found a way to make a bed for themselves out of cushions and moving blankets he'd located in a closet. It wasn't the Ritz, but it was high and dry. The adults stood just outside the room full of landscape paintings. The other bedroom galleries contained some odd modern works that creeped Sammy out. She never was much for horror flicks or anything she deemed scary. Somehow, the beast that was the ARkStorm hadn't caused her to cower in the corner, yet.

"I'll take first watch," began Finn as he gave a final look in at the girls, who'd curled up next to one another. "That strong coffee was the nectar of the Celtic gods. I may be up all night."

Sammy planned on sitting with the girls until they fell asleep. Afterwards, she planned on helping Finn. "Do you anticipate trouble?" she asked.

"Sammy, I don't know. I want to believe the good people of North Arroyo would come together to help one another. However, the stadium is not that far from here, and you never know what desperate people might do."

Sammy's tone of voice reflected her concern. "You mean like break in?"

"Yes, that is a possibility. Certainly, there are plenty of options around us. Actual homes that might be better suited to ride out the storm. However, we should be ready for anything."

He knelt to a crouch, lifted up the right pant leg of his khakis, and retrieved a subcompact 9 mm handgun from an ankle holster.

"You have a gun?" asked Sammy, surprised that he was carrying a weapon. The state had passed a series of strict gun-control measures, making it near impossible to own a handgun, much less carry it in a concealed manner.

"I do," he replied. "I watch the news, Sammy. I see how our society has changed over the years. Too many people do not value the sanctity of life these days. With fewer cops on the street, I chose to protect myself."

A strong gust of wind shook the sprawling home-turned-museum. A large crash startled them both.

"What was that?" asked Sammy.

Livvy called out in the darkness, "Sammy? Is it okay?" Sammy chastised herself for not having at least a candle in the gallery room with the children. She would do that as soon as they determined what had just fallen nearby.

Finn moved down the hallway toward the other rooms and then turned to Sammy, shining his light on her face.

"You let me check it out. Stay with the young lasses."

She nodded and retreated into the gallery. The room, once the master bedroom, was spacious and included several windows facing to the side and rear of the property. She approached each of them and peered through the curtains.

Because it was dark and the rainfall was so dense, she was unable to make out any features around the building. After asking the girls to confirm they were comfortable with her looking through the other upper-level windows, she moved methodically from room to room.

Lastly, at the end of the hall, she entered a sitting room overlooking the other side of the house. She shined her light through the fixed-glass, floor-to-ceiling window. Beyond a large gathering area that was once a swimming pool, she noticed a sizable live oak tree had fallen over the former pool house.

She reached the upstairs landing and called out below, "Finn! I think I know what happened. A large tree fell …" Sammy allowed her voice to trail off when the sound of glass breaking in the foyer alarmed her.

Her eyes grew wide, and she covered her mouth to avoid screaming when she heard men's voices. They were arguing with one another on how to get the door open. She heard one deadbolt latch click, followed by the second. The men hesitated until seconds later, the door swiftly swung open with the help of the wind, crashing hard into the plaster wall behind it. It was dark, and Sammy didn't dare shine the light on them to reveal her position. She hid behind the wall, listening to several sets of feet shuffling inside, their sneakers squeaking on the wet marble floor.

She glanced toward the gallery room to where the girls were. They hadn't made a sound. She peeked around the corner to get a look at the intruders. She was able to make out five or maybe six silhouettes. She gulped.

Where was Finn?

FIFTY-THREE

**Late Friday Night
New Year's Day
American Modern Museum
Pasadena, California**

With his weapon drawn, Finn had exited the rear of the house and eased along the stucco walls, using the roof's overhang to protect him from the soaking rainfall. He, too, came across the fallen tree. Presuming that was the cause of the crash, he looked around the barren hillside, which rose at a steep incline toward the location of the landfill. He smiled when he saw there were no houses constructed behind the museum. Sure, there was muddy runoff that was being easily diverted around the built-up concrete pad that was used as a patio. However, there was no threat of another house tumbling down on top of them like he'd seen toward Devil's Gate.

He laughed at himself as he returned his gun to the ankle holster. He'd never had to fire it other than at the LAPD range while training. He seriously doubted looters were at work at a time like this. Even the bad guys had to save themselves from the ARkStorm first.

Finn returned to the house through the kitchen door and shook the moisture off his body. Standing on a rug, he wiped the excess water from his clothes. He caught a whiff of the coffee, which was still warm on the stovetop. He shrugged. He wasn't gonna worry about his hypertension at the moment. He might not see another pot of coffee for some time.

Just as he made his way to the stove, he heard glass breaking somewhere in the house. The marble floors tended to create echoes, and the driving rain served to distract his sense of hearing. However, the sound of breaking glass hitting a hard surface was unmistakable.

Finn grunted as he once again drew his pistol. He eased through the kitchen into the formal dining room that held a table for sixteen. He approached a wide opening that once led to the living room adorned with a variety of statuary art. He was close enough to the foyer to feel the rush of moisture-filled cool air enter the house when the door was opened.

Finn pressed his back against the wall, nearly knocking over a bust of some ancient dignitary or another. Or maybe it was King William V. He tried to count the dark silhouettes as they entered. It appeared to be two or three adults and two children. They were talking to one another in hushed tones.

They were apprehensive. Not bold. Not intent on causing harm.

Finn had trusted his gut throughout most of his life and career. It had kept him alive and unharmed on many an occasion.

After they'd entered the foyer, one member of the group closed the door behind them. Finn could hear them twist the knobs for the bolt locks. He didn't think it was within the character of looters to lock the door behind them or bring children.

He took a chance.

"Everyone, I would like you to remain calm."

"What?" a man asked.

"Johnny, you said it would be empty!" said a woman.

"Mommy, I'm scared," added a young boy.

"I need all of you to remain completely still," Finn continued. His voice was nonthreatening but stern. "I'm going to shine a flashlight on you now."

He did, and he got his first look at the group. They looked very much like Sammy and the girls. Worn out. Sopping wet. Carrying very little other than the clothes they were wearing.

"Who are you?" asked one of the three women before adding, "You, um, sound familiar."

"My name is Finn O'Brien. I live in this neighborhood."

"The fireman?" asked the only adult male. There was a teenage boy by his side who appeared to be fifteen or so.

"That's right," Finn answered. "How do you know?"

"We were at the party yesterday. At the clubhouse. All of us, in fact."

Relief washed over Finn. The tension was released from his body. However, he had to think of Sammy and the girls before he totally let his guard down.

"Sir, I must ask you, are any of you armed?"

"Like, with a gun?" asked the teen.

"No," the man replied. "Not us. Never."

Finn managed a smile. He still didn't put the

pistol in his ankle holster, opting instead to shove it into the deep pocket of his khakis.

"Sir, what is your name?" Finn asked.

"John Fraser. Most people call me Johnny. My wife is over there with her sister. This is my son, Jack. Two of the kids are mine together with my wife, um, Charlotte's sister's son."

Finn kept the light on them. He glanced toward the top of the sweeping staircase. "Sammy, I assume you heard all of this?"

"Yes," she replied, startling the newcomers.

"Are you okay with them joining us?"

"I think so."

Finn nodded. "Why don't you nice people keep walking into the kitchen over there? We can get acquainted or, well, reacquainted."

As the group passed by, Finn glanced up at Sammy, who was descending the stairs with her flashlight on to avoid tripping. He met her at the foyer, and they whispered to one another.

"They said they remember you from the party," she said, leaning into his ear. "I wanna believe they're safe."

"We'll make sure, but here is the question. Do we want to allow them to stay here?"

Sammy thought for a few seconds. Technically,

she and the girls, along with Finn, were squatters of sorts. "Do we have the right to tell them no?"

Finn shrugged and glanced toward the kitchen. "I suppose I could threaten them to force them to get out. It wouldn't be right, in my mind."

Sammy nodded. "I can't disagree with you. The girls are okay. Sophie is actually sleeping. Finn, I think she's in a state of shock. She's been that way since we pulled them out of the flood."

He walked away from Sammy toward the kitchen and motioned for him to join his side. "Those young girls are our priority. I'll tell these folks they can stay, but they have to remain downstairs. I don't want to do anything to upset Sophie and Livvy."

Sammy patted him on the back. "I'm so glad our paths crossed. You're a good man, Finn O'Brien."

He smiled. He'd received many awards and accolades throughout his career. Sammy's kind words of praise were the sincerest he'd ever heard. He confidently walked into the kitchen and gave the new people the news that they could stay. Sighs of relief and words of appreciation greeted Sammy as she entered as well.

Their numbers had just grown threefold.

FIFTY-FOUR

Saturday
American Modern Museum
Pasadena, California

It was just past midnight, and all the occupants of the museum were awake. Sophie and Livvy had been eavesdropping at the top of the stairs when the new arrivals interacted with Finn. Moments after Sammy entered the kitchen, the two young girls arrived unannounced to see what all the hubbub was about.

In the midst of the chaos around them, the group of strangers managed to make the best of it with a midnight snack for the new arrivals and a treat of sorbet for everyone. Finn reminded everyone that the perishable foods would soon spoil if not eaten, so eat they did.

And they had fun. The kids got acquainted with one another and soon roamed through the museum with flashlights and candleholders. They looked at modern art through the eyes of children, and their remarks were, well, appropriately juvenile. Yet, in the moment, they were enjoying themselves. All of them had traumatic stories to tell. However, now was not the time. They wanted to be kids again, even if their playground was a stuffy museum full of funny-looking paintings.

As for the adults, they hit the mother lode. Johnny, who was a teacher at the local middle school, had led a field trip to the museum once before. He recalled there was a placard advertising an upcoming fundraiser for the museum during which wine and cheese would be served. After they ate, he and Finn scoured the museum in search of the wine.

They were successful. The wine flowed; stories were shared, not just of what they'd been through but also about their lives prior to losing everything. The group was in remarkably high spirits. Perhaps it was denial or even disbelief. After all, what had happened to them was nothing short of biblical.

As the evening wore on into Saturday, everyone agreed their lives would change forever. The mood became solemn as the initial high from the wine brought weariness over the group. The children fought to stay awake, and the adults hit a wall from exhaustion. As Sammy and Finn set up sleeping arrangements for the newcomers, all agreed they'd try to remain in place until the storm passed. They were glad to put the horrors of New Year's Day behind them.

Sammy wore an Apple watch for several reasons, style not being one of them. She'd always been a no-frills kinda gal, and despite the fact she was paid handsomely by her law firm, she hadn't shopped for watches by Cartier or Rolex. The Apple suited her because of the couple's devotion to exercise. It recorded their calories burned, exercise goals achieved, and was, in essence, a minicomputer on their wrists.

Another reason Sammy wore the Apple watch was to monitor her sleep. That night, she entered stage 3 non-REM deep sleep within minutes. She bypassed the typical process of reaching the total state of relaxation during which there was no eye movement or muscle activity. It was a time when it was difficult to wake someone up.

Unless they're jolted awake.

In her sleepy mind, it sounded like a low rumble, not dissimilar to the eighteen-wheel tractor trailer rigs that used to roar down the highway in front of her house when she was a child. She could hear them coming off in the distance, growing louder and seemingly shaking the ground as they approached. Then, with a roar and a whoosh from the displacement of air around their trailer, the big rigs motored by until they were nothing but a faint sound in her memories. Until the next one came.

Sammy didn't want to wake up. Her mind reminded her she wasn't in Pennsylvania, and there were certainly no tractor trailer rigs rumbling by. Yet the fear of missing out forced her to stir awake.

At first, she was groggy and disoriented. She'd forgotten where she was and how she got there. Then, in the dim light provided by a candle in the hallway, her eyes found the girls sleeping together in a corner of the gallery room.

She shook her head, trying to recall the details of the dream she had. She sat up, frustrated that she couldn't recall the reason she'd been forced out of a deep sleep. Then she realized she wasn't dreaming. She heard the rumble again.

It was louder now. She abruptly stood and moved to the windows. The incessant rainfall coupled with the lack of any ambient light made it impossible to see. She rushed into the hallway, where Finn was coming toward her.

"You heard it too?" he said inquisitively.

"Yeah, almost like a quake," she replied. "Are you sure we're safe from a landslide here?"

"I thought so. I mean, there is a slope above us but no homes. It's very rocky and backfilled with an earthen structure built for Glendale's landfill."

Finn had barely finished his sentence when they were knocked off their feet. It was if a giant foot had stomped just outside the house to see how high the structure could be lifted off the ground. Sammy grabbed the railing overlooking the foyer to stand when the house was hit with a massive blow that seemed to move it several feet.

The impact shoved her forward until she somersaulted over the rail.

FIFTY-FIVE

Saturday
American Modern Museum
Pasadena, California

The sudden jolt caused by the landslide striking the back of the museum caught Sammy off guard. It was her inherent survival instinct that prevented her from dropping twenty feet to the marble floor below. She managed to grab the ornate, wrought-iron spindles of the railing and hold on. The house continued to shake as it was battered by a landslide originating at the landfill. Her sweaty palms coupled with the ever-present moisture on every surface caused her to slip as gravity seemed to yank at her dangling feet.

"Sammy!" Sophie screamed. She'd found her voice earlier in the evening after spending time with the new kids in the house. She stood with Livvy. Their faces revealed their abject horror at the sight of their aunt grasping the rail's spindles.

Finn found his footing and rushed to the railing. "Hold on! Can you reach my hand?"

Her grasp was losing the battle with gravity, which had an unfair advantage because her hands were so wet. Her hands had slipped to the base of the spindle, and only the bottom of the railing stopped her from falling.

She tried to pull herself up. One hand first. Then the next. Only to slide downward again. With each try, she almost lost her grip altogether.

"I can't reach!" she shouted to Finn, who was trying various ways to grasp her hands or wrists.

The commotion drew the newcomers out of their sleep into the foyer.

Finn shouted to them, "Johnny, come up here and hold my legs so I can lean over to grab her."

He didn't respond.

Sammy was losing her strength. Her hands were cramping. She'd loosen her grip to flex her fingers before quickly grabbing the spindle again. The last time she tried it, her legs began to sway uncontrollably, causing the kids to shriek.

"Johnny!" yelled Finn louder. "Get up here!"

Johnny looked at his wife and family. He used his arms to direct them toward the front door. He looked at Sammy as he spoke.

"Um, I'm sorry. Sorry. I have to, you know. Come on, kids, we have to go."

They hustled through the front door and into the downpour.

"You cowardly bastard!" shouted Finn. "Karma will get you!"

Sammy's arms were on fire. She was struggling to hold on. She looked downward. It was fifteen feet or so to the floor. If she dropped, what was the worst case? A broken leg or two. Cracked skull?

A death sentence under these conditions.

"We'll help!" exclaimed Sophie, who'd led her sister to the railing. Their little hands reached for Sammy's arms and held her wrists. They tugged in an attempt to pull her through the spindles.

Sammy tried to reassure them and herself. "It's okay, girls. We'll get through this."

"I can try to break your fall," Finn suggested as he frantically looked around for any means of helping her.

Then the girls' attempts to assist gave Sammy an idea.

"Girls, can you scoot over to let Finn in front of me?" Her voice was remarkably calm.

They turned to make contact with Finn and immediately slid out of the way. He dropped to his knees in front of her.

"What's the plan?"

"My hands. I can't do this much longer. I need you to hold my wrists while I try to walk myself to the stairs."

Finn glanced to his left. He understood. She'd stretch her right arm over to the next spindle and follow it with the left. Nine spindles later, she'd be at the stairwell, where she could either walk her way down or swing her legs up.

"I understand. Let's go."

Sammy reached over, grasped the next spindle. Finn took a firm grip on her wrist in case her full body weight pulled her off the spindle.

"You can do it, Sammy!" shouted Livvy. Sophie even clapped her hands like she was watching a sporting event.

Rather than losing her concentration, the girls' cheering emboldened her. *You've got this, babe.* Tyler's words of encouragement that for some odd reason had annoyed her in the past were now loud and clear in her mind. She set her jaw as she picked up the pace. *Yeah, Ty, I've got this.*

When she reached the spindles of the stairwell, Finn quickly moved around to face her. "Try this if you can. I will stand on a step below. You reach for the same level. Understand?"

"Yeah. You'll be able to reach me."

"That's right, missy. When I pull you up, try to gain a footing on the outside of the tread."

Sammy looked up at Finn's weather-worn face. His Irish heritage was apparent by the rosy appearance of his cheeks and nose. His battle scars of fighting fires and saving lives were evidenced by the wrinkles around his eyes and on his forehead. His look of determination gave her comfort that she'd be all right.

Like trapeze artists at the famed Ringling Brothers Circus of days past, Sammy reached as high on the spindles of the stairwell as she could. Finn was ready for her. His powerful grip took hold of her wrist, and those forearms kept strong by his love of weightlifting yanked her upward, catching her off guard slightly.

She struggled to gain a toehold on the outside of the stairwell, but Finn did not falter. After a long couple of seconds, she was on solid ground, with her arms wrapped around Finn's neck.

"Thank you," she whispered as emotion overcame her. He helped her swing one leg over the railing and then the next. They sat next to one another on the step.

With Finn's arm wrapped around her shoulders, Sammy began to sob. "It's okay, missy. You're safe now."

"Sammy, it's okay," said Sophie, who rubbed her aunt's shoulders the way she liked to be comforted by her mother when she was distraught.

"Yeah, Sammy, you're okay," added Livvy as she scooted between Sammy and the railing. Finn slid over to allow the child room to snuggle in next to her.

Sammy took a deep breath and closed her eyes, wishing this nightmare to end and daylight to come. Her arms were shaking from the exertion she'd just put them through. She held her hands out in front of her body as they shuddered uncontrollably, causing them to laugh. As she studied their trembling, she tilted her head.

She straightened her back and sat a little taller on the step. Concerned, Livvy stood, as she thought something was wrong. Sammy gently touched the child's arm to reassure her.

"Hey, look. I've got a cell signal on my watch. There are text messages coming in from Tyler."

"Great!" exclaimed Sophie.

Then Sammy tapped her watch. "No. No. NO! The battery just died. Oh no." Her elation quickly turned to dejection.

And then to primal fear.

The building shook as if a giant bulldozer had steamrolled into the back of the museum. Seconds later, the back walls fell inward, flooding the ground floor with mud and water, with tons of refuse from the Glendale landfill that was poised to bury them.

FIFTY-SIX

Saturday
Fair Oaks Neighborhood
Glendale, California

Tyler had curled up with Carly and Fenway under the eve of the house, ostensibly safe from the burly bruins behind the locked gate. Despite his travails, he was unaware that breaking into other people's homes had become an accepted practice.

Rather than force his way inside the house, he opted to remain in the elements and get some rest. He was restless for the next several hours as he tried to find sleep. Every sound was a perceived threat. Shouts from neighbors startled him. The groan of the earth as the roots of large trees separated from the soil reminded him of the bears that had chased them.

So when he began to hear dings emanating from his watch in rapid succession, he was easily stirred out of his semi-slumber. His Apple watch, other than providing its customary ding notification at the top of the hour, had been silent. Cell towers were down, so he was unable to send or receive communications with Sammy. Nor was he able to receive the emergency warning alerts the county had spent millions of dollars on.

There was no backup system to the cellular towers, leading him to assume that some had been repaired. Regardless, he quickly began to read her messages, which began just before the power went out at Rose Bowl Stadium.

Sammy would never text him during a game, especially one of this magnitude. Yet she was privy to weather and news reports that he was not. Her texts revealed her concern.

Then they stopped right about the time America's heartbeat, the power grid and the communications apparatus, ceased to function.

Tyler was about to roust his pups when he had a thought. He wiped his wet hands off onto his equally wet shirt to allow him to navigate through the apps on his watch. Apple Watch had a feature known as Find People. He and Sammy had set it up when they purchased the devices years ago. It was helpful to find a misplaced Apple device or to simply check on one another during the day when they were apart.

He scrolled down, tapped on Sammy's name, and a blue dot appeared on a map.

Tyler frowned. Confused, he opened the gate and walked onto the driveway of the home, with his head on a swivel. He regarded the threat from the bears as real; however, he believed they'd moved on into the driving rain. He studied his watch, turning slowly until he'd made a complete rotation. He tried to zoom in on her location, which was difficult under the conditions.

He muttered to himself, "She's close."

Tyler returned to the gated entry, thrilled his wife was safe and quite possibly nearby. He rousted the pups.

"Guys, I know where Sammy and the girls are. And it's only a couple of miles. You two up for a long walk?"

Fenway lifted his head, gave Tyler the stink-eye for waking him up, and nuzzled back under Carly's belly. They didn't share his exuberance.

He studied it again before turning his attention

to the house. He furrowed his brow and shrugged before dashing toward a set of double windows facing the street. He picked up a landscape boulder and heaved it inside, shattering the glass. Using another rock like a hammer, he bashed out the rest of the glass, enabling him to climb inside.

"Hello! Sorry about the glass window! It's an emergency!" he shouted to be heard although the interior was deathly silent other than the wind blowing into the living room.

Tyler quickly shut the pocket doors leading into the room and entered the foyer. He quickly opened the doors, and the half-sleepy pups came inside. He'd realized the hunt for Sammy would be taxing on them under these conditions. They would be safe in the house, with food, water and shelter.

"Guys, I need you both to be troopers right now. I've gotta go find Sammy." He patted his leg as he fumbled his way in the darkness toward the kitchen, crashing into furniture and luggage left behind when the owners bugged out.

He rushed through the kitchen in search of a flashlight. He tried every cabinet in search of the junk drawer, that single location for everything that didn't have a more defined spot. There. The flashlight was small, but it packed a nice output of lumens.

The pups were calm, dutifully awaiting further instructions. They were wagging their tails furiously when Tyler found dog food in the family's pantry. He located several serving bowls and hastily filled them with kibble to the point of overflowing. He wanted his dogs to have plenty to eat and drink in case it took him a while to return.

As their voracious appetites took over, the two pups ignored Tyler as they devoured the food. He snuggled on them and promised he'd be back before bolting out of the house.

He checked his watch again. She was still in the same position. He got his bearings again. He'd have to head toward the stadium along the ridge and then make his way down into the neighborhood.

"Straight toward the stadium," he said to himself as he raced down the street toward the sound of the earth moving. Full circle.

FIFTY-SEVEN

Saturday
American Modern Museum
Pasadena, California

"Livvy!" Sammy shouted as the young girl lost her balance and rolled down the marble stairs. Her little body crashed into the rapidly flowing mud and water as it swept through the building. The structure groaned under the immense pressure exerted on its back walls by the flow of rain-soaked garbage mixed with mud that created a massive blob of sadistic papier-mâché.

In the darkened conditions, Sammy was able to see her arms flailing in a desperate attempt to grab onto the chairs flowing along the mudslide. In the blink of an eye, Livvy was gone, sucked out through the front door into the deluge.

Sammy leapt to her feet, slipped, but caught herself by grabbing the stair railing. Her clumsiness provided the time Finn needed to stop her.

"I've got her! You take care of Sophie!"

Finn left her side and, using the railing for support, took the treacherous stairs two at a time.

Sammy stood dumbfounded for a moment as she watched Finn slosh through the mud to exit the museum. The building was shaking, as was her body. She'd almost reached the limit of what her psyche could take. She looked upward, asking God for help. And to give them a break.

The house seemed to lurch forward, bringing Sammy back into the present. Was it gonna be forced down the ravine like so many others? She swung around, expecting to see Sophie at the top of the stairs. The candle that had been burning had been doused by the wind blowing through the house, which caused Sammy to doubt her eyesight.

"Sophie?"

No answer.

"Sophie!" shouted Sammy, her voice panicked.

She scrambled up the stairs and reached the

landing, searching in all directions in the limited light. She shouted the child's name again but received no response.

Sammy rushed down the hallway to the former master bedroom of the museum. Her instincts told her Sophie would return to bed, the only safe place she knew amidst the mayhem. As she reached the room, she forced herself to appear calm. She didn't want to create any more angst in the six-year-old than necessary.

"Sophie, honey, we need to leave, okay?"

Still no response. Sammy inched forward in the dark, convinced that the floor was tilting slightly. She knelt next to the makeshift bed. She thought Sophie was curled up under the moving pads, but it was just a jumbled mess.

Now frantic, Sammy rushed into the bathroom and looked in every corner, including the shower. She tried the master closet, which was filled with boxes. She rushed into the hallway as the roar of debris crushing against the house became deafening.

She was screaming her name as she dashed from one gallery to the next. The building was definitely leaning forward, knocking paintings off the wall and toppling statues off their pedestals.

She quickly glanced over the railing, careful not

to get too close, as her almost falling over was fresh in her mind. She shouted for Sophie again. Mud mixed with garbage had filled the foyer and was halfway up the entry door. Kitchen appliances, statues, and works of art blended with the refuse of Glendale's residents.

It was hard for her to see downstairs, and Sammy feared Sophie might've descended the stairs while she searched. She spun around and ran toward the end of the hallway. The small gallery overlooked the former swimming pool area.

There she was, standing in an eerie, unresponsive stupor. She was staring into the backyard.

"Sophie, honey, I'm here. Please, we have to go."

She didn't move.

Sammy eased next to her, trying to avoid startling the disturbed child. She almost put her arm around her shoulders but chose to crouch next to her as if she'd been invited into Sophie's space. She wanted to look through the child's eyes to determine what had captured her attention.

Now she understood. A wall of mud and debris was pushing on the back of the house. By her estimation, it was twenty feet tall, equally as high as the top floor where they stood.

Sammy's first instinct was to grab Sophie's hand

and drag her down the stairs. Instead, she retreated out of the gallery room to glance over the stair railing again. The landslide had forced its way throughout the lower floors. The entry door was full, as were the side openings leading to the former living and dining rooms of the building. In essence, they were now in a one-story structure.

Panic-stricken, Sammy ran her hands through her wet hair, which was caked with mud. She wanted to cry. She wanted to roll up in a corner somewhere, sobbing until it was over. Yet she couldn't. She needed to save herself and Sophie. She had to put Finn and Livvy out of her mind, trusting the brave firefighter to find a way to save her niece. She had to hope God answered her prayers to protect Tyler and their pups. Her job was right here. Right now.

FIFTY-EIGHT

Saturday
American Modern Museum
Pasadena, California

Finn had successfully rescued many people under all manner of circumstances in his storied career. Even that day, he and Sammy had successfully plucked the two young children out of the swiftly moving floodwaters. However, attempting to chase down a semiconscious child a hundred feet away in a mudslide challenged his abilities.

He wanted to move faster. He wanted to will his legs to displace the mud and garbage as he slogged through the obstacle. On the one hand, it was thick enough for Libby to float atop. On the other, it was too thick for him to make any meaningful progress toward her. All he could do was keep moving, avoid tripping over something under the surface, and keep his flashlight trained on her body.

Even under intense pressure, Finn remained calm. And confident. He'd thrown caution to the wind many times over the years. In fact, he'd been reprimanded on several occasions for risking his life despite a positive outcome. That was who he was.

"Livvy, can you hear me?" he shouted as he felt like he was drawing closer.

Her tiny body rolled over to be facedown and then immediately turned upright again. He could make out her arm waving as she swept around an upside-down car.

Finn set his jaw and pressed forward. The mud was moving faster now. He eased to his right. He tripped slightly as he found the concrete curb of the street; however, he maintained his balance. He could feel the ground underneath him rise slightly toward the house. The shallower section of the mudslide allowed him to pick up the pace.

He was practically running compared to just a moment ago. He focused on reaching the car, which had suddenly rolled over onto its side. The pressure from the mudslide was causing it to tumble.

"Livvy!"

"Help!" Her voice was frightened and meek.

Closer.

Finn pressed on. He reached the car and used its front bumper as a guide to help propel him forward. Another house appeared before him. He pushed ahead, focusing on his footing so he could use the higher ground to move faster.

He called her name again. She responded.

Closer.

Finn stopped and shined his light across the turbulent mudslide, searching for her. He made a long sweep, starting at the overturned car and then down the hill where the street once was. He called out to her.

"Livvy! Where are you?"

He expected her to shout back as before. He just knew he was close to her position because he'd gained speed. Yet she didn't reply.

He tried again. Louder. Instructing her to wave her arms.

Nothing.

Finn quickly assessed the flow of the mud and its direction. He ran toward the center of the intersection. He now realized where he was. The mudslide had carried her back to Linda Vista Avenue. Earlier, the street had been on the precipice of collapsing into the torrential river flowing toward LA. Now the landslide tried to join it.

He rushed through the mud, shining his light in all directions, shouting her name. He never gave up the search. He'd made miraculous rescues in the past, as the media called them. To Finn, he was just doing his job. He persevered, knowing the courageous young girl would not give up on him.

Then he saw her arm protruding just above the surface of the mud, which was more liquified now. As the landslide met the water rushing down Linda Vista, it had dissolved somewhat. Livvy's body had partially submerged, but her head and shoulders were still visible.

He pressed forward. His arms were swinging wildly. Instinctively like he was trying to thrust himself through the ocean.

Closer.

"I see you! Hold on!"

Finn shoved the flashlight into his khakis. His eyes lowered as he became singularly focused on Livvy. He reached out for her before her arm sank underneath the mud, which began to resemble quicksand.

"There!" he exclaimed.

After a deep breath, he knelt down and pulled her upward, fighting the grip the mud had on her tiny body. He joyfully shouted, "I've got ya, missy!" Her arm was limp when he grasped it. He shoved his hand underneath the surface in search of her other arm.

Then he discovered Livvy wasn't breathing.

FIFTY-NINE

Saturday
Pasadena, California

Tyler focused to prevent himself from getting disoriented. Between being in an unfamiliar part of the neighborhood and the raging ARkStorm, which continued to pummel the area with wind-driven rain, it would've been easy for him to stray from locating Sammy and the girls. He'd checked his watch multiple times to study the screenshot of her location on the map. The face of the watch, just over an inch wide, didn't provide him a good look at her location.

He stopped to get his bearings. He wondered if

he'd gone too far down the ridge toward the golf course, which was now the largest river in California. He turned toward LA. He walked between two homes and broke through a gate that was part of a wooden privacy fence.

He suspected the home was abandoned, not that it mattered. He needed to get a better perspective, so he quickly climbed the stairs leading to a wooden deck on the second story. It was difficult to see under the adverse conditions. Frustrated, Tyler paced back and forth on the deck, trying to make sense of his location. He even looked in the double doors leading into the home to determine if anyone was there. Hopefully, he thought to himself, they'd give him directions rather than shoot him as a perceived intruder.

After knocking, nobody answered, leaving Tyler on his own. He left through the home's backyard, kicking the aging wooden fence slats out of the way. He found himself in another backyard and then onto another street.

The sound of a landslide could be heard in the distance. Because he'd spent so much time in the floodwaters and near the dam, he was able to discern the difference. This was not rushing water. Rather, it sounded more like a muffled roar.

He studied the watch again and muttered aloud, "Turn up the hill. Left at the end of the road. Follow the winding road down the hill."

He didn't hesitate as he took off running. His feet sloshed through the standing water, forcing him to be mindful of every stride so he didn't fall. As he navigated through the neighborhood, he didn't have to double-check the screenshot of Sammy's position. He knew where he needed to come out.

His pace quickened as he began running down a series of hairpin curves in the road. Mud appeared everywhere, forcing him to slow down as the faster pace became untenable. Tyler's heart raced from anxiety and hope. He was almost there. He could feel her.

He made the final turn, and his heart sank. The sound of the earth gobbling up buildings and trees was unmistakable. The road he was on had disappeared. It had become a victim of the failure of the earthen dam once holding back the landfill's refuse.

Tyler stared across the flow of mud and debris, using his flashlight's beam to illuminate anything that resembled a structure where he'd presumed Sammy to be holed up. There was nothing. Only debris and a rooftop sliding along with it.

He rushed to the edge of the debris field, contemplating running into it to search for her. He stopped short and ran both hands through his soaked hair. He spun around several times as if he hoped to ask an unseen audience what he should do.

Was she buried? Had she escaped the deluge and found her way into one of the homes behind him? Maybe he was wrong and misread the location on the tiny screenshot.

He tapped his watch face and was about to navigate to the photos when he froze. He tilted his head in disbelief. Inexplicably, the cellular access had returned once again. Tyler furrowed his brow as he forced himself to concentrate. He wasn't sure how long the cell service would be operable.

Nervous, he clumsily tapped on the device, frequently hitting an icon or link other than the one he wanted. Despite several missteps, he accessed the appropriate app. The beacon representing Sammy's watch, and her, was near but on the move.

He slowly began walking along the edge of the landslide, studying his watch while trying to maintain his position in relation to Sammy's. He pushed out of his mind that she'd perished in the landslide, or the watch might've been discarded by her for some reason. Perhaps its battery had died, and she deemed it useless. She probably didn't know Apple continued to record its location for up to twenty-four hours after the battery charge reached zero.

He picked up the pace in an attempt to draw himself parallel to the beacon. Wherever she was within the steady flow of mud and debris, he'd battle heaven and earth to get to her. He picked up his pace again as the beacon began to win the race with the aid of gravity and the weight of the mudslide. He watched his footing as he began to close the gap between them.

As he briskly walked along the edge of the flowing mud, he illuminated the flow again with his flashlight. That was when he spied the remains of a building, its tile roof gently rolling back and forth as it rode atop the mud. She had to be in there.

"Sammy!" he shouted toward the floating roof. It was a wasted effort due to the noise generated by the landslide crushing everything in its path. He tried again. His voice was desperate. Pleading. "Sammy, can you hear me?"

He checked his watch again. The low battery warning had appeared.

"Dammit!" he shouted at the top of his lungs. Then he internally chastised himself for losing his composure. The game wasn't over. Sammy was alive and in what was left of that house. He was sure of it.

Tyler began jogging along the sloped backyards of the remaining houses. At times, he confronted large obstacles such as an overturned motorhome and even a boat on a trailer. He navigated around them, keeping a keen eye on the floating rooftop.

He began to hear noise from the river. He didn't have to form complex calculations to know what could happen. The mudslide was forcing everything toward the river. If he didn't save her, she'd be washed away. He had to get out in front of the debris flow and intercept her.

SIXTY

Saturday
American Modern Museum
Pasadena, California

Landslides are gravity-driven events that oftentimes begin as loose sediment and rocks being dislodged by an intervening disaster, such as excessive rainfall or earthquakes. Once the slurry of mud and water picks up steam, nothing in its path is safe. Trees, cars, buildings, anything can be incorporated into the unstable mixture of earth elements and man-made obstacles. As a landslide gets heavier, it gains momentum, remarkably fast at times. Its weight is unstoppable.

It is the epitome of the *irresistible force paradox*—what happens when the unstoppable force meets an immovable object. In the case of the American Modern Museum, the landslide won with ease.

Before Sammy could return to Sophie, the house began moving. Not all of it, just the upper level. The floor trusses separating the first floor from the second had been knocked loose from the stud walls. The sheathing and marble of the second floor managed to hold the upper level together, allowing it to break free from the downstairs when it dropped several feet before sinking into the debris-filled mud.

Sammy screamed as she was knocked sideways into a wall, landing hard on her injured knee for what seemed like the hundredth time. Sophie cried out, snapping her out of her trance, as she slid along the slick floor and crashed into the base of a marble bust. The head of Medusa, the mythical creature from Greek mythology, fell hard to the floor, scattering plaster snakes in all directions.

"Hang on, Sophie!" Sammy shouted to be heard over the loud rumble surrounding them. She tried to stand but immediately began to wobble as more of the bottom story broke away from the building. It was near impossible to maintain her footing as the remains of the building began to crash into trees and other large debris.

Sammy dropped to her knees and crawled on all fours to Sophie, who was huddled in the corner, with her knees drawn close to her chest. She was sobbing uncontrollably. This was more than a child, or anyone else, for that matter, could take.

Sammy held her tight, rocking gently with the rhythm of the building as it rose and fell like a boat riding gentle waves on the ocean. In a way, it was soothing. Comforting. Surreal.

Until the floor began to break apart. The trusses holding the entire second floor had been under immense pressure from the landslide. The series of pitches and rolls as the remains of the building moved with the landslide resulted in the floor joists pulling away from the subfloor. The marble tiles popped loose, each emitting a loud crack as the plywood subfloor popped the nails loose from its truss.

The center of the second floor was the first to deteriorate. The large open space under it where the foyer once was located did little to shore up the upper level's subflooring.

Sammy kissed Sophie on the forehead and whispered to her, "Stay here."

Her eyes were soaked with tears. "Don't leave me," she pleaded, reaching her hand to grab Sammy's.

"It's okay. I just wanna look outside to see if we should crawl out a window."

Sammy stood and leaned against the wall for stability. She found her way to one window but could see very little. She started to dash to the other side of the room, facing the rear of the house. As she reached the center of the room, a hole opened up in the subfloor, breaking the sheathing and sucking the tiles into the mud below.

Sammy lost her balance, slipped, and fell next to the opening. She desperately tried to move away from the hole, which was growing wider as the floor trusses were pulled away. The house lurched to the left.

"Sammy!" warned Sophie, to no avail. Sammy was knocked over and fell into the mud.

She quickly reached out and wrapped her arms through the diagonal supports holding the top and bottom cords of the truss. As the building moved with the landslide, Sammy's lower body was bashed against anything below her.

She struggled to hold on, her arms weary from using the museum's spindles like she was playing on a jungle gym's monkey bars. Each time she tried to pull herself up, the building would twist or more of its floor structure would be ripped away.

She pulled upward again. She was able to reach the floor. A little more, she told herself. *You've got this babe.* Tyler's words filled her head.

Then her ankle caught on something. It was tugging on her, trying to pull her into the muddy hell below. Sammy tried to yank herself free, even kicking at the unknown object. She kicked again and freed herself. She swung her knee up to the bottom of the truss and flopped onto the floor. She lay on her back for a long second, gasping for air. Her chest was heaving, and she was becoming dizzy.

Then, as she turned her head toward Sophie, who was still crouched in the corner, a man lunged upward through the debris, his arm outstretched in search of a lifeline. His face appeared, covered in mud, desperate for help.

It was good old Johnny, who had opted to run away when Sammy needed help. She was not a vindictive person. Except today.

"Sorry," she muttered. "Gotta go."

With his arm flailing, he slipped below the surface of the mud until the back side of the house ran over him.

Sammy crawled to her knees and made her way to Sophie. The floor was coming apart, making their position untenable. She recalled from when she was dangling from the iron balusters and looking to Finn for help, there was a pull-down attic access located in the ceiling. The floor was disappearing from the landing, but she thought they could make it to the access door.

"Sophie, it's time to be a big girl. I can't do this without you."

Sophie stopped crying long enough to ask, "What?"

Sammy pointed toward the landing. "We're gonna go higher."

Sophie looked through the floor joists at the mud passing under them. She didn't hesitate. "Okay."

Sammy picked up Sophie and instructed her to hold on around her neck. She carefully moved through the room by stepping on the top of the floor trusses and then onto the solid flooring that still remained. When they arrived in the hallway, Sammy immediately frowned when she studied the attic access. It required a ladder to pull the handle down. Naturally, the museum had removed the rope customarily found dangling from the doors in a residence.

She had an idea.

The floor underneath the attic access was still intact. She knelt down directly under it and turned to Sophie. "If I put you on my shoulders, can you reach that handle and pull?"

She shrugged. "I guess so." Her response was noncommittal, but Sammy took it as a yes.

"Okay," Sammy began to explain. She hurried, as seconds mattered. She dropped to a deep crouch. "Climb aboard."

Sophie got settled on top of Sammy's shoulders. She positioned herself under the access door. Sammy rose, struggling to push the extra weight upward with the pain in her knee sending jolts through her lower body.

"I got it," Sophie said happily, clearly proud of herself.

"Hold on tight. This is gonna be a little bit tricky."

Sammy knew the child didn't have the arm strength to pull down the spring-loaded door. She had to walk forward and slowly drop to a crouch until the door opened enough to remain in place.

Careful to keep her footing and not step through a hole in the floor, Sammy began moving. Sophie grunted as she held on with two hands. The tight springs tried to fight the effort. Sophie began to lift off Sammy's shoulders, so she grabbed the child's thighs to keep her in place.

Almost, Sammy thought to herself.

"It's stuck!" shouted Sophie just as her hand slipped free.

The sudden shift in momentum caused Sammy to fall hard onto her knees. Again. Pain shot through her body like a hundred-thousand-volt shock of electricity. *I'm so over this,* she said to herself.

"But not yet." She forced herself to stand and immediately lowered the folded-up ladder inside. "Come on, Sophie. Let's go higher."

The two scrambled up the stairs and moved away from the opening onto a large platformed area. Pink blown insulation was strewn about, and years of dust had been shaken loose from the roof system. Both Sammy and Sophie had sneezing fits, something that was oddly hilarious to them both.

Their laughter was hearty and much needed. She knew there would be more challenges to come.

PART 5
SATURDAY, JANUARY 2

Digging Out

SIXTY-ONE

Saturday
Pasadena, California

"Please, God!" Finn exclaimed as he scooped up her lifeless body and trudged through the muck. His head darted back and forth between the higher ground and the approaching remains of a house. Then a sense of recognition came over him.

Rapidly approaching him were the remains of the eight-thousand-square-foot museum once sprawling with multiple wings and additions. It had been swamped by the force of the landslide, leaving only the upper level intact. The roof tiles had popped off in several places, so the sheathing was bare. If Sammy and Sophie were still alive, their only chance of survival would've been to crawl into the attic's rafters.

When Finn reached the soggy ground, he gauged the speed of the museum's debris field in relation to the raging river below his position. He had to hurry. First, Livvy needed to be resuscitated.

He'd performed CPR a thousand times in practice. Dozens of times in the field. Only on rare occasions was a victim's airway obstructed. In children, improperly chewed foods like hot dogs, whole grapes, peanuts and popcorn were the most common hazards. The upper airway needed to be cleared of the foreign body in order to resume breathing.

Livvy's condition was far different. She had swallowed mud.

Finn tried all of the accepted methods of clearing her airway. He tried the head-tilt and chin-lift methods commonly deployed when there was a foreign object in place. He tried abdominal thrusts as well as back blows to dislodge some of the mud. This resulted in some success; however, she still was not breathing.

He was running out of time. He had no choice but to try to dissolve the mud with more moisture. He peeled off his shirt, tilted Livvy's head back and lifted her chin. He slowly twisted his shirt to wring out the rainwater into her throat. Then he performed the opposite of resuscitation. He placed his mouth over hers, pinched her nose, and sucked the diluted mud out.

It was working. He spit out the mud and tried the normal resuscitation techniques. He knew he was making progress. He repeated the dilution technique. Then he pinched her nose again. With his eyes closed, he sucked the muddy water out of her throat with enough force to clear her airway. He almost choked on the amount of mud she had in her upper airway. Yet a smile came over his face as she turned onto her side and began coughing uncontrollably.

Finn rushed around to her side and comforted her. "Easy, young missy. It's gonna be okay. Try to slow your breathing. Not deep, okay?"

She continued to cough but seemed to comprehend what had happened. She closed her mouth and breathed through her nose, which, oddly, caused her to sneeze. The look on Finn's face must've struck her as odd because she too managed a chuckle. She was gonna be all right.

Finn turned his attention to the remains of the museum, which was floating by. The roof system of the house was close behind, rolling gently from side to side as it approached. He was certain it would hold its structure for several minutes until it hit the steep slope leading to the floodwaters. He had to act.

He crouched down and lifted Livvy into his arms. He rushed up the hill toward the back of a home. The moment he turned to return to the landslide, he noticed the roof twisting, causing the remainder of the roof tiles to pop off the sheathing. It wouldn't hold much longer.

"Help!" a woman's voice shouted from just below him. "Puhleeeeze!"

Finn shook his head, questioning if any of this was real. He rushed toward the sound of the woman's voice. Then a child shrieked.

"Fire department! Call out!"

It was instinctive. A command he'd uttered many times during his days working structure fires. It was effective, as the woman responded.

"Please help! I'm not strong enough to carry her!"

Finn glanced toward the roof structure to confirm its location. He ran toward the distressed woman and child. She was only feet away from the grass. She could've made it on her own, he thought to himself with a hint of incredulity.

As he arrived at the edge of the mudslide and ventured in several feet, he recognized the woman and child. They'd arrived at the museum hours earlier with the rest of their group. They'd also beat a hasty retreat, leaving Sammy hanging in need of help. If he was a vindictive man, he would've left her to fend for herself. However, he couldn't do that.

He quickly escorted them to higher ground and confirmed they were physically uninjured. Then he hissed in the woman's ear, "You left us when we needed you. I shouldn't forgive you for that, but I will. Now, you will do something in return."

She had a look of shock on her face, as her rescuer had turned somewhat hostile. She nodded her head rapidly in agreement.

"There's a little girl who is frightened up there," he said, waving his arm toward the back of the house. "Go to her and wait for me to return. I'll lead you to safety."

"Okay. I'm, um, sorry about earlier. It was Johnny."

"Doesn't matter. Now go!"

Finn left her side and took a deep breath, trying to clear his head. In that brief moment, he became somewhat dizzy from the continuous exertion he'd put his body through. He was retired, a decision put off until the county told him he had to go. He'd worked many long days but nothing like this one. He had to make sure he kept a clear head, and his judgment was not impaired.

As he ran up the hill to intercept the museum's roof, hoping Sammy and Sophie were tucked away inside, he swore he heard the bark and growl of a very large dog or other form of beast. He rubbed his face with his right hand in an attempt to wipe away the hallucination.

SIXTY-TWO

Saturday
Pasadena, California

Tyler stopped again to check his watch, thankful that its battery hadn't been drained. Twice before, he'd attempted to multitask by jogging along the bank of the mudslide and attempting to study Sammy's position at the same time. He'd fallen both times.

He was now out in front of the floating roof after running parallel to the deluge. He needed the perfect spot to venture into the debris field without getting sucked downstream toward the rapids. He hoped his calculations were accurate. There were several parts of a building rolling along the landslide.

She could be in the debris, holding onto anything that floated. Nothing was certain, as visibility was horrendous, and the driving rain caused a significant distraction.

The mudslide was moving swifter as it got closer to the river. The once steady slope to the hill overlooking the golf course had changed as the floodwaters chewed away at the ridge. Now there was a significant drop-off where land met the turbulent water. From what he'd experienced earlier, which was most likely more treacherous now, he doubted the remains of the roof and its rafters would survive the inevitable violent collision.

As Tyler moved into the landslide to intercept, he saw the roof tiles become dislodged from the battens attached to the sheathing. The roof suddenly lurched forward, twisted, and then turned until it hit a vehicle caught on a large oak tree that had somehow not been uprooted.

Tyler ran into the mud, now waist-deep. There was garbage all around him as well as building materials that once were used to construct magnificent homes. Furniture, including a sofa, floated by. Fortunately, there were no dead bodies in his way as he pressed forward.

The roof was being battered by the oncoming

debris. The oak tree's trunk held it in place while the rest of the landslide material tried to push it down the slope.

Tyler pressed forward. Two steps forward, one step downhill. He felt like he was making progress. However, the mudslide was deeper and more powerful at its center. He began to doubt whether he could cross completely without getting tugged under and pulled into the river.

"Sammy! Can you hear me?" he shouted as he fought his way upstream. When he first ventured into the flow, he had been in a perfect position to intercept. Now he found himself too far downhill because the roof had run into the oak. He shouted her name again. "Sammy!"

A Kia came tumbling down the mudslide and crashed hard into the roof, which was now nothing but plywood and trusses. All the clay tiles had been knocked off, joining the flow of mud and debris. The Kia began to beat against the roof system until the plywood began to dislodge from the trusses. The smallish vehicle was spun around and tossed on the garbage heap before it rushed upside down into the darkness.

Openings in the roof system had appeared, although it was too dark for Tyler to confirm whether

Sammy and the girls were inside it. He had to rely on the watch app's coordinates. It was all he had to go on.

"This way!" It was a man's voice on the other side. He could barely make out a shadow of someone waving his arms toward the battered roof.

"I see you!" a woman's voice hollered back.

Was it Sammy? With all the commotion, Tyler wasn't sure.

"How can you not recognize your own wife's voice?" he chastised himself as he continued to wade through the muck. He was fifty yards away when he lost his footing and fell sideways. In seconds, before he could call out her name again, he felt himself being carried away by the current of the mud flow.

He was completely covered in mud and felt like he weighed a thousand pounds. He freed an arm in an attempt to grab onto anything nearby to arrest his descent. Tyler began to think he might be pulled under.

He fought panic. He adopted slow, deliberate movements in an attempt to regain his footing. He removed the clothing from his upper body, which caused him to shiver, but at least he wasn't weighted down. This gave him the ability to stand upright.

Tyler realized he was too far away from where

the roof had now collapsed into kindling. He had to get across the mudslide, but he'd die if he continued this way. Angry, he retreated to the soggy ground before he got swept over the edge.

He lay on his back, his chest heaving, gasping for air. He welcomed the heavy rain to wash away the mud that covered him. He allowed the respite to help him process what was happening. Was that Sammy who'd responded to the man on the other side of the landslide? Now he was sure of it. But who was he? While he was appreciative of him helping Sammy and the girls, could he be trusted?

He needed a break. Something had to go right for him in order to reunite with the love of his life. However, his desperation to find her would be for naught if he got swallowed by the mud or drowned in the river. There had to be a way.

Tyler took another deep breath and jumped to his feet. There was one other way to cross to the other side of the mudslide. Go around it.

He began making his way toward the slope that was gradually being eaten away by the river. He briefly contemplated diving in and swimming along the shoreline until he could climb up the hill. Sammy was the swimmer in the family, not him. He doubted he could find shore before he was swept past the Rose Bowl, where he'd started the day. *Lord knows what downtown LA looks like at this point*, he thought to himself.

No, he'd be patient and find a solution. He found the strength to jog up the hill into the remaining homes in the neighborhood. He sloshed through the streets, looking for anything that might spark an idea.

Then he saw it. It brought back college-day memories of a five-hour trip from hell through the Poconos in Eastern Pennsylvania. It was a life lesson he never thought he'd use again. Today was the day to see what he'd learned.

SIXTY-THREE

Saturday
Pasadena, California

"Hold on, Sophie!" Sammy shouted. She'd stepped across the rafters to look for a way out of the roof system, which had collapsed to the top of the mudslide. It had happened all at once as the second-story walls holding up the roof had blown outward. The ceiling and roof had fallen hard into the mud.

While it appeared to be intact, for the moment, the constant rollicking and abuse it was taking from debris and obstacles worried Sammy. Also, the fact they were trapped inside the floating attic meant they were certainly headed toward the raging river.

They had to get out, and going back through the folding-stair access point was not an option.

She stepped on the trusses' bottom cords and held on to the diagonal boards making up the supports. Her footing was slippery, and her hands were shaking. Yet she still managed to make her way across the attic, looking for holes in the roof through which they could escape.

She'd just reached the far end of the attic when the clay tiles began to pop off from the twisting motion and stress the roof was placed under. Sophie began screaming from the loud noise that, from within the enclosed structure, sounded like gunfire.

"Sammy! What's happening?"

She wasn't sure how to respond other than she needed to make her way back to Sophie. "I'm on my way. Hold tight."

She moved faster than before, partly out of fear and partly from experience at traversing the attic. Keeping her balance, she arrived by Sophie's side before the child completely panicked.

"We're gonna find a way out, okay?" Sammy offered words of reassurance although she knew they were headed for the river.

Then a sudden jolt knocked them off their perch on top of a sheet of plywood nailed to the rafters.

They landed on drywall that managed to hold onto the rest of the roofing system.

"We're not moving!" exclaimed Sammy, somewhat relieved that they had stalled their progress down the slope.

Her enthusiasm was short-lived as the roof system was hit hard by something that caused the trusses to groan.

It was pounded again and again. Like a giant hammer trying to smash it flat. The nails began to wail as the wind began to tug at the roof sheathing. With each twist and turn, the entire attic was coming apart.

Suddenly, the roof ripped open, and the bumper of a vehicle appeared inside the attic. Mud followed, and the space was rapidly being filled with debris and rain runoff.

"What do we do?" Sophie screamed her question. She still had tears to shed, and they were streaming down her muddy face.

A crash startled them both as the other side of the roof broke open. The massive trunk of an oak tree had split the truss system and inserted itself just fifteen feet to their right. The combination of the tree acting as a wedge and the vehicle pummeling the roof like a sledgehammer caused the roof sheathing to break loose. One four-foot-by-eight-foot panel after another tore away from the trusses, sent flying into the air by the wind.

In that moment, Sammy became convinced they were gonna die. Then she heard a voice. It was Finn.

"This way!" he bellowed.

She turned her head in the direction of his voice and saw his silhouette on the edge of the mudslide, waving his arms. He was not that far from where they'd crashed into the tree.

She lovingly took Sophie's face in her hands. She needed the young girl to remain calm. "Come on. Let's get out of here."

They walked together along the remaining trusses, which were barely held together by the last of the roof's structure. At the gable end of the attic, they stepped through into the mudslide, with Sophie on Sammy's back, her legs wrapped tightly around her aunt's waist.

She saw Finn, who immediately entered the flow of debris to help. He took Sophie and cradled her in his arms while Sammy wrapped her arm around the two of them. Together, they trudged through the last of the muck until they were clear.

Seconds later, before they could catch their breath, Livvy came toward them. She ran so fast she fell on her backside and began to slide toward her sister. The two of them ended up crashing into each other, hugging with no intention of letting go.

Through their exuberance, they heard a blood-curdling scream from the house up the hill. A woman and her child came running, waving their arms and pointing behind them.

Finn, Sammy and the girls ran to meet them. He shouted his questions as he ran.

"What? What is it?"

The woman was so distraught she couldn't bring herself to speak. She pointed back toward the house. Just as she managed to scream to explain what had frightened her so badly, Finn saw for himself.

Two black bears were lumbering toward them, ferociously barking and growling, pounding their skull-sized their paws on the soggy grass. They were hungry and pissed off.

A bad combination.

SIXTY-FOUR

Saturday
Pasadena, California

Tyler had some experience riding the rapids. While in college at Penn State, he and some buddies had spent a weekend in the Pocono Mountains near the Lehigh River. Tyler, who'd played all kinds of sports, including outdoor activities like bungee jumping and ziplining, had been excited at the prospect of whitewater rafting with the guys.

The springtime trip came after a period of heavy rains in the Poconos. That, coupled with a relatively inexperienced bunch of guys in the raft, resulted in a near-death experience for one of his friends.

While they were riding an intense section of the rapids toward the end of the five-hour excursion, one of their group, who was battling fatigue, got knocked over the side of the raft when it smashed against a boulder. The sudden change in the dynamic resulted in the entire raft slamming repeatedly against the rocks, knocking out two other rafters, including Tyler.

They were all wearing helmets as protection against more serious injuries. Nonetheless, two of the guys broke bones, and a third dislocated a shoulder. Tyler fared better, with only scrapes and severe bruising; it could've been worse.

He'd only gone rafting, well, canoeing, on one other occasion following that weekend. It was in Florida, the flattest state in America. There was not the risk associated with whitewater rafting like in the Poconos. The trip along the Crystal River was more likely to be disrupted by alligators coming off the bank or snakes falling from the trees.

When Tyler spied the bright yellow kayak strapped to the top of an overturned Subaru SUV, his eyes lit up. He'd never kayaked, but he couldn't imagine it was more difficult than whitewater rafting. The kayak had a single opening and a double-bladed paddle. Rather than being seated and paddling with a single flat paddle, he'd have to kneel and keep both sides of the paddle in motion.

From his recollection of the orientation by the instructor, a kayak was more challenging because it wasn't as stable as a canoe. However, he could move faster and make sharper turns. The canoe's wide berth prevented it from tipping over, but turning was akin to an eighteen-wheeler making a right turn on a city street.

None of that mattered as Tyler diligently worked to unharness the kayak and its paddle from the Subaru. Once it was free, he dragged it along the wet grass until he reached a point near the floodwaters that wasn't as steep as other locations.

Tyler was undertaking this task solely on gut feeling as to what was the proper technique. His common sense would have to carry him through the ride, which, if it worked out, would be short. He only wanted to go a couple of hundred yards to the other side of the landslide. It he overshot the bank, he could always double back.

He set the kayak near the water, perpendicular to the shore. Because the ground was so soggy and the rain provided continuous moisture, he felt like he could board the kayak on the bank and ease his way into the water, using his paddle as support.

He got started. He thrust his hips forward while using the paddle to push off the ground. Within seconds, the bow was at the edge. With one final thrust, he made sure the entire kayak found the river at once; otherwise he'd be turned over before getting started.

He was away and flowing downstream. Then he struggled to master the paddle stroke and suddenly found himself sideways to the current. By a stroke of luck, a hollowed-out log struck the front of the kayak and turned him downstream. He was moving swiftly now as he approached the point where the landslide met the river.

He was not prepared for the turbulence the mud and debris crashing into the water would create. If the wind-generated waves didn't topple him over, the splashing water being displaced by the mudslide would.

He confirmed his paddle blades were properly oriented before he began making quick, forward strokes in the water. He needed to get away from the turbulence, even if it meant that he ended up farther away from shore.

A part of a house landed in the water, creating a wave that crashed into the choppy river. Tyler turned the kayak downstream and paddled furiously to get away from the wake that would surely swamp him.

He paddled faster to avoid the landslide. He was past the Rose Bowl and approaching partially submerged buildings. He had to steer the kayak toward shore, which took a bit of a learning curve. Once again, by sheer luck, the stern of the kayak received a nudge from floating debris. He made a sweeping turn and pointed the bow toward a part of the bank where the land jutted out into the floodwaters.

With sheer determination, he drove straight for the shore. He was prepared to crash the kayak and swim to safety. However, he remained upright. Tyler paddled furiously, racing until the kayak beached itself on the muddy bank.

He couldn't get out of the vessel fast enough. He intentionally tipped it over and crawled onto the mud. He lost his footing as he tried to scramble upward, causing him to slide back into the water. He repeated this twice before he was able to dig his feet into the muck to get a foothold. Using roots from trees that had been torn from the earth by the ARkStorm, he pulled himself to higher ground, where he collapsed.

He struggled to catch his breath as he pushed up

on his elbows. His chest heaved up and down with every effort. His adrenaline was surging, causing his heart rate to reach unfathomable levels for the athletic trainer who prided himself on his own cardiovascular training.

"Calm down, buddy," he encouraged himself as he forced himself to slow his breathing. "Slower. You've got this."

He glanced at his watch. Its black display looked back at him. The battery charge had finally given out. He looked toward the sky and allowed the rain to pelt his face, begging for the early light of dawn. Surely, the sun would be rising soon.

Or would it?

SIXTY-FIVE

Saturday
Pasadena, California

"Run!" Finn implored the women and children by waving his arms toward LA.

The bears responded as quickly as Sammy and the rest did. The moment they started, the prowling bruins sensed prey was near. Finn had no option but to engage them.

"Hey! You beasts! Over here!"

He found a galvanized trash can lid near the flowing debris and a golfer's seven iron that had lodged in a sapling on the bank. He ran toward the bears, who were lumbering along the soggy ground in pursuit.

He shouted again and then began beating the trash can lid with the golf club. This had an instantaneous effect on the massive animals. Confused, they had to choose between prey and a potential predator. Clumsily, they came to a sudden stop, digging their paws and claws into the once well-manicured lawn.

They slowly turned toward Finn, a solitary target in closer proximity than the running prey. He continued to bang on the galvanized lid, allowing Sammy and the others precious seconds to get away. Once he had the bears' attention, reality set in for the retired wilderness firefighter who'd helped rescue bears like these in the past but now found himself needing to be rescued.

"Now what, lad?" he muttered to himself.

He glanced behind at the flow of mud and debris from the landslide. The roof that had brought Sammy and Sophie to near where he stood was starting to dislodge itself from the oak tree. He had an idea.

The bears were closer now but slowing their pace as if they were having second thoughts about their priorities. He pounded on the trash can lid again, yelling at them to draw them closer.

They ran now, once again emitting threatening barking sounds and ferocious growls. Finn dropped his tools of distraction and ran toward the mudslide. The roof had twisted toward the bank to the point he could get on the remains of the structure, which resembled something ol' Tom and Huck might've sailed down the river.

Once he had a footing, he yelled at the creatures again. They'd taken the bait. The two entered the mudslide hesitantly at first, side by side, within feet of the roof. Strangely, Finn whistled to them in the same singsong tune millions of dog owners had done in years past.

It kept their attention until they were climbing onto the fragile roofing system with him. Their extra weight caused one end of the structure to sink, immediately freeing the remaining part from the grasp of the oak tree. In a flash, the entire wreckage was floating atop the landslide toward the edge of the solid ground. Just ahead, much like a waterfall, the liquified earth and everything it carried with it took a sudden drop before plunging into the river.

There was no turning back for Finn. He'd successfully drawn the bears away and possibly sentenced himself to death in the process. He knew he didn't have a prayer in fighting off two of the wild animals. Maybe he could have played dead, and they might've left him alone. However, it would've just taken one swipe with their massive paws to cut him open. His reaction to the pain would've been immediate, and the ruse of playing dead would've been over. At least this way, he'd have a fighting chance.

Then the dynamic changed. One of the bears lost its balance on the roofing system and slipped into the landslide. The soaking muddy water swept it past the heavy, awkward roof, which frequently caught itself on other debris as it rode atop the flow.

The other bear seemed to understand the predicament its partner was in. Finn recalled from assisting in several bear rescues the words of several experts he'd interacted with. In the moment, Finn's recollection of the expert's words was as if she were standing on his shoulder to remind him.

"These bruins may not always act smart, but their intelligence is remarkable," she'd said. "They are extremely curious, powerful animals as well as surprisingly fast sprinters, agile climbers and excellent swimmers. Don't forget, they have an extraordinary sense of smell to assist with their voracious appetite."

Finn looked toward the bank. It was still in reach for him. The maneuver would be risky and certainly a test of the bear's agility. It was better than rolling over the muddy Niagara Falls ahead.

He took a deep breath, steeled his nerves, and ran toward the bear along the remaining roof trusses and plywood sheathing that held it together. Finn sensed the bear turning in his direction as he abandoned his curiosity about his mate. The bear struggled to find a grip on the roof. Finn seemed to have an acrobatic ability that had eluded him for the first sixty-two years of his life. He pushed off the edge of the roof and jumped at least ten feet until he landed partly in the mud. His upper body fell forward from the momentum, causing him to face-plant in the water.

Without looking back, he scrambled on all fours up the bank to get away. By the time he paused to look back, the roof and the bruin that sailed atop it were disappearing over the edge into the river.

Finn rolled over on his back and stared into the rain. He suddenly started to laugh, a release of nervous energy that was befitting his personality. In times of stressful situations, he'd been known to break the tension by telling old jokes from the mother country, as he used to call Ireland, always making a point to lay on the thickest Irish accent he could muster. He'd cracked up many a group of firefighters and rescue teams as they fought to save lives. This time, he'd saved his own.

As he lay there, allowing the rain to rinse off his face and body, savoring the moment, he didn't hear the sound of feet rushing across the muddy ground toward him.

SIXTY-SIX

Saturday
Pasadena, California

"Hey, are you okay?" asked Tyler as he slowly approached Finn. The fact the man was breathing and seemingly in good spirits didn't stop Tyler from approaching him with caution. The only people he'd encountered thus far were either helpless or panicked. Finding someone lying in the rain only a few feet from the landslide gave him reason to pause.

Startled, Finn sat upright until he got his bearings. "Oh, sure. Absolutely. It's been a whale of a day."

"I know you," said Tyler as he and Finn made eye contact for the first time.

Finn's face reflected his recognition and excitement for his new friends. "The football coach? Sammy's husband?"

"That's right. You remembered. Are you hurt?"

"No. Not at all. I have some good news for you, lad."

"You do? Do you know where Sammy is? And my nieces?"

Finn extended his hand, and the two men shook. Finn squeezed hard and continued pumping Tyler's arm. "I do. Well, um, not quite at this very moment. But they're close. I've been with them most of the night."

Tyler's eyes reflected his emotions as he spontaneously hugged Finn. The two men shared a hearty, backslapping embrace for a moment. Then, with a puzzled look on his face, he drew away.

"Whadya mean? They're close? Where?"

Finn pointed toward the houses and urged Tyler to follow along. He summarized what had just happened. "When it all began, I sent them running in this direction toward safety. I'm not sure where they went, exactly."

Tyler also told Finn about the encounter he'd

had with a couple of bears at the top of the ridge. They wondered if it was the same duo, not that it mattered, as the vicious creatures had just washed into the river. Tyler peppered Finn with questions about Sammy and the girls. Were they safe? Frightened? All of the things a loving husband and uncle would want to know.

Mentally exhausted and just a little sore, Finn led the way as they attempted to enter the nearby houses. The doors were locked or barricaded. Tyler swore he saw movement inside one of the homes after he'd pounded on the door. No one answered, so they shouted for Sammy, raising their voices to be heard over the downpour of rain.

Nothing.

They'd walked well past the stadium when they approached a modern block and glass home with the front door left ajar. Inside the all-glass front façade, Finn saw the dim glow of candlelight.

"Let's try this one," he said to Tyler. "One if by land, two if by sea. Right?"

Perplexed at first, Tyler shrugged, not understanding Finn's reference to Paul Revere's ride. Then he understood. There was only one candle burning in the living space.

Despite his confusion, he sensed Sammy was

close. He picked up the pace, assisted by the drop in slope from the street to the garage. His voice reflected his hopefulness.

"Sammy! Sophie! Livvy! Are you here?"

As he crossed the yard toward the entryway, Sammy burst out of the house, followed by the girls. Her long legs enabled her to hurdle over the shrubbery bordering the sidewalk. In just seconds, she'd crashed into her husband, knocking him onto the wet turf as if USC defensive lineman Elijah Rushing had made the tackle himself.

The couple embraced one another and kissed repeatedly. The words *I love you* were spoken more than a dozen times even though they weren't necessary to drive home the point. Neither would ever admit they'd feared the other had perished in the catastrophe. There was always doubt they'd reunite. Yet there they were, rolling in the grass, enjoying the moment.

Sophie and Livvy joined in the celebration. As they did, Tyler assured Sammy their dogs were out of harm's way. Then they thanked Finn for everything he'd done to keep Sammy and the girls safe.

The sound of a house succumbing to a landslide in the distance forced the joy of reuniting to be set aside for the moment. The storm was still raging, and they needed to seek cover. Before they went inside, Sammy turned to Finn and Tyler.

"It looks like a pretty good spot to ride it out, but I've thought that before. The house is solid block except for the front. It has lots of food and water, too. Are we gonna be safe?"

Finn looked around, feeling a slight tremor under his feet. The millions of cubic feet of earth flowing a quarter of a mile from them was a concern as well as a new landslide.

"Let's give it a try. Everyone needs to regroup, and the wee lasses could use some nourishment and a nap, I imagine. However, if your husband is willing, we'll take turns keeping watch."

"Not a problem. Let's go inside. I'm tired of being sopping wet."

"Sounds good," said Sammy as she ran her arm through his. Tyler escorted her inside, where he was introduced to Johnny's wife and child. Sammy had withheld her knowledge of coward-turned-deceased Johnny's fate until she talked to Finn. She couldn't deal with the woman's emotions until Finn had joined them.

Once inside the spacious home, the group gathered in the living room. At first, Sammy felt an odd sense of guilt that the mud-soaked clothing everyone was wearing would ruin the white upholstered furniture. Before they sat, she and Johnny's wife went through the house, looking for clothes for everyone to change into. The family of six had plenty of options, as it appeared the couple's children ranged in age from six to high school.

Before they returned to the living room, Sammy took it on herself to explain to the woman what had happened to her husband.

"I want you to understand that everything happened so fast. At the time, he could've ducked and allowed the building to pass by. I just wanted to let you know that he was alive at that point."

She shed a few tears but was nowhere near as distraught as Sammy expected. "Johnny and I have been through a rough patch lately. This was his weekend to watch our son, but he didn't show up yesterday. He ended up partying last night and forgot to call, he said. Then his way of making it up to our boy was to take him to Hooters to watch the Rose Bowl. I think he planned on watching the waitresses and drinking beer."

Her chin dropped to her chest as she struggled to admit her husband had eyes for other women, if not more. Sammy gave her a hug, happy the two of them had already changed into dry clothes. In fact, they were wearing matching Juicy Couture tracksuits. Sammy had chosen navy, and the woman had chosen black. They shared a moment during which Sammy convinced her to focus on the mental well-being of her son. There would be time later to deal with the probable death of his father.

After everyone changed clothes, Sammy and Tyler volunteered to prepare some snacks and pass around the drinks. The man of the house had built an elaborate man cave on the basement level of the sprawling rancher. After a brief inspection of the downstairs, Finn quickly claimed it to be his new abode.

"He must be from the UK," said Finn, referring to the abundance of décor and mementos adorning the space from the United Kingdom. Finn was especially enthralled with the variety of beer in the large, glass-front refrigerator. Newcastle, Harp, Guinness. Finn wanted to sample them all, chilled or not.

He started with a Guinness and lit every candle he could locate behind the bar. Soon, the space was illuminated enough to reveal a tournament dart board affixed to the wall. Tyler laughed to himself as Finn suddenly immersed himself in his surroundings, seemingly ignoring the continuing threat they faced. For the moment, Tyler thought the hero of the day deserved to be alone.

Tyler perused the options. He grabbed a bottle of Grolsch beer with its signature swing top. Then he reached for a bottle of sangria. It was red with white polka dots. Like the Grolsch, it also had a swing top to cap the bottle.

He made his way back upstairs, leaving Finn with his beer and darts. While Finn appeared intent on losing himself in several pints of ale, Tyler just needed to take the edge off. He'd feel better when the light of day arrived, even if it wasn't sunny. At least he'd be able to see their surroundings.

Upstairs, he found Sammy sitting alone with the girls, munching on the snacks they'd prepared. He looked around the room for the woman and her son. Sammy noticed his arrival and the concerned look on his face.

"Sit tight, girls," she said as she eased off the deep sofa. She nodded toward Tyler to step toward the kitchen.

"Something wrong?" he asked, studying her face.

"Well, it's possible her husband, the boy's father, died in the landslide. I told her what I knew because I thought she had a right to know. I also suggested she wait until later. Because he could still be alive, I thought it would be best to wait and see if he turned up. You know?"

Tyler looked at the ground and nodded. "You did the right thing. After what they've probably been through, why go there without knowing all the facts. So, um, where are they?"

Sammy pointed over her shoulder with her thumb. "They stepped out onto the covered porch. She didn't want to upset Sophie and Livvy in case her son lost it."

Tyler opened both bottles of alcohol and retrieved glasses from the cupboard, when something hard crashed into the living room's floor-to-ceiling windows. Tyler pushed past Sammy to get a better look at what had caused the commotion. Then the girls screamed in unison and leapt off the couch.

Blood streamed down the outside of the window, along with unidentifiable parts of the woman, who never finished telling her son about his dad.

SIXTY-SEVEN

Saturday
Pasadena, California

Tyler ran toward the girls and ushered them toward Sammy. He pressed his face against the glass and cupped his hands to block the ambient light emitted by the candles. He witnessed what might've happened to him and their dogs on the ridge. The bears were mauling the woman and her son, one powerful swat at a time.

"Can you help them?" she yelled from around the corner of the wall separating the kitchen from the living area.

"No. It's too late," Tyler said solemnly, shaking

his head in disappointment. Everyone should've been warned to stay inside, but he thought it was obvious.

He began to turn toward Sammy when he noticed the woman had left the front door slightly ajar. He walked over to shut it; however, suddenly, it slammed open, causing Tyler to spin around and land hard on the floor. One of the bears, using its sense of smell, busted through the door in search of more prey.

Tyler quickly crawled away, shouting instructions to Sammy. "Downstairs! Warn Finn!"

The bear stood on its hind legs and roared as its massive body filled the doorway. Tyler crawled backwards, locking eyes with the fierce predator as it slowly approached him.

He felt Sammy and the girls rush by to descend the stairs, their feet clamoring on the hard surface as they disappeared into the darkness.

Tyler leapt to his feet. In a perfect fluid motion, he placed his hands firmly on the railing and jumped over. He dropped ten feet to the landing below, sticking the landing like a gymnast, causing the already hostile bear to roar with disapproval.

The commotion encouraged the other bear to abandon its meal and enter the house. It immediately went to the snacks on the coffee table and swatted at them in disgust. Its snout rose in the air, sniffing the smell of humans. The two bumped into one another as they slowly walked along the railing leading to the lower level.

Tyler remained stoic, standing in a dark corner of the landing to determine the bears' next move. As he watched, Finn called to him from below.

"Come on down. We can leave through the back and lock them inside."

Tyler started down the steps, and the house suddenly lurched sideways and down, causing him to lose his balance. He landed hard on his backside and slid down several steps until Finn reached out to him.

Without warning, the house began to sink. Not inches, but many feet. It was if an elevator had fallen a couple of floors before arresting its drop. Then the house tilted again.

The candles that were burning in the man cave had been knocked to the floor and were immediately doused by water that was rushing in through the glass patio doors. Mud began to ooze inside, rising rapidly with the floodwater as the house settled.

"Sinkhole!" exclaimed Finn. He'd seen it before. This was his first time being consumed by one.

They were startled as parts of the upstairs collapsed, tilting downward as gravity took its toll. Tyler rolled the rest of the way downstairs to join the others on the lowest level of the house. He fumbled around in the dark, trying to find his way to Sammy and the girls. Only the girls' shrieks guided him.

"Sammy! I'm here!"

"Come to my voice," she shouted. "We're near the bar."

Finn left the room and headed to the far side of the house. While he was downstairs earlier, he'd wandered around the space and found a storage area made of solid block with a steel security door. It had all the indications of a panic room, a safe space built by wealthy residents of Southern California as crime spiraled out of control and made its way into the suburbs. Within the space, there was a wrought-iron, spiral staircase that rose to the garage.

Feeling his way in the dark, he confirmed the room was still intact, leading him to believe it was reinforced with solid concrete within the block walls. Sloshing through the rapidly rising water, he felt the spiral staircase and gave it a good shake. It was slightly loose but usable.

Finn retreated from the room to get the others. The water was higher in this part of the basement, likely because that side of the house had sunk deeper into the depression created by the water dissolving the soft soil.

"Tyler!"

"We're here," Tyler replied calmly. "Finn, the bears are somewhere upstairs. We can hear them."

In the completely dark space, Finn bumped into Tyler, causing both men to flinch. Finn tried to remain calm.

"I have a way out that will avoid the threat above us. There's a spiral staircase that leads into the garage. It may be partially or completely below ground, but it's safer than what we're facing if we go up these stairs." He pointed toward the stairwell.

Sammy asked, "Why don't we swim through the back? Won't we come out somewhere?"

"I think we've been pulled into a sinkhole," Finn replied. "This water may be part of the flooding that's found its way through rock formations. There is no backyard anymore." Finn's voice trailed off as he struggled to be honest about their situation without further frightening the young children.

"Lead the way, Finn. Let's try the stairs you mentioned."

Sammy took the girls by the hands. "Everyone,

hold hands. Finn is gonna take us to a place to get out of the water."

Sophie and Livvy firmly grasped one another, something they'd done many times since this began. Sammy took Tyler's hand, who in turn placed his hand on Finn's shoulder. They made their way past the stairwell opening, where the bears could be heard angrily destroying the house.

They reached the spiral staircase. Finn patted Tyler on the back. "Take the lead. I'll make sure everyone gets up."

"Sounds good." Tyler started upward, and Sammy got Livvy in line to go next. He turned slightly and said, "One at a time. This feels kinda rickety."

"It does?" questioned Finn. "I just checked it and thought it would hold."

Tyler had reached the top and pushed the door open that led to the garage. He explained, "It's bolted to the concrete floor up here. The landing has twisted, causing the stairs to pull away from the lag bolts."

"We have to make it work," he shouted up to Tyler. The house sank a little more, giving them a new sense of urgency. "Girls, hurry!" Finn instructed.

As Sammy supervised them winding their way up the iron stairs together, Finn turned to check the water levels in the bar area. The house was tilting farther to one side. He could tell from his stance and the fact the water was nearing the top of the doorway entering the safe room.

He turned his attention back to their escape. Sammy was climbing upwards now. A small amount of light seemed to make its way into the garage, giving Finn hope that this side of the house would provide them a way out.

Just as Sammy arrived at the landing, the house lurched again, turning it sideways even more, which knocked Sammy to the floor. Finn was now immersed in water. He struggled to find a way to stand, inadvertently stepping through the doorway that would have plunged him several feet down the slope into the man cave.

Sammy gasped and then screamed. The concrete beneath her fell apart in chunks. She crawled toward the garage door, where Tyler got a firm grasp on her forearm. He pulled her closer until she could grab the doorjamb to hold on. Instinctively, she turned to look for Finn.

He was gone, and so was the spiral staircase, which had broken free of its anchor bolts.

SIXTY-EIGHT

Saturday
Pasadena, California

"Finn!" Sammy yelled for her friend, who'd saved her life over and over again. She leaned over the concrete landing, which was crumbling under her weight, swinging her hand around in the dark in search of Finn or the staircase. As more of the broken concrete began to crumble, she crawled backwards into the garage, where Tyler waited.

"What happened?"

"The landing fell apart, and the staircase broke loose. Finn's not responding. I'm afraid it fell on him, or he's pinned underneath it."

Tyler started toward the door leading to the safe room. "I'll find him."

Sammy grabbed his arm. "No, let me try again. Besides, I'm the better swimmer. Can you find your way out?"

"I think I already did," he replied. "I swear, Sammy, I think the sun might be out. There is a little light coming where the front of the foundation was. The damn house is tilting sideways. If we can find some tools in here, we might be able to dig through the mud and crawl out that way."

Sammy held her breath to focus her hearing. "I hear water trickling in somewhere."

"At the front. That's how I found the opening. It's only a little bit splashing on the garage floor, so I don't think it will flood us. Probably just rain."

Sammy leaned into him and gave him a quick kiss. "Get yourselves to safety. I'm gonna try to help Finn. Ty, I owe him. Do you understand?"

"I trust you. Go!" He spun around and fumbled his way through the garage in search of a shovel.

Sammy returned to the landing. She called out Finn's name again. This time, he responded.

"I'm here, lass. I've tried to break free of this thing, but it's got me pinned against the wall."

Sammy dropped to her knees. "I wish I could see

you. How much of your body is above the water level?"

"Just my head. I can raise my arms, too. The water's rising, Sammy." His words hung in the air. He could drown.

Her heart raced. "Okay. Okay. Let me think."

"Listen to me, Sammy. There's nothing you can do. This thing won't budge. Go to your husband and get those precious young lasses out of here to safety. This is my time to go."

"No, it is not!" she insisted. "There's still time. Let me find a ladder and a, um, something to pry the stairs away from you."

"Sammy, it's embedded in the concrete wall. This iron is too heavy."

Finn's words of protest fell on deaf ears. Sammy had already returned to the garage as he spoke, in search of a ladder. She also needed a tire iron or some type of sturdy pole.

In the dark space, she felt her way around the walls to find where the owners of the house stored their tools. After several minutes, she began to curse them.

"Who doesn't have a ladder? Or a rake? Or any tools, for that matter?" Then she scowled as she answered herself. People who can afford to pay someone to do everything for them. She and Tyler would never be like that despite their increased incomes. If they could do it themselves, why pay someone else was their way of thinking.

She rushed back to the landing overlooking the safe room. More of the concrete had fallen away, making her footing treacherous. Holding the doorjamb with both arms, she called out to Finn, "How are you doing down there?"

"It's up to my throat, Sammy. There's nothing you can do. I want to leave this earth feeling at peace."

Sammy sat on the edge of the landing, staring down into the darkness. Tears streamed down her face as Finn spoke.

"I loved our community," he continued. "My wife and I never had children. She was my everything, and I was hers. When she died suddenly after the pandemic, I'd never felt in more pain. I've had bones broken. Skin burned. Multiple concussions. But the heartache of her unexpected death was more than I could handle."

Sammy was sniffling as he spoke. She wiped her nose on the tracksuit jacket's sleeve.

"Finn, I can't let you die. I'm a great swimmer."

"No!" he fired back. "You have a husband and

family who need you. I won't let you risk your life for me." He paused for a moment and then told a story.

"There was a time when I knew this moment would come. After the second station fire ended a few months ago, I stood up on this very ridge, proud that I'd helped save our neighborhood from the blaze that wanted to consume it.

"I'll never forget the eerie silence other than the occasional snap or pop of a dying ember. Yet off in the distance, from somewhere I could never determine, I heard music playing."

"Music?" asked Sammy.

Finn managed a laugh. "Well, it was really a single instrument. It reminded me of the story of the emperor Nero playing the fiddle as Rome burned. Only, I prevented Rome from burning, and the music I heard came from a saxophone, not a fiddle."

Finn started into a coughing fit as water entered his mouth for the first time. He didn't have much longer. Yet he continued talking, as it seemed to keep him calm as he prepared for his inevitable death. He stretched to jut his chin above the surface.

"To this day, the sound of that saxophone haunts me. I'd give anything to know what song they were playing."

"'Hallelujah.'"

"What?"

Sammy gulped as she began crying again. Her voice quivered as she became filled with emotion. "The song was 'Hallelujah.' I was playing the saxophone that day."

He didn't say anything in response. Only, long silence.

Until Sammy impulsively jumped into the water to save Finn.

SIXTY-NINE

Saturday
Pasadena, California

Tyler saw a ray of sunshine. It was not a mirage. It was not wishful thinking. It was not delusion. It was an honest-to-goodness ray of sunshine peeking over the horizon. It lasted but a fleeting moment before disappearing behind the dark and dreary clouds that had beset California for weeks. However, it was proof positive that the sun was still doing its job. It had just been a bit lazy of late.

The rain had let up, too. Of this, he was certain. For twenty hours, his body had been soaked to the bone by the incessant downpours. One storm after another had invaded California's shores until yesterday when the mother of all disasters arrived. It was as if a thousand years of storms came all at once.

He couldn't take his eyes off the raging river that flowed below where he and the girls stood mesmerized. Its depth was nearly as tall as the Rose Bowl. Its girth was more than double the size of the golf course his home once looked upon. The interstate highways system in the distance, once bustling with traffic, had tilted and slid down the ridge as the raging waters gobbled up everything.

With the coming daylight, Tyler thought the nightmare was over. They'd wake up, laugh it off, and go for a jog. The shivering bodies holding his waist were a grim reminder that there was still work to do before this bad dream went away.

"Girls, I'm gonna need you to help me out," he began as he knelt next to the cold and exhausted kids. He pointed toward the edge of the road at the top of the driveway. A pickup had been abandoned on the side of the street, with two wheels pulled into the adjacent yard. "I need you to please wait over there while I go help Sammy and Finn. Can you do that for me?"

"What about the bears?" asked Livvy, a legitimate question. Tyler glanced toward the house, which was now turned on its side as one end sank deeper into the sinkhole than the garage end. The front entrance was almost completely covered in mud and landscape material.

"I'm pretty sure they're still inside the house. But just to be safe, let me get you inside that truck. Would that be okay?"

They both nodded. Tyler took them by the hands and hustled them up the slippery slope toward the four-door Ford pickup. The doors were unlocked, and the keys left in the ignition. Tyler chuckled at the owner's nonchalance about the possibility of theft. The street on both sides of the vehicle had washed away. There was no place for a thief to go.

After they were settled in with the windows partially rolled down, he rushed back toward the hole in the foundation. He'd grown concerned that Sammy hadn't emerged from the garage yet. Had she found a way to rescue Finn? Was she in trouble? Or was she too distraught to leave him behind?

Tyler slid feet-first into the mud and down the chute they'd created when they dug out of the garage. He maneuvered his body so that he easily fit through the crack in the home's foundation. At the bottom of the slide, he grabbed the walls to keep from falling inside. The house had tilted more since he and the girls left. He immediately wondered if the earth would swallow it whole.

Before entering the pitch-black garage, he shouted for his wife. "Sammy! Are you okay? Can you hear me?"

No response.

He tried again, his bellowing reverberating off the enclosed, mostly concrete space.

Again, nothing.

He ran his hands through his partially matted hair. For a brief moment, he closed his eyes to recall the layout of the garage area. Without light, he'd felt his way around the entire perimeter of the two-car garage. He could recall where the storage room was located that he was dangling his feet over. The entrance to the landing above the panic room was directly across from him. However, because of the building's tilt, he'd have to make his way downward toward the home's garage door leading into a utility room and then climb his way up toward the panic room landing.

Tyler took a deep breath and got started. He stumbled several times as he struggled with the slope. The final time, he slid down the slippery, polished concrete floor and landed hard against the block wall of the foundation. As he kept moving, he shouted for Sammy, who should've responded.

Unless, he thought to himself. Tyler shook his head in disbelief. It was too dangerous for her to jump into the water to save Finn. Besides, neither had the strength or the leverage to remove the iron staircase that pinned him down. If she did go after Finn, how would they get out?

He made his way to the opening and pulled himself inside using the doorjamb. Sammy wasn't there. Tyler shimmied closer to the edge of the concrete slab, which had almost completely disintegrated. The dark, murky water had risen significantly since he'd spoken to her last.

Filtered light had entered the garage from the hole he'd crawled through. It provided him just enough light to see the water's surface. It was still except for a few ripples caused by the concrete aggregate falling from underneath his weight.

There was no thrashing. No arms waving for help. However, there were no bodies floating on top due to drowning. They were both alive, somewhere, inside the house.

Tyler had an idea. If they were stuck underwater within the basement or even in the upstairs living spaces, they'd be trying to climb to the highest point of the structure. It would be dark, and their ability to see would be nil.

He pushed his body out of the opening and slid down the garage floor to the wall where the back door was located. He knew this might be risky for him, as two ornery bears could be on the other side. However, with the door open, Sammy and Finn might gain the benefit of the filtered light entering the garage.

He tried the door and was relieved when the knob turned. He didn't want to kick it in, potentially causing a commotion that might draw the bears after him. It was going to be difficult enough to claw his way back to the opening without having a couple of bruins swatting at his legs.

He cracked the door, allowing it to open slowly. He listened intently for any sounds of movement on the other side. And for growling. It was quiet.

Tyler held onto the knob, slowly allowing it to open fully. The utility room was dark, but dry. The water hadn't risen to that point.

He grimaced. Was it worth the risk? Should he call out to Sammy? What if his voice drew the ire of the bears? What if, by drawing them towards him, he blocked Sammy and Finn's only means of escape? Should he go in to rescue them?

The questions caused his head to ache. It was one of the most difficult decisions he'd made in his life. Tyler debated inside his mind until it hurt. Finally, he made a decision.

He slowly lowered himself into the utility room, using the washer, dryer, and cabinets like a three-rung ladder. He was able to get to the doorway entering the back side of the kitchen. Then he froze. Something big and burly was tearing through the refrigerator and kitchen cupboards.

SEVENTY

Saturday
Pasadena, California

Sammy plunged downward into the darkness until her feet struck the concrete floor. She immediately slipped due to the tilted angle and fell on her back. From the start, she was having difficulty breathing from the impact. Yet her determination and perseverance kept her going.

She blindly swung her arms around in front of her to make contact with Finn. However, all she managed to do was rap her knuckles against the iron staircase, sending a jolt of pain up her arm into her shoulder.

Then Finn grabbed her forearm. It startled her and sent a wave of relief over her at the same time. She couldn't see him, and the silt-filled floodwater caused her eyes to burn, so she'd closed them.

After assessing the tilt of the staircase and where it had Finn pinned, she moved her body into position so that her feet were pressed firmly against the wall and her back was against the side of the stairwell.

Finn, who'd remarkably held his breath for more than a minute now, sensed what she was doing. He twisted his back so that it was flush against the wall next to her feet. He grasped one for the stairwell's treads as if he were getting a firm grip to perform a bench press at the gym. He imperceptibly nodded, knowing full well Sammy couldn't see him. Somehow, he felt he was able to communicate his readiness to her.

In near unison, Finn pushed with his chest and upper-body muscles. Sammy forced her legs to push against the wall, grunting as she performed the equivalent of a deep squat. As she grunted, the air in her lungs escaped through her nose. It was nearly depleted. She willed herself to push a little harder, and then she felt it.

The movement seemed miniscule. Maybe an inch. It was all Finn needed to hastily extricate himself from the hulking staircase. He dropped toward the floor, his legs now free of the stairs.

Sammy slid to the side, narrowly escaping the spiral structure, which bounced back just enough to cause her back serious injury. In a fluid motion, she used the stair's treads to propel herself upward, where her head broke the surface.

She gasped for air, searching in the darkness for Finn. Seconds later, he also breached the surface. He'd been underwater for at least a minute longer than Sammy, yet he didn't struggle to catch his breath like she did despite being twice her age.

She nervously laughed. "Why aren't you winded like me?"

Finn reached out to her until he found her arm holding onto the stairwell. "I'm a trained rescue diver. I've been PADI certified for most of my life." PADI was an acronym for Professional Association of Diving Instructors.

As Sammy calmed her nerves and recuperated from the efforts underwater, Finn slowly moved around the confined space, looking toward the landing above them, or what was left of it. In the darkness, he could still make out the distance between the water's surface and their potential escape route.

"Are you injured?" she asked finally.

"It's gonna hurt tomorrow. Bruised, but nothing broken. The biggest problem was that my lower legs were going numb from the lack of circulation. I kept trying to wiggle my toes and roll my feet around their ankles. Soon as the water went over my head, that part didn't matter."

He moved around the top part of the staircase so he could be closer to Sammy.

"What kept you going?" she asked.

"I was praying for forgiveness before I died. Then my mind wandered to where I could hear my wife reaming me out for not trying harder to survive. Then, in the midst of her mental tongue-lashing, you came plunging past me."

Sammy looked up to the garage entry. It was too far to reach. The staircase had dislodged from the landing and tipped toward the far end of the room past the door, so it was no help. To make matters worse, it partially obstructed the entry to the panic room. They couldn't maneuver furniture into the space to climb up.

"The water was rising fast, which is why you fell under in the middle of our conversation," she noticed. "Now it seems to have slowed down."

"I'm afraid you're right. The thought just crossed

my mind we'd wait here until the floodwater fills the room and pushes toward the garage level. I think the sinkhole stopped swallowing the house, and, um, maybe the rain has let up."

Sammy furrowed her brow as she thought about their options. "First of all, I'm pretty sure Tyler and the girls got out of the garage through a hole in the foundation. If they didn't, I'm certain he'd be up there looking at ways to drag us out."

"There's another way into the garage, of course," interjected Finn.

"The garage door leading into the house. I saw it through the laundry area."

"Exactly. I don't know how long we'll have to swim underwater, and it will be completely dark, not that it matters."

Sammy interrupted him. "Yeah, I tried to open my eyes underwater. My eyeballs will itch for days."

Finn changed his grip on the staircase and kicked his legs to ensure there would not be a problem using them. "I believe we'll come across pockets of air as we swim through the house. Allow your natural buoyancy to carry you upward in case you need to refill your lungs."

"I can swim several minutes underwater. How about you?" asked Sammy.

"Three or four, comfortably. Being a nonsmoker and not terribly chubby helps."

Sammy was quiet for a moment and then relayed her thoughts. "See if this is what you remember. It's not that complicated. Through the panic room doorway, we head straight toward the bar. The stairwell will be on our right. We can use the railing to pull ourselves to the first landing, make the turn, and then up to the living room."

"That's correct. I believe it will be the most difficult leg because we won't have any air pockets to assist us. We'll actually be going deeper into the sinkhole before turning the stairs. It's possible the kitchen might be out of the water."

Sammy closed her eyes to regain the visual of the home's layout. The bedrooms were mostly located on the other side of the house from their present location. She wondered if they'd be crushed under the weight of the sinking house.

"All right. Even if it isn't dry when we reach the living room, it's a fairly short swim down, um, up the hallway toward the laundry room. The kitchen will be on our right and the pantry on our left as we swim toward the garage." She pointed above their heads.

Finn laughed. "This will be a lot of work to get to a point just ten feet above us."

Sammy noticed the water level had dropped ever so slightly. They didn't have the option of rising with the tide, as they say. In fact, she was concerned that the water was seeping out of the house, potentially allowing more mud to find its way in.

They needed to hurry.

SEVENTY-ONE

Saturday
Pasadena, California

With Finn leading the way, they began their descent into the depths of the submerged house. Sammy immediately noticed how thick the water was with mud and much finer silt granules. She didn't dare open her eyes. It would've been a fruitless exercise and would've likely caused her eyeballs permanent damage.

Finn moved methodically through the open space that was once an extraordinary entertainment room. The décor and furnishings were reminiscent of sitting in one of England's finest pubs. Now it was mostly covered in mud, and the vintage décor was floating aimlessly through the muddy water.

Finn arrived at the opening to the stairwell, where they planned on making their way to the upper floor. He waited for Sammy to bump into him to reveal the problem. He took her hand and slowly guided it around where the opening should've been.

The doorway-sized entryway was blocked by mud mixed with some rubble. It completely filled the opening. For a minute, the two of them clawed at the mud in an attempt to ascertain if an opening could be created. More silt filled the water and surrounded their bodies. If they continued, it would be easy to get disoriented.

Finn tapped on her shoulder, grasped her hand and tugged her slightly. She understood and followed him as he returned to the panic room. At the entry, he waited to make sure she was behind him before they both shot upward toward the surface for air.

"I can't believe this," said Sammy, her words coming out in between deep breaths. "How thick is it?"

Finn shook his head. "I don't know. Actually, based upon how I think the house turned as it sank, it doesn't really make sense. That area should be clear, and at this point, we should be making our way past the kitchen."

Sammy felt around. She gauged the water's depth in relation to the stairwell by how much of the iron center post protruded above the surface. It hadn't changed in the brief time they'd been away.

"We only have one option, and that's to dig it out," she suggested. "If we work together, we can shovel the mud out of the way with our hands, return here to refill our lungs, and continue."

Finn injected humor to calm their nerves. "Wash, rinse, repeat. Right?"

Sammy laughed. "I always thought that was stupid. No woman, especially someone like me with long hair, would torture herself by washing twice. I think the shampoo companies came up with that bright idea to sell more shampoo."

"Me too," said Finn. He really hadn't thought of it that way. He imagined the process of digging through the mud might result in an endless loop of repeating the same steps until they break through the barrier. "Are you ready to give it a go?"

Sammy answered cheerily. "Let's do this."

Before Finn dropped below the surface, he admonished Sammy to be careful and not overexert.

Rather than get in trouble, always save enough air to get back to the panic room.

After attempting a fist bump in the dark that missed wildly, the two dropped below the surface and swam toward the stairwell with confidence, having made the round trip once already.

They tore at the mud, sending it flying into the man cave, where it dissipated or fell toward the bar, the lowest part of the room. They returned to the panic room briefly for air and then continued the dig. They washed, rinsed and repeated, as Finn put it, four times before they were able to create a hole big enough for Sammy to shimmy through.

She was able to dig mud toward her while Finn did the same on the other side. He needed a larger opening to squeeze through. Sammy was on the end of her timeframe to remain underwater, so she grasped the handrail to propel herself to the upper floor to refill her lungs with air. Her head breached the surface with a rush as she began to panic slightly.

It was just as dark upstairs as it was in the basement. She gasped for air, breathing rapidly to rejuvenate her empty lungs. After she calmed down, she heard a commotion in the kitchen. It was not simply canned goods being removed from the cupboards as the house continued to tilt. One of the bears was angrily ripping the room apart with its powerful paws and sharp claws. Sammy closed her eyes, took a deep breath, and forced herself underwater again.

She pulled herself down, once again using the railing as an aid. Finn was close to making his way through the hole. She dug underneath his chest and then tugged on his arms. That made the difference.

She'd planned on guiding him up the stairs so he didn't make noise when he finally reached the air above them. However, he was close to choking on the muddy water and rushed past her. She tried to keep up but couldn't. Seconds later, she arrived by his side, and her head shot above the surface.

Finn was paralyzed from fear. The brave firefighter was facing down the bear, which had heard him thrashing about when he came up for air.

Sammy breathed steadily and whispered to Finn, "I think his vision might be impaired from the dark space. And for some reason, his sense of smell has failed him."

Finn was recovering from his state of shock. "It may be because we're partially submerged and covered with mud. I'm not positive he saw me."

"Here's the problem," began Sammy. "We have to crawl uphill on a tile floor to get to the garage. He's gonna be a few feet away in the kitchen."

Sammy rose out of the water a little more to look for any signs of daylight coming into the living room. Her watch display had disappeared hours ago, it seemed like to her, but she felt it was close to dawn.

She eased half her body onto the floor at the top of the stairs and looked toward the garage. It was brighter than earlier. She wasn't prepared to say the sun was out, but certainly, daylight was fighting its way through the cloud cover.

Suddenly, a shadow eclipsed the light. Light. Dark. Light. Dark. It was if a sheet or blanket hanging in the utility room was flapping in a breeze that didn't exist under the earth.

"Sammy!" It was Tyler speaking to her in a loud whisper. He was being cautious. "Bear in kitchen."

Her heart leapt. They needed a break to get out of there. However, she wasn't sure how Tyler could help.

"I know," she whispered back. She held her breath to focus on the bear. He apparently didn't hear them speaking to one another.

She continued to whisper, "Ty's up there. In the laundry room."

"Okay. Okay." Finn thought for a moment before continuing, "I've been listening to the bear. I'm not sure he's rummaging for food. I think he's having trouble standing or walking. Either he's hurt, or the slick floors are like ice, with the only difference being his claws can dig into ice, not marble floor tiles."

"What does that mean?" asked Sammy.

"I'm not sure he can get to us," he replied somewhat convincingly.

Sammy looked toward Tyler, whose silhouette was barely discernible against the diffused light coming from the garage. She closed her eyes to concentrate. It was a two-step process. She turned her body toward the garage.

"I'm gonna go for it."

"Tell me what you're thinking, lass."

Sammy reached behind her and patted the wrought-iron spindles making up the stair railings. "I'll use this as a ladder to extend my reach to the pantry door. I'll pull up to that point and then use the doorjamb as a way to reach the utility room entry. I'll pull my way up to there, maybe with Ty's help."

Finn nodded and continued to whisper, "If the bear senses your movements and tries to rush you, I'll slap the floor with my hand to grab his attention. It may be all it takes to throw him off balance."

"He'll slide right back into the kitchen," added Sammy.

"It looks good on paper," he said. "What could go wrong?"

"Everything," Sammy replied. She patted him on the back and eased herself completely out of the water. She stayed perfectly still for a moment to allow excess moisture to drip off her and to gauge whether the bear was alerted to her presence.

It wasn't, so she got started. Sammy was diligent with each movement. When she was able to reach the pantry doorway, she used her upper-body muscles to pull upward, avoiding the kicking motion most people use when doing pull-ups.

She stopped her climb and crouched in the doorway. From her perch, she studied the bear's activity in the limited light. Their assessment was correct. It was trying to climb out but couldn't get any traction on the floor. In between attempts, it'd take out its frustration on anything within its paws' reach.

"Come on. I'll help pull you up," she said to Finn in a normal voice.

Finn continued in hushed tones, "Sammy, what are you doing? The bear!"

"He's got his hands full. Let me help you to this point. Then Ty will pull us the rest of the way."

"Are you sure, Sammy?" asked Tyler from above her.

"Yeah, he's stuck in there. The only way around would be through the dining room, which is submerged."

Finn added, "Fishing is one thing. Deep-sea diving is another when it comes to bears."

He scrambled onto his hands and knees to quickly move to Sammy's position with the aid of the stairs and the doorjamb. First Sammy and then Finn joined Tyler in the utility room, where he led them into the garage. After a brief embrace, they made their way toward the light shining through the broken foundation.

They were so close now. So close.

SEVENTY-TWO

Saturday
Pasadena, California

"This way," instructed Tyler as he crawled up the chute he and the girls had created. The opening was a little wider, as water runoff had eroded the mud and washed it downward. They each helped one another, Sammy pushing Tyler's feet when he slipped. Once the couple were both above ground, they reached for Finn's arms to drag him into the daylight.

Moments later, the three of them crawled along the rain and mud-soaked lawn as far from the sinking house as possible. The girls screamed in delight as they saw the trio emerge. They exited the truck and began running down the hill with far too much momentum to stop. Tyler and Sammy stood to intercept them before they tumbled into the sinkhole.

The tears flowed again. For the first time in what seemed an eternity, they could see each other's faces.

"Mud puppies," quipped Finn as he struggled to stand. "We all look like a bunch of muddy puppies."

Tyler barked. The girls squealed in delight. Finn panted like a pup.

And Sammy looked toward the sky, wondering if it was truly over.

The skies were gray, not black. The rain was, well, normal. Not a deluge. The wind was blowing but not howling. In the distance, the sound of rescue helicopters approaching gave her hope.

Had the ARkStorm moved on, or did it run out of energy? Or was it merely taking a respite? Maybe it was reloading for another trip to the California coast?

Sammy stood a little taller and adopted a defiant pose as she saw the new river rushing by. She followed its path toward the city, where imposing skyscrapers once dotted the landscape in the midst of a million homes.

The towering buildings were barely visible. The

homes, covered by water, were not. The Pacific Ocean had washed ashore, and the river that roared through the Crescenta Valley had merged with it into one enormous body of water.

Sammy suddenly found herself reflecting on their future. They had survived, but barely. She didn't intend to stick around for the next wave of storms, if any. When they first arrived in La Cañada, she'd heard about the so-called Big One. She was assured there would be warnings about earthquakes. Well, this was the Other Big One, and there was no warning. She'd had enough. It was time to go before some other form of shit hit California's fan.

"Hey, Sammy, look what the girls found," Tyler said, who was in good spirits. He held up a Disney Monopoly board game. "Wanna play? I'll even let you win."

Sammy scowled and set her jaw. No more self-loathing. It was time to kick her husband's ass for teasing her. She chased him around the soggy yard just as a sheriff's rescue chopper settled overhead. They were being taken to safety, after they gathered up the pups first. Tyler's punishment would have to wait 'til later.

During the ride, they were able to survey the damage. Neither Finn nor the couple were surprised their homes were gone. Every street on the west side of the river had sustained damaged if not disappeared altogether.

The same was true for the lower parts of Los Angeles County. Hundreds of thousands were presumed dead or still missing. The roadways were so clogged that vehicles couldn't move, resulting in a mass exodus on foot. Many walked along Interstate 15 toward Las Vegas. Others were diverted to a massive tent city built at Edwards Air Force Base northeast of the city. Even more fled toward Arizona on Interstate 10.

The refugees could go anywhere, the pilots informed them. Finn said his goodbyes on the chopper and asked to be dropped off at the nearest staging area for search and rescue teams. He was gonna return to the fire department whether the county liked it or not. He and Sammy hugged for a long time until the pilots grew impatient with them. They promised to keep in touch, assuming their old phone numbers were still assigned after all this was over.

The pilots then ferried Sammy, Tyler and the girls to Edwards AFB. They rode in silence, allowing the staccato thumping of the rotors to put them to sleep. When the pilot announced their approach,

Sammy looked at the thousands of tents that had been set up in the desert. Even the base's dry lakes were filled with water.

The chopper unceremoniously dropped them off on a helipad. They'd barely reached the edge with the help of an escort when it took off to pluck more survivors from the ridges overlooking the river.

It took an hour to be processed. They received basic clothing and toiletries. They were told the next meal wouldn't be served until dinner but were provided a box of bagged fruit and some almonds.

Once they entered their assigned tent filled with sixteen cots and a dozen strangers, the reality set in. They were homeless. Penniless. And clueless as to what the future held.

Yet they were alive. In the end, survival was all that mattered. Houses, cars, and stuff could all be replaced. Lives could not.

EPILOGUE

**Three Years Later
Central Pennsylvania**

Life went on for Sammy and Tyler. They gradually recovered from the emotional trauma inflicted upon them during the ARkStorm. They would never forget.

The couple fled California, literally. Once Tyler's brother and sister-in-law made contact with them at Edwards AFB, they rented an SUV and drove cross-country back to Central Pennsylvania. There was no choice, as there was no home to return to.

It took more than a year to receive the insurance

proceeds for their loss. Every home insurer in the state went bankrupt, which required the federal government to issue a record-setting bailout to cover their policies. The state of California went bankrupt as well. The economic loss was measured in trillions of dollars.

The cost of the rescue and recovery effort was astronomical. Hundreds of thousands of people died. Tens of thousands were never accounted for. The rebuilding of what was left cost billions more.

Scientists assessed the damage to the state in ways other than social, economic, and physical consequences, or even loss of life. They studied the environmental impact the new lake had on California. They calculated the amount of rainfall and melted snow was equivalent to twenty-two Mississippi Rivers in terms of water volume. The weight of the water was enormous, changing the face of the state as mudslides continued for the next year or so until the land stabilized.

As for the state itself, the geographic transformation was beyond belief. A lake split California in half. It stretched three hundred miles from Sacramento through the Central Valley into Orange County. Los Angeles remained under water, as erosion lowered it to below sea level. At first, the state and federal government attempted to build a levee system similar to the one in New Orleans. The next winter, a series of atmospheric rivers rolled across the coast and obliterated the partially constructed levees. Any construction within LA and Hollywood was swamped as the enormous waves washed ashore.

Not to be deterred in achieving a lavish lifestyle, the stars of Hollywood purchased available land along the ridges bordering the newly formed lake. Life went on as California gradually rebuilt. Nonetheless, many thousands, like Sammy and Tyler, vowed to never go through something like the ARkStorm again and moved to safer locales.

Finn officially unretired and assumed his old role as a deputy chief. However, after a few years, once California began to recover, he retired again, and he moved a cabin with a view of Mammoth Mountain. His home was a remote cabin nearly ten thousand feet above sea level. Once a year, he got together with Sammy and Tyler, during the summer, when there was no threat of an ARkStorm. At ten thousand feet, Finn wanted to rest assured he wouldn't get caught up in another catastrophic event.

After the briefly played Rose Bowl during the storm, the NCAA declared USC to be the winner mostly out of sympathy since the school had been totally destroyed. Months later, the Penn State University coaching staff discussed the game and the effort Tyler had made to prepare the USC team in peak physical condition. They learned of his personal loss due to the storm and offered him the position of assistant athletic trainer of the football program. Three years later, he became the head athletic trainer, and with his help, the school was headed to the Sugar Bowl to play Tennessee.

As for Sammy, her law firm was dismantled as a result of the catastrophe, not that she intended to return anyway. She longed for a simpler life, which included a law practice that did good things for people as opposed to being engaged in the cutthroat business of mergers and acquisitions.

She joined a firm in Harrisburg, Pennsylvania's state capital, that lobbied the state legislature and the United States Congress to preserve lands for gaming and fishing. It was a singularly focused practice, which enjoyed her expertise in negotiation. She was instrumental in creating state and national parks throughout the region.

As for having children, they reset their five-year plan until they'd both settled into their new jobs. Carly and Fenway were still their constant companions despite the fact they had grown older. The family enjoyed spending every available moment together and having their nieces, now middle-schoolers, come to visit. Sammy had mentioned to Tyler there was something to be said for getting that kid fix by borrowing the nieces for the weekend now and again. He replied he was amazed they'd agree to do anything with him and Sammy after what had happened during the ARkStorm.

So the family lived happily in rural McVeytown, Pennsylvania, buying some farmland from their uncle, Farmer Joe. They found a new path into the future, one filled with the activities they loved and one that hopefully didn't ensnare them in a catastrophic natural disaster.

As for California, a state whose beauty was unsurpassed on many levels, time would tell how it fared.

THANK YOU FOR READING ARKSTORM!

If you enjoyed it, I'd be grateful if you'd take a moment to write a short review (just a few words are needed) and post it on Amazon. Amazon uses complicated algorithms to determine what books are recommended to readers. Sales are, of course, a factor, but so are the quantities of reviews my books get. By taking a few seconds to leave a review, you help me out and also help new readers learn about my work.

Sign up to my email list to learn about upcoming titles, deals, contests, appearances, and more!

Sign up at BobbyAkart.com

THANK YOU FOR READING ARKSTORM!

VISIT my feature page at Amazon.com/BobbyAkart for more information on my other action-packed thrillers, which includes over forty Amazon #1 bestsellers in forty-plus fiction and nonfiction genres.

READ ON to see what's coming next and to learn the backstory behind the writing of this novel.

WHAT'S COMING NEXT FROM BOBBY AKART?

FRACTURED, a standalone disaster thriller in the CALIFORNIA DREAMIN' universe.

California is a land divided by an 800-mile-long rupture known as the San Andreas Fault. The state's heart, the Central Valley, hasn't experienced the fault's full fury, at least not in modern times.

Until now.

A standalone disaster thriller from international bestselling author, Bobby Akart, one of America's favorite storytellers, who delivers up-all-night thrillers to readers in 245 countries and territories worldwide.

"Akart is one of those very rare authors who makes things so visceral, so real, that you experience what he writes."

Several years ago, an ARkStorm, a once-in-a-thousand-years flood event caused by a series of intense atmospheric rivers, flooded the Central Valley of California from Sacramento to what was once Los Angeles.

The weight of the water was equivalent to the volume generated by the Mississippi River times twenty-two. It challenged an already fragile seismic system consisting of hundreds of active faults.

"Bobby Akart is a genius at creating disaster scenarios."

The ARkStorm, the Other Big One, was leading to another epic catastrophic event, one that would rip the state apart. What was once deemed a slow and silent rupture of the famous San Andreas fault line

WHAT'S COMING NEXT FROM BOBBY AKART?

has changed dramatically since the ARkStorm. It has awakened.

One person saw it coming. However, nobody would listen. Mac Atwood warned that an earthquake along these stressed fault lines wouldn't just rattle homes. It would rip the state apart, sucking the lake and the land around it into the earth.

"You are there. Feeling what they feel. Anger, joy, love, mourning. You feel it all. Not everyone can write a book like this. It takes a special writer to make you feel a book."

If only they had only listened.

This modern-day, fact-based novel will have you whispering just one more chapter until the end.

REAL WORLD NEWS EXCERPTS

SOCAL SEES RECORD RAINFALL AS STORMS BRING FLOODING, EVACUATIONS AND POWER OUTAGES

~ *LA Times, March 15, 2023*

Californians deal with surging rivers, sliding rocks and flooded towns as unprecedented rainfall hits Southern California.

More than a dozen locations along major rivers were overflowing as the high-impact storm moved south through the state.

At least 90 flood watches, warnings and advisories were in effect statewide, as were avalanche warnings in portions of Mono and Inyo counties and the Lake Tahoe area, according to the National Weather Service, which said the storm would "create considerable to locally catastrophic flooding impacts below 5,000 feet elevation."

About 336,000 households across the state were without power as of Tuesday afternoon, according to data compiled by the California Governor's Office of Emergency Services.

In Central California, officials said flooding wasn't the only risk in the area. Major utility lines run through levees under California Highway 1, and several wastewater treatment facilities were downstream.

"If the water continues to erode through the levees such that it reenters the river system … it could overwhelm the river system downstream of Highway 1," where the wastewater treatment plants sit, said Mark Strudley, executive director of the California Regional Flood Management Agency.

If the water overtops or seeps through the levees, Strudley said, "we may end up releasing untreated sewage to the floodplain, to the river and then ultimately to the drinking water aquifers."

REAL WORLD NEWS EXCERPTS

CALIFORNIA IS FACING ITS 12TH ATMOSPHERIC RIVER THIS WINTER AFTER A HISTORIC DROUGHT

~ CNN.com, March 20, 2023

An atmospheric river is like a conveyor belt of moisture that originates over the tropical water of the Pacific Ocean. They can carry more than 20 times the amount of water the Mississippi River does, but as vapor. As these storms pummeled the state in quick succession, the soil became over-saturated and vulnerable to flooding and mudslides.

California is bracing for yet another powerful, atmospheric river storm this week, continuing the onslaught of major weather whiplash after a years-long, historic megadrought.

Many welcomed this winter's heavy rain and snow since it was so desperately needed to replenish the state's severely drained reservoirs and depleted groundwater.

But the storms kept coming. California is now

facing its 12th significant atmospheric river since the parade of strong storms began in late December.

"This is an unusually high number of storms this winter in California," said Daniel Swain, climate scientist at the University of California at Los Angeles. "No matter how you slice it, no matter how you make these formal definitions, this is unusually many."

CALIFORNIA'S ATMOSPHERIC RIVERS ARE GETTING WORSE

~ *Wired.com, March 25, 2023*

As climate change makes storms warmer and wetter, the state's flood control system is struggling to keep up.
The parade of storms that has struck California in recent months has dropped more than 30 trillion gallons of water on the state, refilling reservoirs that had sat empty for years and burying mountain towns in snow.

But climate change is making these storms much wetter and more intense, ratcheting up the risk of potential flooding in California and other states along the West Coast. That's not only because the air over the Pacific will hold more moisture as sea temperatures rise, leading to giant rain and snow volumes, but also because warming temperatures on land will cause more precipitation to fall as rain in the future, which will lead to more dangerous floods.

The family of storms that descended on the state this week only underscored this danger, shattering snow records and overtopping levees across the state.

"There's a cascading chain of impacts," said Tom Corringham, a researcher at the Scripps Institution of Oceanography at UC San Diego. "As you push the rivers harder, as you push the flood protection system harder and harder, you get sort of exponentially increasing impacts. You flood the whole floodplain, or a levee breaks, and that's where you get the really catastrophic events.".

Corringham's research shows that because a slight increase in flooding can cause rivers to overtop levees and spill out into floodplains, the risk of flooding increases exponentially even with a moderate increase in the wetness of an atmospheric river. As a result, it won't take much planetary warming to lead to widespread flood devastation—

the results may be visible over the next few decades, or even earlier."

SCIENTISTS WARN CALIFORNIA'S FLOODS MAY BE A SAMPLE OF MEGAFLOODS TO COME

~ *NPR.org, March 26, 2023*

UCLA climate scientist Daniel Swain warns what Californians have lived through this winter is only a taste of what's to come. Swain says, "As disruptive as this year's events have been, we're nowhere near close to a plausible worst case storm and flood scenario for California."

Dr. Swain is clear about the links between climate change and the increase in extreme flooding. In a study last year, Dr. Swain looked at the worst-case scenario - a weekslong parade of extreme atmospheric rivers which California did not have this year. Dr. Swain found the warming climate has already doubled the probability of a megaflood. Such catastrophic flooding could create more than $1 trillion in damage. Hundreds of thousands could die.

Swain said, "It could happen next year, or it might not happen for 100 years. Or, it could happen every year. A thousand year flood event happened in the early 1860s. It can certainly happen again."

AUTHOR'S NOTE

April, 2023

The media and pundits refer to it as "California's trillion-dollar mega disaster no one is talking about." To them, it's all about the money. Natural disasters that strike the United States are always measured in terms of economic loss, whether through property damage or lost business revenues.

But, what about the toll it takes on humanity? People die when hurricanes come onshore, or tornadoes sweep across the Midwest or up Dixie Alley. A nor'easter brings bone chilling cold and massive amounts of snow to New England causing incalculable harm to citizens of the region. Their homes are

AUTHOR'S NOTE

lost. Their pets vanish. They try to survive in despair waiting on a government response.

Disasters typically associated with the West Coast include devastating earthquakes and out-of-control wildfires, but there's an epic disaster that could be far worse than both -- and it could happen at any point. Scientists refer to as an ARkStorm, a thousand-year flood event that is considered The Other Big One compared to a rupture of the San Andreas Fault, the so-called Big One.

An ARkStorm, often mistakenly associated with Noah's ark in the Bible, refers to a series of atmospheric river storms resulting in a thousand-year flood (the "k" in the scientific term). California would be swallowed in as much as fifty feet of rain. Massive flooding would hit nearly every major population center in the state.

It would cause thousands of landslides, major dam failures and decimate the state's entire agriculture industry.

It might sound like a scene from a post-apocalyptic movie, but this type of storm is not only possible, it's happened before.

California's deadliest and most-destructive natural disaster in recorded history hit the state in the winter

AUTHOR'S NOTE

of 1861 and 1862. Dr. Lucy Jones, a seismologist at the U.S. Geological Survey, or USGS, has spent the better part of her life helping communities and leaders prepare for inevitable disasters. Here's what she's said:

"My family came to California in the 1870s. And the really biggest storm was the 1860s, and I had never heard of it. The deadly storm of 1861 and 1862 fundamentally changed California. The flood flooded a quarter of the homes in California. It destroyed one-third of the taxable land of California in that year, and it bankrupted the state. It actually drove the cattle trade out of California."

UCLA Climate Scientist, Dr. Daniel Swain, contributed heavily to the research behind this novel. He'd relayed his thoughts on the mega storm of 1861-2.

"This was a multiweek, extreme precipitation and flood event that essentially filled up a significant portion of the Central Valley with flood water, creating an inland sea, supposedly 40 miles wide and 150 miles long. Roughly 1% of the state's 400,000 people died."

Both Dr. Jones and Swain were involved in the creation of the USGS study known as *The ARkStorm Scenario*. For a decade or more, both scientists have been sounding the alarm about what could happen if a similar storm happened today.

"Our model that we did we called the ARkStorm. It was actually raining for about 25 days. And that was enough to flood one-quarter of the property in California," Jones said.

The *ARkStorm Scenario* model serves as a warning to local and national leaders about a climate catastrophe that will become reality one day. "This is very much a trillion dollar-type disaster that we're talking about. So this is on a really high level, in terms of what the long-term consequences would be from California," Swain said. Further, the model predicts "substantial loss of life" and at least one-and-a-half million Californians would have to be evacuated from their homes.

What I found remarkable was this point. Both Jones and Swain warned that a storm like this is not a freak event -- it is inevitable. Tree rings and rocks show six mega storms more severe than the 1861-2 storm have occurred in the last eighteen hundred years.

As Swain has pointed out, recent evidence suggests a catastrophic flood event of this nature happens about once every two-hundred years,

AUTHOR'S NOTE

meaning in theory the next ARkStorm could happen at any point in the next forty years.

A note of caution. If I've learned anything in my life devoted to the study of catastrophic events, our planet doesn't follow a schedule. Whether it be the eruption of the Yellowstone Super volcano, or an earthquake along the New Madrid seismic zone, or an ARkStorm, it could happen at any time. Even tomorrow.

Which is why I've adopted the mantra:

Because you never know when the day before is the day before,
Prepare for tomorrow.

A BRIEF OF HISTORY OF THE HISTORIC FLOOD OF 1862

K, STREET, FROM THE LEVEE.

INUNDATION OF THE STATE CAPITOL,
City of Sacramento, 1862.

Published by A ROSENFIELD, San Francisco.

A BRIEF OF HISTORY OF THE HISTORIC FLOOD OF 1862

The Great Flood of 1862, as it was called, was brought on by more than forty days of constant rain, leading to thousands of deaths. The region that was underwater in 1862 is now home to many more people than it was then — it's home to some of California's fastest-growing cities including Bakersfield and Sacramento. Back then, the state's population was about 500,000, but today it's nearly 40 million. In addition, a fourth of California's 800,000 cattle either drowned or starved. Flood waters in that disaster created an "inland sea" three hundred miles long and sixty miles wide in some places.

Intense rainstorms pummeled central California "virtually unabated" from Christmas Eve 1861 until January 1862, Scientific American chronicled in a 2013 story on "The Coming Megastorms."

"Thousands of farms are entirely under water – cattle starving and drowning," wrote scientist William Brewer (author of "Up and Down California in 1860-1864") in a letter to his brother, cited by Scientific American. "All the roads in the middle of the state are impassable; so all mails are cut off. The telegraph also does not work clear through. In the Sacramento Valley for some distance the tops of the poles are under water."

In Southern California, beginning on December

A BRIEF OF HISTORY OF THE HISTORIC FLOOD OF 1862

24, 1861, it rained for twenty-eight days in Los Angeles. In the San Gabriel Mountains the mining town of Eldoradoville was washed away by flood waters. The flooding drowned thousands of cattle and washed away fruit trees and vineyards that grew along the Los Angeles River. No mail was received at Los Angeles for five weeks.

The Los Angeles Star reported that:

The road from Tejon, we hear, has been almost washed away. The San Fernando mountain cannot be crossed except by the old trail ... over the top of the mountain. The plain has been cut up into gulches and arroyos, and streams are rushing down every declivity.

The plains of Los Angeles County, at the time a marshy area with many small lakes and several meandering streams from the mountains, were extensively flooded, and much of the agricultural development that lay along the rivers was ruined. In most of the lower areas, small settlements were submerged. These flooded areas formed into a large lake system with many small streams. A few more powerful currents cut channels across the plain and carried the runoff to the sea.

In Los Angeles County, (including what is now Orange County) the flooding Santa Ana River

A BRIEF OF HISTORY OF THE HISTORIC FLOOD OF 1862

created an inland sea lasting about three weeks with water standing 4 feet deep up to 4 miles from the river.

In February 1862, the Los Angeles, San Gabriel, and Santa Ana Rivers merged. Government surveys at the time indicated that a solid expanse of water covered the area from Signal Hill to Huntington Beach, a distance of approximately eighteen miles.

At Santa Barbara County, the narrow coastal plains were flooded by the rivers coming out of the mountains. The San Buenaventura Mission Aqueduct that was still drawing water from a tributary of the Ventura River for the town of Ventura water system, was abandoned due to the damage in the area that became the separate Ventura County in 1873.

In San Bernardino County, all the fertile riverside fields and all but the church and one house of the New Mexican colony of Agua Mansa, were swept away by the Santa Ana River, which overflowed its banks. A local priest rang the church bell on the night of January 22, 1862, alerting the inhabitants to the approach of the flood, and all escaped.

In San Diego, a storm at sea backed up the flood water running into the bay from the San Diego River, resulting in a new river channel cut into San

A BRIEF OF HISTORY OF THE HISTORIC FLOOD OF 1862

Diego Harbor. The continuous heavy downpour also changed the look of the land, the previously rounded hills were extensively cut by gulleys and canyons.

The event was capped by a warm intense storm that melted the high snow load. The resulting snowmelt flooded valleys, inundated or swept away towns, mills, dams, flumes, houses, fences, and domestic animals, and ruined fields. It has been described as the worst disaster ever to strike California.

ACKNOWLEDGMENTS

Creating a novel that is both informative and entertaining requires a tremendous team effort. Writing is the easy part.

For their efforts in making this novel a reality, I would like to thank Hristo Argirov Kovatliev for his incredible artistic talents in creating my cover art. He and my loving wife, Dani, collaborate (and conspire) to create the most incredible cover art in the publishing business. A huge hug of appreciation goes out to Pauline Nolet, the *Professor*, for her editorial prowess and patience in correcting this writer's same tics after sixty-plus novels. Thank you, Drew Avera, a United States Navy veteran, who has brought his talented formatting skills from a writer's perspective to create multiple formats for reading my novels.

ACKNOWLEDGMENTS

Thank you, Kevin Pierce, the beloved voice of the apocalypse, who brought my words to life in audio format.

A few years ago, we met a couple who have become close friends. Their names? You guessed it. Sammy and Tyler, together with their fur babies, Carly and Fenway. There have been many friends and acquaintances who've found their way into my novels as named characters or inspiration for those in the story. I have to say, this has been incredible fun including Sammy and Ty in ARkStorm. Dani and I truly admire these two. It was my honor to create characters in this novel who have some of the real personality traits of our friends. When the shit hits the fan, we know we can trust them as we hope they know we'll have their back. Thank you both for being such good sports and providing me lots of material to bring the fictional Sammy and Ty to life!

Now, for the serious stuff. Accurately portraying a thousand year flood event and the aftermath required countless hours of never-ending research and interviews of some of the brightest minds in the world of climate science.

Once again, as I immersed myself in the science and history, source material and research flooded my inbox from around the globe. Without the assistance

ACKNOWLEDGMENTS

of many individuals and organizations, this story could not be told. Please allow me a moment to acknowledge a few of those individuals whom, without their tireless efforts and patience, ARkStorm could not have been written.

Many thanks to the preeminent researchers and engineers at the United States Geological Survey and the UCLA Center for Climate Science for their research and climate models.

A shout-out must go to Jeffrey Mount, a senior fellow at the Public Policy Institute of California. He is an emeritus professor of earth and planetary sciences at the University of California, Davis. A geomorphologist who specializes in the study of rivers, streams, and wetlands, his research focuses on integrated water resource management, flood management, and improving aquatic ecosystem health.

This story couldn't have been written without the research done by Dr. Lucy Jones and Dr. Daniel Swain.

Dr. Lucille Jones is one of the foremost and trusted public authorities on earthquakes, Jones is referred to by many in Southern California as the *seismologist-next-door* who is frequently called up on to provide information on recent earthquakes.

ACKNOWLEDGMENTS

She is currently a research associate at the Seismological Laboratory at Caltech and chief scientist and founder of the Dr. Lucy Jones Center for Science and Society. She was previously at the USGS from 1985 to 2016, where she conducted research in the areas of foreshocks, seismotectonics, and the application of hazards science to improve societal resilience after natural disasters.

At the USGS, she was also part of the team of scientists that developed the Great Shakeout Earthquake Drills, during which millions around the world participate in annual earthquake safety drills.

Dr. Daniel Swain is a climate scientist in the Institute of the Environment and Sustainability at the University of California, Los Angeles, and holds concurrent appointments as a Research Fellow in the Capacity Center for Climate and Weather Extremes at the National Center for Atmospheric Research and as the California Climate Fellow at The Nature Conservancy of California.

Dr. Swain studies the changing character, causes, and impacts of extreme weather and climate events on a warming planet—with a particular focus on the physical processes leading to droughts, floods, and wildfires. He holds a PhD in Earth System Science from Stanford University and a B.S. in

ACKNOWLEDGMENTS

Atmospheric Science from the University of California, Davis.

Finally, as always, a special thank you to my team of loyal friends and readers who've always supported my work and provided me valuable insight over the years.

Thanks, y'all, and Choose Freedom!

ABOUT THE AUTHOR, BOBBY AKART

Author Bobby Akart has been ranked by Amazon as #25 on the Amazon Charts list of most popular, bestselling authors. He has achieved recognition as the #1 bestselling Horror Author, #1 bestselling Science Fiction Author, #5 bestselling Action & Adventure Author, #7 bestselling Historical Fiction Author and #10 on Amazon's bestselling Thriller Author list.

Mr. Akart has delivered up-all-night thrillers to readers in 245 countries and territories worldwide. He has sold over one million books in all formats, which includes over forty international bestsellers, in nearly fifty fiction and nonfiction genres. He has produced more #1 bestselling novels in Science Fiction's post-apocalyptic genre than any author in Amazon's history.

ABOUT THE AUTHOR, BOBBY AKART

His novel *Yellowstone: Hellfire* reached the Top 25 on the Amazon bestsellers list and earned him multiple Kindle All-Star awards for most pages read in a month and most pages read as an author. The Yellowstone series vaulted him to the #25 bestselling author on Amazon Charts, and the #1 bestselling science fiction author.

Since its release in December 2020, his standalone novel, *New Madrid Earthquake*, has been ranked #1 on Amazon Charts in multiple countries as a natural disaster thriller.

Mr. Akart is a graduate of the University of Tennessee after pursuing a dual major in economics and political science. He went on to obtain his master's degree in business administration and his doctorate degree in law at Tennessee.

With over a million copies of his novels in print, Bobby Akart has provided his readers a diverse range of topics that are both informative and entertaining. His attention to detail and impeccable research has allowed him to capture the imagination of his readers through his fictional works and bring them valuable knowledge through his nonfiction books.

ABOUT THE AUTHOR, BOBBY AKART

SIGN UP for Bobby Akart's mailing list to learn of special offers, view bonus content, and be the first to receive news about new releases.

Visit www.BobbyAkart.com for details.

OTHER WORKS BY AMAZON CHARTS TOP 25 AUTHOR BOBBY AKART

The California Dreamin' Duology
ARkStorm (a standalone, disaster thriller)
Fractured (a standalone, disaster thriller)

The Perfect Storm Series
Perfect Storm 1
Perfect Storm 2
Perfect Storm 3
Perfect Storm 4

Black Gold (a standalone, terrorism thriller)

The Nuclear Winter Series

First Strike
Armageddon
Whiteout
Devil Storm
Desolation

New Madrid (a standalone, disaster thriller)

Odessa (a Gunner Fox trilogy)
Odessa Reborn
Odessa Rising
Odessa Strikes

The Virus Hunters
Virus Hunters I
Virus Hunters II
Virus Hunters III

The Geostorm Series
The Shift
The Pulse
The Collapse
The Flood

The Tempest
The Pioneers

The Asteroid Series (A Gunner Fox trilogy)
Discovery
Diversion
Destruction

The Doomsday Series
Apocalypse
Haven
Anarchy
Minutemen
Civil War

The Yellowstone Series
Hellfire
Inferno
Fallout
Survival

The Lone Star Series
Axis of Evil
Beyond Borders

Lines in the Sand
Texas Strong
Fifth Column
Suicide Six

The Pandemic Series
Beginnings
The Innocents
Level 6
Quietus

The Blackout Series
36 Hours
Zero Hour
Turning Point
Shiloh Ranch
Hornet's Nest
Devil's Homecoming

The Boston Brahmin Series
The Loyal Nine
Cyber Attack
Martial Law
False Flag

The Mechanics
Choose Freedom
Patriot's Farewell (standalone novel)
Black Friday (standalone novel)
Seeds of Liberty (Companion Guide)

The Prepping for Tomorrow Series (non-fiction)
Cyber Warfare
EMP: Electromagnetic Pulse
Economic Collapse

Printed in Great Britain
by Amazon